Etherium book one:

THE DAUGHTERS OF GOD

Abernathy

It was an infernal place.

While there may have been a chandelier of gold alloy hanging from the parlour roof, The Happy Huntress only ever observed the glistening bodies of man and woman sinning under the warm glow of its light.

Yes, it may have had silk-thread curtains to cover the windows as well as satin sheets atop the bed but these luxuries were still just tools to shroud and cushion the two – or sometimes three or four – hedonists as they wrinkled out the mistress' ironing.

For there was not enough mahogany upholstering nor salted window sills in the world to properly bring up the status of such a place of work; The Happy Huntress was simply infernal.

But can a den of sin be called so without any guests?

Because the people around Whitley Moor, who liked to think their town nice and consecrated, were the ones keeping the candles lit. On one night you might find a zealous preacher reading scripture to all from a street corner and on the very next

you might find him in the lap of Harlot Abernathy, the business woman who runs this fine establishment.

It would amuse some to hear this story, as is seen by the extra bills he thrusts into Harlot's hands every night to ensure their meetings remain clandestine. To her, however, he was the tamest guest at her boudoir.

One of her favourites was of course the butcher's boy. At only sixteen, he came to the parlour on a winter's evening after some delirious teasing by his classmates. None of them had touched a woman like they had claimed to have but that did not stop them from winding this poor lad so round the bend that he felt forced to Abernathy's doorstep.

She might have dismissed the boy on the spot but not for her emptied stomach. Between that, the flashing memory of her piling medical bills and the boy's promised payment of discarded meats from his father's shop, she found herself welcoming him inside after all.

Once in bed, he was shy but eager. It almost brought her to instruct him, especially when he had to keep stopping everything to prevent an untimely climax. But every time she found herself egging to help him, she quickly closed her mouth with realisation that she did not in fact care at all. He paid for the half-hour, he would get the half-hour, however he liked it.

And he did. For fifteen minutes. After which, he would lie there on the bed intertwining their fingers and grinning like a fool until the other fifteen minutes were up. And after that he left. And She thought, with an unexpected sadness, that she would never see him again.

When the next Saturday approached and the next seven O'clock came to pass, he was once more at her doorstep this time with two hefty pre-payments frozen by the blistering winter air into his hands. After the door opened he made that fool's grin at her and without a word in return she let him in.

It wasn't until his six or seventh visit that she would come to admit her growing fondness. Not because he was getting better at it or that he was attractive in any way, no he was too young for her mature eye, but because it was this time, or that, when he finally started to fill those fifteen minutes silence at the end of their sessions. The silence where he grins some more while she conspicuously stares at the ticking over hands of her elegant wall clock.

"Is your name really Harlot?"

He rolled over, unaware that his hands moved to cover his nakedness, and asked the first question of a series to come.

She laughed at him. "Of course not, lad. What mother would curse her daughter so?"

"So tell me how your mother blessed you!"

She parted her lips and narrowed her eyes and pondered why he would even ask that. She was always the first to know that physical intimacy strummed the heartstrings of men – even before they knew it themselves - so much so that they would fall in love with her from time to time. It was even known that

Harlot might take advantage of this to withdraw more money from them, sometimes even playing it into their sessions to make them last longer. Or shorter.

So each time the butcher's boy knocked on her door, she grew more and more scared that his young heart would swoon too close to the sun. And besides the lovemaking, Harlot was not so disenchanted that she couldn't recognise her own beauty: she had thick, black curls and puffy cheeks marked with freckles. She was not fat, not by any means, but not slim either. She was skinny with just enough meat to stop her ribs from poking through. This made her grateful for her full face - that others might have despised having - as well as her strong legs that gave muscle where fat was lacking. Although that last aspect may have been a product of 'exercise' rather than a natural gift.

All of this is why she was silenced in the moment after his retort – but just for a moment – as his curiosity struck her to realise that he had not an ounce of romance for her in his heart. It would have offended her, actually, had it not been so amusing.

"She blessed me Amy," was her response. The boy thought on this with a scrunched expression before asking her if that was true. She answered by pointing out that the half-hour was up. Courteously, he left without another word.

The next week, when he came with a near-ruined cut of aurochs, he would go on to ask her the same question as if their previous discussion had never happened. This time she answered again except this time she answered that her mother had named her Sarah.

The boy frowned but still left on time as graciously as the last week.

And so it went. He grew to be seventeen and then he grew to be eighteen and then he even grew to be more skilled. Whether he had lain with any others during his tenure at her house of decadence, she did not know nor care, for each time he came, he paid in deft and he went without a word over the mark.

It wasn't until one winter night that his repeated question changed, for the first time in their two years of patronage. He turned to her, no longer ashamed to let his body be seen, and asked as he interlaced their fingers: "why do you not use your real name?"

That week's alias choked up her throat as she caught a second too late that he had asked something different.

"Oh. Because it's better not to, is all."

"Better how? For business? Is it lustier, is it safer, is it... more fun?"

"No, boy, not for any reason like that."

"Do all of you use a persona?"

"All the whores from here to Northend do anyhow."

He simply stared at her, his eyes big and yearning. She looked over his shoulder to see that the time was ticking over the half-hour but decided not to point it out.

She sighed, "it is because a woman could not pair their name with 'whore.' Whether in a parlour or a damp and dark alley; whether for little or for riches; whether they are down on their luck or making a good living... no woman could utter the open secret that Amy or Sarah or whoever is in fact a whore."

"Is Abernathy a whore?" he asked sincerely.

"Yes," she uttered, "but I am not Abernathy."

The butcher's boy stood up and dressed and then looked down at her form on the bed. "And so *you* are not a whore," he surmised.

His leaving that night was the last time Harlot ever saw him. She would like to say she was sad to see him go but all she confessed to was sadness that her quality meat for the week was gone.

And she never found out why this had happened, either. Whether he had found a new lass to call his own or his father had caught him, she did not know. This begs the question, why did she cry the next Saturday when he did not knock on her door? Why did she drink just a few glasses extra the following Saturday after that? Why did she always keep her seven O'clock open just in case; an eye always watching the hands tick over the half hour? And why did all of this tumult in feelings of anger?

In the end, as she dozed off into the lull of sleep, she realised that she knew fully well why he left. Their musings had reminded him that he and her both were humans. And alike in their humanity was ever the smallest flame of pride.

So she let herself grow that anger. He got to leave and take over his dad's shop all the while she let any kind of men walk in and out of her door.

She let in the preacher time after time.

She welcomed the men who had not seen clean water in weeks.

She worshiped the boys who somehow kept finding new diseases to spread to their manhood – diseases that would eventually allow her medical bills to pile up *again*.

Only for men with new ways to hurt her for their pleasure to come in and hurt her *again*.

As her thighs bruised and her hair knotted and her feet ached *again* and *again* the butcher's boy just got to leave.

It was a matter of contempt for her that ate her heart out every day. It wasn't until the anniversary came, of his leaving her, that she would finally find her own spark of pride.

On another winter night.

Harlot Abernathy never forgot a face – a matter that ensured her business thrived more than others – so she was certain that this evening's face was entirely new.

"Welcome, sir," her sultry tones teased him through the front door. When it shut behind him, locking out the winds of winter, he became enveloped in warmth, his soft skin losing its frost. She tilted her head and draped her body over any arm of furniture or corner of a desk - as if she herself were décor – and let his eyes wander hungrily across her form.

Quality service like that came at a high price, but for this man she began to feel uncharacteristically charitable. A discount, perhaps, for the handsome chap in the tailored suit. Yes, it was very rare that her eyes too would wander, but it was not unknown.

"I want the hour," he purred. His lolled mouth indicated an intoxication with her; she had him and was happy for it. The handsome men never did want the full hour so that night would truly be a new one, one to see her uncharacteristic discount for certain.

And, at last, when he stepped forward into the candlelight she realised who the man was. She did not comment, for fear of scaring him away, so she let their secret remain open – but this was the mayor's son. Never had someone so esteemed walked through her doors 'till tonight.

She pondered why he might be there as she undid his waistcoat, only to have her mind hitched by his aftershave. She tried to ask herself what kind of women this man took when he felt like it, if not for his moonlit, pale chest drawing her attention.

In slimness and elegance, his shirtless form sat on the edge of her bed ready to be orally delivered as a prelude to his ravaging. She was sure that she would not block it out like usual and instead let herself enjoy the occasion of being had by a man who knew what grooming meant.

In taming her excitement, she managed to slowly tug at the hem of his breeches before taking a teasing finger to the buttons. What writhed underneath was begging to be free, already drawing damp spots on his trouser's groin.

At last, in a slow hunger, she unearthed it, only to find that the man was not concealing what she initially hoped he might be. It sprung out, excited and in motion: a red tentacle that tapered to a blue-green tip.

"My god!" Harlot cursed as she fell back onto her arse and scuttled away. When she hit the wall with her back she pointed at it with wide eyes but could not find words enough.

"Suck it," he cooed still high on his arousal.

His terse instruction quickly brought forth her words after all. "*Out*," she commanded.

For her whole life, Harlot Abernathy had not let her real person, her identity, slip to a client. That moment was the closest she had come as it was not the whore who shunted the mayor's son from the parlour that night, but a woman scared.

"*Now*," she repeated looking up and down between the man's angering visage and the aquatic limb between his legs. The appendage was thick, girthy, about seven inches and wriggling independently in place. Each time she looked at it she was too disgusted to remain focused. Each time she looked away she was too curious not to look back.

He said some cruel words to her and made crueller threats as he dressed and removed himself. It was all just blanked out though as she mentally located her salt and any crosses that she had in any drawers, all ready to line her doorway and hang up in the windows respectively.

She did so after he left and then returned to her bed to pray. With the image of his curse flashing in her mind, she forced herself to think on something else. Where she unwillingly landed was on a visit from her sister three winters ago. For her sister's situation back then was not dissimilar to his.

She had shown up on Harlot's doorstep that day with tears in her eyes and woes about her latest boyfriend. Harlot had warned her time and time again: 'don't fall in with beggars.' 'Do not court thieves.' 'Certainly don't go marrying the man who raped you.' Every time she failed to listen; always turning up weeks later with news of a break up.

But that time, three winters ago, was different. Her latest partner had been a man of honesty, at least he sounded as much, until the sister revealed that they broke up when she caught him at an orgy lit by red candles and purveyed by infernal creatures.

She ran, never speaking to him again, and came straight to Harlot's door. Harlot took a disinterested interest in her sister's poor decisions and offered her a place to stay as she always did. But then her sister revealed that this time truly was different. This time she needed help.

Harlot laughed and explained that holy matters were foreign to her never mind an exorcism or what have it. Her sister carried on though and illustrated the problem by simply removing her shoes.

Below were not the dainty feet she had always taken care of but instead two cloven hooves edged by blood-red fur. After staring at them for long enough, Harlot finally looked up to see that her sister was sobbing and her lip was trembling with a beg for help.

That night, she put her sister up in a public house, with excuses about lots of clients booked, while she darted to a church the next street over.

She never saw her sister after that. She still had three days of opportunity to but based on what the local priest had told her about such a condition she decided that it was better off remembering her sister as she was and not by what she would become.

Even that memory managed to flood her with guilt and hate and pity. Even to the present day as it all resurfaced at the sight of the mayor's son...

For he too must have been laying with spirits; with daemons!

Ancercy, that priest had called it. Ahn-ker-see. It was a phrase that bubbled to the front of her mind each time she found a disease down there for fear that ancercy might be diagnosed.

It was uncurable and consuming. It was more than just a monstrous deformation – it was a complete daemonification of the human form. It was a total reduction of the intelligent mind to that of a beast's.

When she went to bed that night, the night after shooing away the mayor's son that is, she couldn't help but hear the noises of ancercy taking her sister away again. It was an echo from the past still scratching at her ears.

It was a whole song, really. The roaring of those night hunters that came for her sister complimented the screeching of the beast they found and killed. Those hunters with their tall hats, silver weapons and garlands of herbs – they fought tirelessly as the beast - as the sick girl - scratched at Harlot's parlour door. Whether she, or it, or however, was looking to kill a nearby citizen or seeking asylum in a relative's home, Harlot never knew. Either way, the song was eventually cut off. A last grunt, a final stab and a diminishing growl ended the lament of Harlot's sister... whatever she had become was snuffed out by Belgrave's finest.

That whole matter turned around well in her mind, despite her fears that the mayor himself might turn his evil eye to her establishment, as she realised that she had finally managed to find reprieve from the matter of the butcher's boy.

In her bed, in the cool nighttime sheets, one spirit weighed on her and another lifted as she realised that she was no longer angry at him. Just like that. It went away as she hugged at her old pillow and soothed herself to the clock's ticking for she could finally say that she had a matter of pride for herself, however small.

Harlot Abernathy would not sleep with men who had ancercy.

The swelling feeling warmed her journey to sleep. And while that warmth may have slipped away from her in the morning as she recalled what happened, and let her fear of the mayor chill her instead, she still had that pride buried somewhere.

For now.

It won't be long until she her mind changes. Soon, she will increasingly wish that she had just slept with the handsome man. For all the bother, even if it is ancercy, might have been a mercy compared to how her life unravels after the fact.

Culver

Mary grimaced as she walked the group of fifteen or so men through the grounds of her esteemed university. As the department head she was expected to show new students on the course what life was like in the ecosystem of higher education.

And like every year, she grew increasingly disappointed that each one of them turned out to be male. It disheartened her. She found herself having to remember that while she did fight to get women in education it was really a bid to get everyone in education.

It was a reminder that helped her to grin and bear as all fifteen or so of these men proceeded to ignore her tour and giggle at the statues on display with their marble penises. Yes, she decided, even these people deserved equal opportunity to education.

"And here are the famous gargoyles of The Spire. They have been looming above our doorway for near seven centuries now." She smiled and waved a gesture at the stone edifices of large, bear sized birds that hung in rows of three all the way up the university's structure.

The Spire was the name of the tallest building in Okhram; a giant tower which was linked to the imperial palace via a single, massive copper chain. Each ring that made it was an oval the size of a tall house, all linking in an oxidated green rope that stretched far into the distance. The structure itself was made of grey stone bricks that had withstood the test of time. It towered up in a perfect cylinder and peaked in a circular brim that housed an observatory. That was topped by a cone of purple tiles for a roof that stood atop six stilts around the balcony area.

While all the five kingdoms had a central tower like The Spire, not all of them served the same purpose. In Belgrave it was a palace, in Northold it was a mighty forge. Of course here, in Okhram, it was the university.

"I'm sorry, miss, but I've got to be honest with ya... they look a bit shit, don't they." The crowd chortled along with the comment. Mary inhaled a patient breath and counted down the time to her lunch break where some special bread, cheese and wine were waiting in preparation specifically to help cope with introduction day.

"If you're referring to the damage to the statues than yes, they are very weathered." It took great effort for her to put on a cheery voice, "originally, they were accurate portrayals of reavers; slim yet large birds with black feathers as sharp as metal and eyes as red as blood."

One of the men in the crowd sniggered while another piped up, "yeah we know what fackin' reavers are!" The crowd erupted again. Mary just continued.

"The original idea was that the gargoyles would keep reavers away. They are territorial birds - the theory goes that if we purport a large gathering of them through statues all across the spire then the real ones in the forest would be too intimidated to attack!" The boys' focus began to drift away again as her words fell on unhearing ears, "unfortunately, the plan backfired. Local reavers saw the large flock as a threat and instead moved to attack. They quickly lost interest, though, when they realised they were stone - but that didn't stop their steel beaks from damaging the statues a great deal before they did. Today, we remember that night as... we remember..." she trailed off. She could have been saying anything at all and it wouldn't have mattered.

So she deigned to walk away. To just let them roam if that's what they want. And with an impatient exhale, she did. As she walked through the entranceway she weighed her punishment – a five minute slap on the wrist – against another horrid fifty-five minutes of touring. She decided it was worth it.

It nearly brought tears, however, when she looked over her shoulder to see that the flock had not taken the hint. And these tears were tears of hysterics as she held herself back from openly laughing in their faces. They thought she was still giving the tour! Of all the unworthy entrants to The Spire, this year's were the worst.

She made up her mind to just continue through to the end, the rest of the tour being made bearable for the humour of that moment. She went on up flights and flights of stairs giving humble commentaries on all the rooms or statues they passed.

Whenever someone spoke or asked a question, she just ignored them instead choosing to rattle off a list of memorised facts and nothing more. When fifty-five minutes had finally elapsed she found great satisfaction in dragging them all the way down the stairs they had climbed and watching as they realised that this would be their life for the next four years now that they had enrolled.

Once she was back in her own office, hidden in her well-deserved solitude, she pulled out that lunch she had been drooling over as her reward for seeing the whole thing through. She would have given herself the reward either way but now she felt she had earned it.

As she ate, putting soft cheeses between hard crusts of fresh bread, she thought to ask God that she might witness something quite as funny as she had that day and perhaps even the opportunity to laugh aloud at it next time. As the afternoon unravelled, so did her stress, both melted by the good food and humorous thoughts.

When her head was cleared and she had sipped with melancholy on her glass of wine, she began the self-indictment portion of her reflections. Her comedic prayers would not be answered, she thought. She even went on to scold herself for the slip of thinking that maybe these boys weren't worthy of being here earlier. If anything, she was rather glad indeed to find that they would be shaping themselves in those halls of learning rather than halls of decadence. There is nowhere else in the world she would wish for young people like that to be.

Two knocks came to her door then with a man's voice begging enter. It took her a second to respond as she resurfaced from her reverie.

"Just a moment!" She called back. She needed a second to brush the crumbs off of her shirt and hide the wine in the wide drawer at the bottom of her desk. It was not against policy to drink alcohol on school grounds – technically – but it was incredibly unprofessional.

She had also known the Magister of history there to be a man whose water glass is filled, rather, with gin, and so she never let the guilt get to her.

"Put the blood down," the man's voice came again as he entered without quarry. Mary rushed to shut the drawer as her hand drew to her heart in shock. She sat down, relieved, when her eyes fell on the face of the one colleague she could truly refer to as a colleague and not another rival. Mary would even go as far as to use the term 'enemies' to describe the other misers who taught there but they were all far too old to be anything of the such.

"My lord, Ahmar, you are much more unprofessional than I fear I am sometimes, you know that!" She hissed, only teasing of course. Ahmar used his shoulder to push the door open as he presented her with a silver tray of coffee. He ignored her jibe as she appeared to soften at the sight and nod for him to enter.

The pot in the middle of his refreshments was tall and had a thick spout. It was made of pewter and had a wooden handle that matched those holding the tray. As Mary continued to talk,

Ahmar would pour the thick, brown beverage into two antimonial cups; they weren't the finest the university had to offer, but they'd do.

"I swear on all that is good, next year I shall not tour them around again. I would even offer my wages up if they'd rather hire *staff* to do it. I am not staff, Ahmar. I'm not!"

The man gingerly smiled at her over the rim of his cup. The steam seemed to brighten his dark cheeks, bringing red to his smile. And he didn't answer, he just listened. Mary liked that about him. She also liked how that face of his was very pretty but would not dare to let that particular thought known.

So instead she just sighed and slipped into an ever so un-ladylike slump as she blew to cool her own drink down.

"Why the coffee?" she had to ask.

Ahmar finished his first daring sip of the burning liquid and smiled. Again. Ironically, this was the part Mary found hard to like about him: he was always smiling. She thought that his brown-ish skin – a western complexion – was sweet and that his soft, dark hair was enviable. Her own hair was a cascading river of deep browns but his hair was black in a way that no one from Engelland's could be.

He was sat there in his lecturer's clothes, the deepest of purple blazers and pure black trousers that matched his shoes. While she sat there in what can only be described as a frock. A deplorable piece of pocketless clothing that made her yearn for trousers like her colleague had.

And still it was his smile that she detested most.

So as he kept beaming away, her eyes only narrowed.

"I thought you might need it after a day with the youth. Now, don't look at me like that. You were one of them too once, you know."

"I wasn't quite like that," she complained.

"No," he agreed, "but you certainly looked just as rough."

"Oi!" If not for the scalding drink she might have hit him on the arm while he chuckled at her expense. She knew that her features were more dinner-lady-like and less nursery teacher than most ladies and so she was just the more envious of the taller, slimmer man. It also made her ever more the unrequited admirer. Who could confess to a man whose first words for her face were always 'rough.'

"I also came for another reason."

"If it's for the food I've eaten it all," she put her hands up to say guilty but not sorry.

"No, no. I came to say that theres a man looking for you downstairs. Royal office, or something of the like."

"Oh," she leaned in. "What did he look like?"

"Silver," Ahmar nodded, "yes, silver hair and very angry. But eyebrows-angry not face-angry. And he had a short cape over his shoulders. A white shirt. Black trousers too- and listen here: he had a belt of wands."

Mary bit her lip. She had no idea who this could be - and the wands unnerved her of course - but a royal officer was not a reassuring guest to have.

"I'd better go and find him then."

"No need, Miss Culver," the door swung open to another uninvited man as the described person entered with his word. "Please, do sit back down."

She did, after having half risen to leave before. And then in her nervousness she leant towards Ahmar instead while purposefully bumping their knees together feel the platony of his touch.

"Of course. May my associate remain?"

The man looked at him. "No."

Ahmar knew what that meant. "I'll see you later, yes?" She didn't like how quickly he stood up to go but still gave a nod of assent to him. He smiled. He left, giving nervous glances at the other man who was now standing in the centre of the room like he owned it.

As Ahmar went, and the stranger watched him, Mary took a quick look to confirm that indeed five wands of varying shades of wood hung around his waist.

"Interested in becoming a witch, Miss Culver?"

"Sorry, sorry," she said, looking back up at him. His face was expressionless yet still maintaining a degree of disdain.

As she sat there, awkwardly so, while he pulled something from the inside pocket of his half-cape, she started to remember what it felt like being a student again. In this moment there was an older man looking down on her, his head full of knowledge and hers wanting to know it.

"I am Victor Redding, auger to the throne." What he pulled out was his letter of marque stamped with the reaver crest of House Iris. You could tell it was a reaver and not a crow or a raven by its wider, thicker beak and narrower eyes. She also believed him purely on the premise that he looked exactly as auger to the throne should: a witcher in uppity clothing.

He proceeded to furl the identification papers back up, slowly as if he were waiting for something from her.

"Right, of course. Apologies, my lord, how might I assist you?" Satisfied with the formalities, he tucked the paper back into its pocket and stood with his hands clasped.

"I have been lead to believe that you are the magister of worship here, is that correct?"

"Yes... my lord."

"The department head of study of the sacrosanct... In turn, that would make you just as much an expert in infernal dealings as hallowed ones, correct?"

"In theory, my lord, yes." It was illegal to study the infernal never mind host an expert on the matter. Mary was one of the very few people privileged enough to access the few unburned texts on daemonology for the sole purpose of divining more knowledge about God from them.

Victor sighed, "in theory will have to do. You see, we need an expert on dark arts but did not want to turn to cultists or the mad. At least not right away."

"Um, 'we,' my lord?"

"The royal court. The *immediate* royal court. The gentry will know not of these dealings and whether you help or not, you will keep your silence on everything we are discussing, is that clear?" His tone never changed, not really, but his words always carried a weight. The same is said to be true of a knight's words or a bishops. The weight of the crown, she supposed.

"Yes, of course. But might I inquire into what exactly you are asking of me? My lord?"

He considered before answering. "Are you versed in the consequences of laying with an infernal creature?"

"Damnation, you mean?"

"I mean ancercy."

"Oh. Yes, I am versed enough."

"And in your opinion, magister, do you think that a human might be able to... weaponize or deploy degrees of ancercy on an area of their choosing?"

She was taken aback by such a suggestion. Any idea she had of standing back up after her initial intimidation of the man was dashed by her newfound shock as she thought on the question.

She could only continue to do so for a few moments more though, as soon enough the question as to *why* he had even asked became rapidly more prevalent.

"Is there an enemy attempting to do so, m'lord? I have heard of a mayor's son in Belgrave-"

"It does not matter why."

"Of course... um, in that case, I believe that upon closer inspection of how - specifically - ancercy is spread, then we could isolate that factor and potentially weaponize it, yes," she stared at him with shaking eyes. He didn't reply until she added, "... my lord."

The auger grinned right away. This unsettled Mary deeply for it was a shallow grin that stretched the wrinkled skin on his face.

"Mary Culver, how would you like to assist the throne in a matter of great importance to the future of Okhram?"

Lobelia

Let it not be said that the palace of Belgrave did not know how to host its guests.

When the ambassador of Weyland approached the large double doors he could not help but scowl at the pomp of their royal green coating and gold rings of accentuations. He had no real reason to despise it as much as he did, it was more so the fact that these doors would only be the beginning of the worst day of his career. As guards pulled these doors open for him, he pre-emptively gave another curse - this time to the leagues of stairs he would have to climb to reach the throne room. Instead what he found was a neatly decorated foyer that surrounded a glorious platform of wood – a platform of wood edged with a railing of finely crafted banisters. It had dark chains protruding up through to the darkness above and was manned by an attendant with a disciplined face.

When two other members of staff came behind the ambassador to push the great door to a close, the platform attendant took his own turn and moved to open a gate. It was the kind of gate that blended into the bannisters of the wooden platform, the kind you could not tell was there until the skilful worker had pushed it open.

He was tentative to take this invitation, having never visited the central tower at Belgrave before, but still took his self in stride when he did decide to step on. As he walked to the centre of this device, emblazoned by his lord's demands, he kept his chin up and did not think once to engage in small talk with the servants.

Once satisfied, the attendant rejoined him on there by closing the gate and letting the latch fall down. It was also wooden, antique cherry by the looks of things, and blended with the gate into the whole structure as if the railings went on undisturbed. After that, he moved to the back corner behind the ambassador and made three mighty raps of his jet black cane against the platform surface.

Nothing happened for a second as the echoing sound weltered into the high ceiling. And then a sickness came to the ambassador's stomach as suddenly he noticed the entrance getting lower – for he was rising.

The device was being hauled, with great merits of synchronisation as well as strength, up by some serving men hidden behind the walls or rather, inside them. They were lugging with great strain to the time of a soft drum to ensure that each of the four corners were not only hauled up with the same force but with the same speed too.

A lifter of the royal house was a task not left to the untrained and was one of the most important roles to play in the palace of House Lobelia.

But all of that was behind the scenes. The Wey ambassador was simply left with a feeling of awe as he climbed past floor after floor of the steeple-like structure.

Each one of these floors had the perfect square shape surrounded by independent railings to allow them to pass up and through it. They also had gates, should the rider wish to make a stop at any one. What was curious to him, however, were the multitudes of isolated tunnels they rose through and glances at stairs leading up to rooms he could not see.

And while at first he had not cared at all what may lie hidden in the rooms closed off from guests, his mind was changed when he came to witness a room with rails of the finest gowns in the kingdom. And again when he saw a guarded room where jewels lay in great glass cases. And once more when, nearly at the top, he saw a collection of cabinets with scrolls and dusty desks – although uninhabited at that time it was clearly the office of Belgrave's own royal auger, a position desperate to be filled.

So when he had risen to the top and out into the sunlight, he had to wonder what might be so valuable to hide that it takes precedence over wardrobes and jewels and esteemed offices.

But as his eyes adjusted to the midday sun shining through the poles that held up the green-tiled roof, he set his view on the throne where her majesty sat.

He saw her there, hands folded in her lap with a great brown and white gown on and saw that despite all the stories and dire warnings of courtesy she was just as real as he was. And when his mind thought again on what might possibly be hidden in those coveted palace layers he realised with great stupidity that they were simply just bed chambers.

"Ambassador Carthey," the queen noted, "how did you like your first use of my lift?"

He stepped forward through the gate; opened once again by the attendant. He came to the end of a green carpet, accentuated by gold thread, and knelt before the throne.

"Your majesty," he bowed his head, "never have I experienced such a means of travel. It was... enlightening." He stood up again and looked on her dour expression. Besides her throne, which was all silver and black, was a diminutive copy where her daughter sat clearly bored beyond her mind. Nearly fifteen and still being forced to watch the day's proceedings must have been deeply tiresome.

"Hm," the queen agreed. "And if we may get down to business, what dare I ask is so urgent that your king has sent you straight to my doors and not to the embassy? The embassy that the Weys insisted be built out of fairness, might I remind you."

"I am reminded," he replied. His voice was deep, and unsure. He was meant to carry his lord's demands, and he had all the way to the throne room, but the problem seemed to come from having to voice them.

He looked behind the two royals and saw two guards in black suits of armour with green tunics stretched over the top. On them was the golden emblem of the aurochs: mighty with its strong horns; the crest of house Lobelia. In their hands were mighty glaives: they had strong, steel blades with smaller, protruding edges around them like the petals of a flower.

"And the urgent matter that brings me here... the urgent matter, ma'am, is the matter of your disposition on the religious divide."

The queen's eyes narrowed, "everyone in Belgrave subscribes to The Holy Paradigm. Every Engel in the empire does."

"But not all of them are Extenic."

"I am aware." Her voice grew deeper.

In her opinion, the church didn't need all the bells and whistles of reaver shaped lecterns and oil paintings of scenes from scripture. Just faith and a cross or two. She especially like the bit about being allowed to divorce.

And she would let her people who think the same be free to do so.

"In which case, you must be aware that Extenic following is the faith of your emperor? Is the faith of the Weys?"

"End your pitiful questioning and relay your master's words, messenger."

Carthey swallowed. He felt very small. "The king is displeased that his ally is not performing liturgy in God's language. He believes it would be wise to cut ties... with infidels."

As the insult left his lips the queen stood in regal efficiency from her throne. At the same time her guard advanced two paces. The thudding of their sabatons resounded and shrunk the ambassador further. Still, he remained in place, small but all the fiercer as her majesty's words lashed him:

"The Bill was not written in 'God's language' it was written in ancient Calarian. Nor does the right to preach, the right to commune with the lord and the right to worship your rightful place in the paradigm belong solely to the Calarian speaking clergy."

She stepped down from the platform of her throne and came to be face to face with Carthey, her guards a few paces behind.

"And in the spirit of free worship, you will know that my kingdom is not Revolutist as you imply it to be. I simply do not enforce a right way to worship, just the people's way. If Revolutism is on the rise, then perhaps the people have spoken, ambassador."

He scowled at her. Were it not for the fear of her knights, he would shout and demand her to respect the proper means of worship. Instead, his acid words dripped: "your *kingdom* is nothing but the weakest constituency of a dwindling empire. You would do well not to challenge your remaining allies as you have done today."

"What is your master's word on this particular alliance?" Her voice was strong but quiet, weighed against the man's emotion.

"The Weys are defecting to House Carnation. We will do trade with the empire through our northern boarders and forge strong ties with a kingdom that knows the path to salvation."

The queen scoffed as the man turned and rejoined the lift attendant. The black cane struck the platform's wood twice this time and, after the echoes fell down to the bottom, the platform began to descend - slowly and carefully lowered by the staff within the walls.

The queen returned to the throne, "I can't quite imagine a salvation that requires one to lionise an innumerable amount of saints," she shuddered dramatically to make her daughter giggle, "ghastly business."

Princess Lolita had remained stoic throughout the whole exchange, as to learn the ways of politicking and not interfere, but she did still enjoy watching her mother stand up for the citezens. The high-held Carnations may find pride in their rigid military and astutely climbing profits but it is the common man's favour that nurtures a Lobelia. Lolita, who had grown up on stories of dashing knights, handsome princes and heroines from far off lands, saw her mother so brightly as if she were a fairy tale herself, thanks to her upholding of the family doctrine.

It was a fact that lent itself well to Lolita's position as the female child of the monarch, for her older brother – the heir – would usually receive all the attention of the court and of the staff and of the adoring peasants, (especially the women.) But not of their mother. She had love in droves and could give it equally not just to her people but both her son and daughter too.

Lolita also loved how alike they were; the same small faces and elegant noses, the same caramel blonde hair and the same slightly lower voices than the other women. Their masculine blood was favourable with the sons of course but that did not mean that the daughters disliked being known as handsome, especially as the passing of time had proved that it always earns a mate eventually.

After a few minutes of waiting in the throne room and stretching out the aches that a royal seat brought on, the pair heard a threefold thud from the entrance hall below and prepared for their next appointment.

"Mum," Lolita asked, a question coming quickly in their reprieve.

"Yes, dear?"

"Why didn't you tell Ambassador Carthey about Victor?"

The queen's nose scrunched in distaste, "tell him what? That as a show of my good faith, the crown hired an overtly pro-Extenic man to be our auger only for him to run off at a moment's notice to those rancid Irises in the west."

Lolita pursed her lips, "yes... that."

Her mother smiled away any negativity for her daughter's sake and leant over to cup her left cheek. "Oh, sweetheart. If I were to defend against his attacks that would only dignify them.

No, it is better to let the matter rest. If they wish to leave than they wish to leave, I shall not fight to remain friends with a king who can't comprehend that his job is to serve the people, not the other way around."

Lolita smiled wide again as she pictured her mum painted deftly on the cover of a bed-time book with a noble title for its heroine.

Quickly, the pair fell into more regal positions as the queen retracted her hand from her daughter's face. The platform had returned.

This time, of the two on the platform, the attendant alighted first to announce the guest, this one actually being expected.

"A potential witcher, ma'am. Cyrus Magellan." The man walked in and performed a very, very low bow of honour. Lolita leaned over quickly to whisper to her mum.

"I would have much preferred we get a witch to perform my baptism."

Her mum sighed, "as would I, if that's your wish. However scrying is a wholly male endeavour."

"Mmm," Lolita grunted as she returned to her seat. She watched the man before them rise and then she pondered a future, one perhaps revealed during this baptism, where she becomes the first far-seeing witch.

"It's an honour, to perform this most gracious of ceremonies, your majesty. Your highness." He then gave another neck bow to Lolita.

She tilted her head at him, pleased that he showed her the proper courtesies, unlike most guests of the court. She liked his hair, too. It was yellow, properly yellow, and in a cloud of short curls that made him look rather like a dandelion. And his face was young, forties at the latest, but wrinkled only by experience; handsome.

His clothes were another matter entirely. The man's long coat and leather boots were the deepest black colour while his breeches were as yellow as his hair. It was obvious from the outside that the purple satin inside his coat housed a myriad of thick tomes and his belt, in accompaniment, stored ten wands in total, five on each side of his waist. And while his shirt was the ordinary white of a good gentlemen's, his nails were painted in the same deep purple as the satin of his coat. He cut an interesting figure although it was not unlike a witcher's usual eccentricity, so he remained acceptable in the queen's presence. For now.

"An honour indeed," she replied, "Magellan was it? Was your father Ivan?"

He already fell nervous, "yes, ma'am."

"Oh!" She clapped, her sharp demeanour switching in an instant, "Ivan Magellan performed my baptism not twenty one years ago!"

"Oh-ho, that's- that's fantastic," he chuckled with relief, "yes, he mentioned it to me before. It is truly an honour that you remember even his name."

Ignoring the pleasantries, she stood up and urged the lift attendant over. He marched to her side and bowed his head in waiting. "Cancel all other pagan interviews, this man will do the job."

"Yes, ma'am," the attendant made a mental note and returned to his post at the lift.

When the queen sat back down she whispered to herself that she didn't even know Ivan had a son. All she heard was that there was some dreadful business not long ago involving a church and a fire in Summerset. An incident that had killed the senior witcher dead.

Lolita didn't mind that her mother had done this without asking her. The queen did that a lot but Lolita liked to think herself a good girl and would often graciously accept her charges.

"And do you still operate out of Summerset? From that little shop by the post office?"

While the queen addressed the witcher and the two engaged in familiarities, a small brown bird flitted from the sky to land on the attendant's shoulder. It was a mocking pigeon, a messenger bird augmented with the ability to relay spoken messages over long distances. Due to the name, a lot of people believe that mocking pigeons are literally mocking the sound they hear but a more accurate description would be that they are simply a means of transportation for a magickaly remembered message stored inside them. The joys of witchcraft.

After listening to this one's message, the attendant nodded to the bird, dismissing it. As familiar conversation went on, the man walked over to the queen and stood by her throne waiting patiently for her to address him.

"Yes, Manford?"

"A message, ma'am. It appears that there is yet a second uninvited guest." At her approving nod he leant forward to whisper the message in her ear. The queen nodded as he talked then rolled her eyes when he finished.

"Right. Well he can wait until I'm done with Magellan."

"Very good," Manford returned to his post and prepared to rappel down to relay the message before he was stopped again.

"Oh wait, Whitley Moor?" She pointed at the witcher, her long finger nail focusing on him, "that is a border town, is it not?"

"Astute as ever, ma'am. Whitley neighbours Summerset on the border of Weyland."

The queen sneered at the mention of that god forsaken, or rather raptured, country and returned her eager hand to her lap. "Yes, well as long as you are our witcher for the time being, you might be able to help in this matter. Come to my side and address the guest with me."

A confused Cyrus' face turned red. "Y-yes ma'am," he stammered as he awkwardly moved to her side. He stood with his hands folded in his lap on the other side of the throne to Lolita. Briefly, as the attendant went to fetch the new guest, his head turned to look at the princess opposite him. He saw that she was grinning and giving him a thumbs up. He smiled back, quite unsure on what royal protocol said about responding to a gesture like that.

Standing up straight again he remembered the two guards stood behind him and the thrones. While they were not in his peripheral, he could still certainly feel the weight of their presence at his back as if their very shadows were armoured and bearing down on him.

Eventually, after much sweating and anxiety for Cyrus, the attendant returned. This time he brought an older man with him – with white hair and a plump moustache – who stepped forward once the second the gate was opened and begged audience with the queen.

"Your majesty!" He fawned, bowing so low down that it would have hurt a fit man's spine never mind a sixty-something's.

Manford cleared his throat and shut the lift's gate, "the mayor of Whitley Moor, ma'am. One Theodore Rushings." The mayor returned to a rigid form after a painful display of groans as he straightened out his back. He was short and wore a light brown, three piece suit. He would have looked like a fuller man on any other day but on this one his puffy face seemed to sag with malnourishment as his eyes shook with tears.

"It's my son, ma'am. He's been overcome with a terrible case of ancercy, or so he says. Not even a whore will lay with him now and word is starting to spread throughout the community! I am in dire need of a cleric."

The queen just raised an unimpressed eyebrow at the man. She turned to Cyrus and shrugged her shoulders, very regally mind you, at the witcher. His cheeks flushed again but still he stepped forward. He cleared his throat and spoke, "if I may, mayor. I may be a pagan practitioner but I can tell you without a shadow of a doubt that there is no cure for ancercy. I am terribly sorry."

The mayor's eyes went wide and his face swelled red. He looked ready to pounce on the colourful gentleman before he remembered his company.

"That is all well and good, *sir*," he spat, "but I am here to beg for the queen's mercy and seek audience with a priest. Or-or perhaps a bishop!"

Magellan opened his mouth to respond but closed it again waiting instead for the queen to steer the conversation. She didn't. She was leaning back and simply thinking on the matter. As she did, the two men stood patiently with their hands behind their backs, although Rushings looked ready to pop if he had to keep on like this.

Eventually she clapped her hands together again.

"I've just had the most fabulous of ideas!" She turned to take a surprised Lolita's hands in her own, "how about we go to Whitley Moor. We can holiday in the mayoral halls and try to help Theodore while we're there. Then on your birthday we can ride to Summerset and you shall be baptised in the same cathedral that I was!"

"Th-there's a cathedral so close to the border?"

"Dear, there are cathedrals all across the continent. Now what do you think?"

Lolita knew what she said wouldn't matter. And again, she found herself admiring her mother's desire to help others. So she sighed and she smiled and she agreed.

"Let us travel to Whitley!"

Culver

Mary was stuck in her office. Hours had gone by since the auger had left and still she could not decide her stance on the contract.

- The employed will secrets keep.

A foreboding line of legalese that trapped her from talking: a great issue for the simple fact that Ahmar was her greatest confidant. What would she do could she not confide in him?

A sigh left her lips. All the frustrated ones had long since gone and now all she could spare were sighs of fatigue.

At least she had the view. From the window behind her desk she could see the gardens on the eastern side of The Spire. The whole grounds formed a gorgeous pattern that circled the university and at this vantage she saw a third of it, in all its purple glory.

They were all irises, of course, planted in concentric patterns that honoured the royal house.

She thanked God that she could not see the pathway taken during those students' inauguration as it would surely dampen her lamenting.

- All work of the employed will be pending review of the royal auger of House Iris. The party of the second half will carry all the authority of the amethyst crown in this matter.

The pressure would be ungovernable, she had decided.

She had worked hard, her whole life, to achieve the rank of magister. That position is not just cherished for its authority but also its tenure. She was safe, happy even. Despite her battles, she was comfortable here. For even her battles were ones that she had chosen to fight.

This? This contract was not part of her choice. But who else could Victor turn to? In all of Okhram, there is no higher authority on the holy arts than her.

- The matter outlined, in which the employed will be working, will remain beyond the ecclesiastical realm.

Noone outside the church, anyway.

After all, the archbishop would be the primary candidate or perhaps the bishop ordinary. This line of thinking ended up bringing her mind to the next logical question of why exactly the church was not involved. Ignoring the fact that they would supersede her knowledge and ability, they would surely approve of something the crown wishes, however underhanded, and work for her majesty without question.

It would not be the first time. If ever there were a matter that Mary was the authority on it would be just that: accountability of the church.

No, the only reason that the queen could possibly wish to keep this matter a secret is if her will went against the church itself.

Or the empire.

Mary chided herself for even thinking such a thing and decided to get back to the immediate matter.

- The employed's primary objective hereafter is gathering the means to weaponize the sexually transmitted disease known commonly as 'ancercy.' For all intents and purposes, the definition of weaponize is...

The list went on to define all the ways in which she was bound to do precisely what as instructed. This caused her mind to fall into pits and dark places where she imagined that loopholes or traps could exist in this contract – ones that the auger might exploit to betray her at the last moment of duty.

In wondering why she might propose to imagine something so cruel she remembered that the matter as a whole seemed underhanded. She got angry, then, that she simply could not let this matter go: what is her majesty Queen Charlotte Iris up to?

Mary began pacing. She walked back and forth across the length of her office with the three unfurled sheets of contract flapping in her hands as she scoured them again and again for rhyme or reason to simply figure out what the ulterior motive there was. And when that proved to be as fruitless as it had been all day she eventually turned to her shelves. Lined with tomes of the past and essays on history, she thought that the answer may lay in a previous royal stunt.

But the volumes, if they even knew at all, succeeded no information to her. And just as she groaned in defeat at their lack of wisdom, the door opened in time for Ahmar to witness her throw her arms in the air.

"Hello again," he smiled sheepishly. She glared back at him.

Then her eyes went wide as the presence of the highly confidential royal documents on her desk returned to her mind and sent her in a frenzy.

"Wait there!" She commanded while tucking the papyrus into her safe drawer, the one at the very top-middle of her desk, and locking it just to be sure.

"Sorry. Are you still going over the contract the auger gave you? I can come back."

"No, no. Do stay. I need a second mind…" She sighed and pulled a trunk over that she had used to store old books and quills. She sat atop its closed lid with a thump and offered the desk chair to her friend.

"Thank you." He sat down and gazed out of the window. While all offices had a nice view of the surrounding gardens, his was five floors lower than hers and much less nicer for it. He appreciated whenever he got the chance to see this sight - all the while Mary was appreciating the sight of his hair blowing in the gentle gusts of spring.

She sighed again. For the first time today her sigh was a longing one.

It is a great shame that Ahmar is too dense to detect this, however: "Oh, right. Sorry, Miss Culver. Please, how can I help?"

She smirked when he called her that.

"Well, I believe that what I am tasked with is... wrong. And even worse, I fear that the reasons I am being tasked with this are more immoral than that. I'm scared, Ahmar, and leaning on simply doing nothing at all."

His mouth parted softly to form a small 'o' as a silent gasp left his lips. He leaned forward and placed a hand - a gentle, kind, caramel hand – on top of hers that was resting on the desk. A blush dusted her cheeks as their eyes met in the small space between them.

"Oh, Mary. Irregardless of the situation, never ever in your life should you do simply nothing at all."

She swallowed, "I think that is what I am most afraid of."

"What?"

"Myself. Every avenue that's open to me feels like I am becoming a worse person because of it."

"Treason. Heresy. Inaction," he listed, earning a harder glare from her this time. But it softened just as quick for he was right.

Who was she to become? And what right did bloody Victor Redding have to march in here and change her life like that in the first place?

"It is said," she muttered, "that the call to arms finds us all one day." Ahmar laughed at that and she brought herself to smile. "I guess I should answer it, shouldn't I?"

"That's kind of what I'm telling you."

"But what if!"

He put a finger to her lips to silence her. "Here's a 'what if' for you. What if you, the esteemed Mary Culver, turn this down and the matter ends up in the hands of an actually bad person? An actual heretic, an actual traitor? What if, by doing this yourself, you aren't serving any dark purpose but controlling it and maintaining some light in there?"

She bit her lip. He made a good point. She hated when he made a good point. "That's two 'what ifs,' genius."

He grinned and tilted his head at her. "So tell me what it *will* be."

She bit her lip and nodded. "I'll do it, I think. I agree with you. If this is going to happen, whether I like it or not then I shall see that it is at least done in a way that I do like."

"Good girly."

She nodded her resolution again and thrust the key into the drawer. She started to open it, ready to dip her quill in ink and sign the bottom line before she realised that Ahmar was still present.

"Um, I believe you shouldn't be seeing this."

"No, yes of course." He stood up and looked down at his friend. She was smiling so vulnerably and her eyes were wide. He wanted to shake her hand or congratulate her or maybe say his farewell now. Instead he panicked and leaned down to kiss her on the forehead.

"Good luck, Mary," he mumbled before making a quick escape.

* * *

The entrance hall of The Spire is known as somewhat of a joke to the staff and students there. It is decorated in a disproportionately fine manner whereas the rest of the offices and lecture halls maintained more practical appearances.

While, say, Mary or Ahmar's offices were coloured the same grey as the stones that make the tower up, the foyer saw lavish wallpapering in patterns of brown and beige. Whereas the lecture halls had arched windows with no curtains and glass that pooled at the bottom, the entrance hall had brilliant red hangings over renovated, frosted windows with stained glass crosses in the centre.

To people on the outside, people like the auger who sat patiently on a velvet lounger, it promoted an idea of grandiose that would not be shattered until, too late, when a student had already enrolled.

Of course, the auger had already peered past that veil and was simply waiting for his potential new employee to return with some good news. It had been hours, unfortunately, but he was content in losing his consciousness in a deep meditative trance while he waited. He sat cross-legged on a plump sofa with his eyes closed and his mind directed at a floating charm before him.

It was a pentacle, silver, hanging on a thick, black thread. It hovered in a mild up and down bob as he concentrated on keeping it there. It was a pointless exercise that offered nothing to him but protection in a room where he was perfectly safe – he simply decided that practice would be a good way to pass the time.

And it was until he found himself awoken.

"Hello? Hello, Mr Redding was it?"

A voice penetrated his focus and brought him back to the awakened realm. His eyes first turned to the grand clock on the wall above the entrance to note how long it had been since he started before he turned to see that it was Mary's western friend who had roused him.

"You dare disturb my practice?" he snarled and let grimace show aplenty. Ahmar just thought him naturally grumpy and let the animosity slide away.

"Sorry, I didn't realise. I just wanted to say that I'm going now, but it was nice to meet you, my lord."

Victor continued to sneer. He didn't say anything; just stood up and looked down at the shorter man.

"Right then. Just wanted to say... well goodbye. And please be fair to Mary she... she is a good woman." He gave a bow of his neck and left with a smile.

The auger considered what exactly he might say to illustrate his disdain for being instructed, in any manner, by a lesser man but was interrupted by the arrival of the woman in question with precisely the signed contracts he desired.

She held them out proudly and kept her chin high as she returned them to him, "I would be honoured to assist the crown in this matter, my lord."

He looked down at them and finally abandoned his musings to retrieve the documents and store them within his shoulder cape.

"Yes. Very good."

Mary let her arms relax. "Is everything alright, m'lord."

"I was just thinking that after this ordeal is over it might be the auger's next task to investigate the integrity of this university and the kind of... rabble, they employ as staff."

"Oh I could not agree more, my lord. There are some people here who would completely undermine my authority simply on the matter of my sex. Me. The magister! Can you believe that?"

He dismissed her naivety, "on another matter, now that you are under my employ it will be Redding. I already tire of 'my lord,' frankly."

Mary let another anxious breath out, glad for the informality.

"Of course, Redding. In fact, I am ready to begin right now, if you have a transport?"

"The auger's carriage is on the road. Follow me and share your proposal."

She nodded and let him lead the way. As they went, Mary made no effort to tell people she was leaving. Despite the academic term coming to a start, there were no schedules in circulation yet so she had organised a cover with Ahmar for any of her potential lectures. In fact, she had named him the substitute magister while she was away – a fact she was delighted to imagine would piss the other staff off to tears.

"Do you remember that I mentioned a mayor when we spoke? One who, rumour has it, has a son infected by ancercy?"

"Yes. How did you come to hear such gossip?"

She turned red at his last word, "um, I actually try to keep tabs on all happenings in our empire's churches. So when I was talking to some new students - just arrived from the Weyland border - they had said that priests were becoming increasingly annoyed by the Mayor of Whitley Moor as he had spent days begging at their doors for assistance."

"Assistance in the matter of his son?"

"Yes. As it turns out, a lot of people on the border, in Whitley, Summerset and Leechacre, are seeing rising cases of ancercy."

"Hm. And you think there is a correlation with the proximity to Weys?"

"What? Of course not. This is because of their distance from the central tower – the palace. The further away a town lays from the economic centre, the lower its average income."

The auger let out a deep 'hah!' "So the cause is not foreigners, it is the poor."

Mary furrowed her brow. This man lacked a severe degree of reality that irked her to the bone and started to make her rethink her prior cooperation. "Well, like you say. It is correlation, not causation. The poor who cannot afford a cheap whore might attend a gathering of cultists to lay with a daemon instead. Or just summon one themselves."

"They could marry and lay with their *wife*," the auger suggested.

Mary opened her mouth to continue enlightening him to what life was like for real, actual people before reminding herself that it was too late to renege on their agreement.

And as such, they would have to get along.

"Redding, my point is that there are rising cases in these towns so it would go unnoticed should we... experiment."

"I see," he trailed off. "I like your cunning, Miss Culver. And I accept your proposal." They arrived at his carriage. It was a deep, red box with two horses at the front: one pure black and another bright white. A patient driver was stood holding the door open for them as they approached.

Gallantly the auger stood aside and gestured for Mary to enter first, a motion that made her feel ill. She did still enter first, though, sitting on the blood coloured cushions of the pure black, wooden seats.

He followed her in and the door was closed behind them while the driver remained at the window awaiting his instructions.

"Which of the border territories do you propose we perform your experiment in?" Victor inquired with more eagerness than made her comfortable.

"Well. It does not matter, I suppose. But if we could observe that mayor's son it would be a great help. And we could lodge at the mayoral hall. So, Whitley Moor, I suppose."

Victor nodded at the driver who moved to take the reins without a word.

"Whitley Moor it is," the auger said giving Mary another one of those dreadful grins.

Lobelia

Queen Katherine's carriage was a truly royal affair.

Pulled along by three brown, muscled stallions, it was as much a living room as it was a mode of transport. Rather than two cushioned benches the queen and her daughter Lolita sat opposite each other on two veritable chesterfields. They were green, of course, a deep emerald green that complimented the ebony wood of their vessel.

A diamond shape of nine miniatures hung in silver, oval frames on the wall opposite the door with a sizeable square window on each side of them for the two passengers to look from. The portraits themselves displayed the Lobelia lineage of five kings and one queen dating back to the founding of the five kingdoms; the remaining three frames were empty awaiting a picture of Lolita's older brother on the day that he would ascend to the throne - and then his progeny after that.

Whispers say that on the day of the coronation of the ninth monarch, their emerald crown will fall into the hands of another great house and the portraits would be replaced. Lolita knew that not to be true, though. After all, her mother's spirit would surely fight off any offenders from beyond the grave with more strength than her bravest knight.

She also knew it to be nothing more than superstition just because it is a superstition. Surely, when the ninth portrait is filled they would just change the pattern to fit more in, right? Maybe she had to work on her whimsy...

She imagined, then, what the carriage might look like a thousand or two thousand years hence with a portrait on every empty space of the wall they can find; each like an eye watching the passengers. She looked down to see the green and gold woven rug laying on the wooden floor – she toed it to make sure it was still there and not replaced by a million watching eyes of her ancestors. She shuddered.

"Are you alright, dear?" Katherine asked.

Lolita nodded, "just a bit chilly. Countryside air."

Katherine mumbled her agreement. "I cannot imagine how the lesser houses live in those estates. I would much rather be surrounded by leagues of buildings than acres of field. A hideous living – and for people who enjoy *horses* of all things."

Lolita giggled, "do not let Kilmartin hear you. He very much loves keeping the royal steeds."

"Then let us be glad he shares our appreciation for urban living."

The two smiled widely together.

Outside their carriage they could see that they had just travelled into the Summerset countryside: the trees were becoming droopier and the grass much taller as they approached the moorlands of Whitley. As much as the pair could stand staying here they both agreed that to take a trip further south to Leechacre was a step too far.

While they had enjoyed a holiday one year in an auntie's home in Pool - the neighbouring harbour town to Leechacre – that had very much been within their urban prerogative. The latter town was rather a miserable spotting of villages amongst wet fields and a depressingly rocky beach. Nothing like the imperial harbours at Pool.

"While we have the time, I was wondering if I could ask you about something, mother." Lolita was rarely shy but she kept on nervously poking at the carpet with her foot as she spoke.

"Anything, sweetheart."

"Could we discuss the baptism?"

Her mother smiled, "we have not had time to go through the specifics together, have we?"

Lolita shook her head. In the past few weeks there had been no mention of it at all until suddenly, two weeks before her birthday, the queen had started telling Lolita all about interviewing witchers and choosing gowns and finding a suitable cathedral. All the princess found was that she had no time to ask any questions.

"Well its nothing to worry about. Not really. The main bit is the submersion, laying down on your back and then tipping your head so that just your eyes are dipped in without letting your whole nose go under. Like we practiced, remember."

"Is holy water all too different to regular water?"

"It is only lighter in colour. The big difference is that it can be filled by the Lord's presence. It is through these means that you will meet the whisps."

"Why is it a pagan practitioner who performs it then? Will the archbishop be present?"

"Of course he will." Katherine sighed, having put this conversation off for a reason. "Witchers are needed to perform a royal baptism because divination is... not holy. But not unholy either!"

"Oh," Lolita frowned. "Do not all girls receive this then?"

"Just the special ones," her mother answered, "everyone else gets a regular, Bill-approved baptism. Not that ours defies the Bill either, of course!" Her mother laughed nervously, "the Bill of God describes the old kings witnessing their destiny at the hands of a pagan. The only difference now is that we employ them to do it rather than enslave them. Most of us, anyway."

"Have you read the Bill? All of it?"

"Honestly? Yes. Every word. And I am sorry that this is how you must find out but after your baptism you will be enrolled in classes to study our scripture as well. A rather boring but necessary business."

Lolita smiled her good girl smile. "No, it sounds exciting. Or interesting, anyhow."

"And for the baptism; are you scared?"

"I don't think so. I believe in my future; I'm not scared if it's good or bad."

"Good gi-"

"I am scared of the witcher though…" The words came out in a whisper. Her mother's face softened and she moved across the carriage to sit by Lolita's side and wrap her arms around her shoulders.

"Oh, honey, whatever for? Has he done something? Has any witcher done something to you?"

"Nothing like that I… I just do not understand his work. Or any witch or witcher or other practitioners of magic."

Ketherine pulled her lips together to stifle a laugh, "oh, honey." She removed herself, stood up, straightened her dress and returned to the sofa on her side of the carriage. She sat in her usual portrait-like pose with her hands in her laps and adopted a teaching voice.

"You should not say 'magic' it is immature."

"I believe I heard Mister Magellan call it magic."

"My point exactly." She cleared her throat. "When a paladin smites his foe or when an exorcist banishes a spirit. When a bishop ordains a minister or a priest delivers communion. These are times that are," and she continued reluctantly, "no different to when a witcher might cast a spell." Lolita's expression caused her mother to put up a hand and command her to wait until she was done. "First off, you are a lady. You will use the proper terms, not 'magic.' If it is smiting, exorcism, ordainment or even transubstantiation – you will call it as it is."

Lolita nodded quickly.

"A person can do these things, whether it be holy, pagan or infernal, because of the element of the realm. The church would call it faith. To some it is the earthblood and to foreigners it might be mana. But in the proper tongue we call this force-"

"Ether," Lolita finished.

Katherine gave a coy smile, "now where did you hear that word?"

Lolita looked embarrassed. "When God made the realm He dubbed it Etherium to mean world of ether," she recited the Bill perfectly. "That, and I remember it from one of the tales you would tell me."

The queen's few seconds of being impressed by her daughter faded with a scoff. "Of course, The Princess Privateer. I knew that book would rear its head again one day. Now listen, ether and casting is not a topic for a young lady to discuss so you will leave this conversation in the carriage, do you understand?"

Lolita nodded again. Her mother's face remained coy as she broke the silence once more, "since when have *you* been reading the Bill, anyhow."

Lolita smiled, "I don't. Sometimes Aaron reads it aloud to me while the maids do my hair."

Katherine frowned. "your brother should not be in your chamber while you change. It is improper."

"It is just while my hair is styled!" She protested, "it takes so long sometimes and is so dreadfully boring."

Her mother shook her head, "that is all well and good but you best hope that Anna is not one to gossip with the other staff. The last thing we need is the servants thinking that our family does things by halves."

"Do not worry, I trust my lady's maid dearly." It was Lolita's turn to sound teacherly, "and is it not respectable that I am learning our creed?"

Her mother tried desperately not to smile in that moment. After deliberation she decided, "I should certainly hope to hear good things from your faith teacher in a few months then."

Lolita grinned and their caravan continued on throughout the daylight hours.

Culver

"I had not imagined that when you said you had a matter to attend to before we began the experiment that you quite meant *shopping*, Victor."

Mary had been scowling from the moment they entered Union Square. It was an overcrowded collection of market stalls all covered by varying colours of cloth to protect from the elements while stocking large, precarious piles of produce. There were men behind them all shouting at passersbys to get the freshest vegetables this side of Belgrave while some even claimed to have fruit that was handpicked in exotic lands. What these people really had was pineapples and that did not amuse a scholar or a royal officer.

Although she did want to know quite how they had got them so far south and still all the fresher.

"Redding," the auger corrected. "And of course you hadn't. It is not of a woman's mind to think further than her own scope."

She bit her tongue to stop it lashing. "Still, the mayor's office was more than happy to feed as well as house us. Unless you are saying that you enjoy the culinary arts."

He scoffed, "that is a job for chefs and wives." He turned to look down on her, "and do you genuinely believe that that man's kitchen is stocked with anything but lard?"

"I can't say I have ever met Theodore Rushings in person, *Redding*."

"Then you might think to prepare your peripheral vision," he chortled.

'At least he makes himself laugh,' Mary thought as she continued to follow behind him and carry his woven bag of various healthy foods. Even she had to admit it was admirable to see him care for his body just as much as his soul. Even if it looked silly to see such a grandstanding man compare the sheens of two perfectly identical apples.

"I should like an onion too," he said as he handed the copper crows to a jolly woman behind a pile of orchard fruits. "Actually," he said looking her in the eyes, "might you know where I can procure roots here?"

The woman seemed to blush, "oh, um, yes m'lord. That would be Gary's stand by the fountain, m'lord."

"Excellent."

"However, m'lord, he is indisposed today."

Victor shot a look of grave disappointment at her that could shake the bones of any weaker being. "A merchant not working on a Monday? Has some new book of The Bill been released that I am not aware of wherein the Lord did have a lie in the day after he rested from creating the realm, hm?"

The seller choked on her words as she looked back and forth from the two customers and begged her own voice to say anything at all. Eventually Mary stepped in to thank the woman for her help and steer her boss away from the situation.

"Look, we can 'procure' an onion or two tomorrow. You have plenty here for days of feasting. Now please can we get on with the experiment, *m'lord*."

He did not seem impressed with her impotence.

"Fine. But I will hold you to your word on the onion debacle should I have to drag you back here by your hair, do you understand?"

Her bottom lip quivered, "yes, Redding."

"Good. Go on then. Lead me to this cabal you claim lies hidden beneath the streets." She stared him down for a second before thrusting the bag of food into his hands and storming out of Union Square.

She led him down the ways of Rincer Street and Sutton Drive and past the dead end of Mardon Crescent. They followed an alley that cut through Annum's Lane and finally led them to a church on the corner of Rewbridge Road. It was one of the quainter ones, clearly Revolutist in its minimalist décor. Just rows of wooden pews and a measly platform with a bare lectern. But the inside was of no concern to them as they instead made their way around the back to where a cellar entrance lay. It was in the floor and was locked up tight with a rusting chain and padlock.

Once there, Mary made a proud expression and put her hands on her hips. She stood there, waiting for the impending questioning as the auger moved his judgemental expression back and forth between the lock and the woman.

Eventually he spoke, "am I being led to believe, Miss Culver, that there are devil worshipers at work on consecrated ground? Well?"

Mary's body slumped, "well, yes, actually. I'm certain."

"And why are you so certain?"

"Because when we arrived at the Mayoral hall I approached William Rushings and asked him where he summoned the devil that he had so openly lay with." A furious expression began to rise on Victor's face as Mary let a tangent run, "and then he pointed out that it was his dad who spread the whole business about town, not him, and then-"

He interrupted her by tightly gripping her arm and pulling her close to his face so that she might not misinterpret his words; "I most certainly hope that you did not let slip our task here. That would be in violation of your contract – an act surmount to treason!"

Her eyes went wide, "n-no I lied to him, Redding. I told-told him that we were here to cure ancercy. That is what were up to. I gave him a noble lie, Redding, that is all."

He kept his vice grip on her arm as he analysed her and pondered the validity of her decision. Eventually, he let her go and she rubbed the sore area diminutively. "That lie will serve us well. Fine, we shall operate under that bluff for now. But do not presume to act so vehemently without my permission first, do you understand?" As the question left his lips he took a step toward her. She recoiled, leaning her bruised arm away from him.

"Yes, Redding," she replied.

"I think we should return to 'my lord,' for now."

"Yes, my lord," she mumbled. She looked down at her feet and stood there in silence until he spoke again.

The auger turned his attention to the padlock on the door and let his finger trace the wands on his belt.

"After I break in here, what are you proposing we do, exactly?"

"A-actually, my lord, if I may," she took a step toward the door and he moved aside for her. "William already showed me how I might gain access. Secret club knock and all that."

She stood before the lock and took a deep breath in. She held out her left hand with two pointed fingers and then pressed them to her lips where she whispered into their tips. The words she said were Calarian:

Nigrum cor Mara, et ortu stellam orientalem.

Secundus adventus aeternitatis et os bestiae.

The tips of her fingers blackened as she pulled them away. When she moved to push them against the cold metal of the lock, their darkness slipped into it leaving her fingers the normal, pale colour again. From there, the chains turned translucent as if they had become a spirit themselves and the door was now viable to pass through for the next five minutes.

Between the heavily Extenic witcher and the honourable magister of worship, the spoken words were clearly understood – unfortunately to both of them, they didn't translate into anything particularly exciting and so they went on without another thought on the matter.

"I will go in alone," she said, "If I am permitted to. I believe they would not be trusting to an auger, my lord."

He grunted his assent.

"Once inside, I will use our established bluff, no doubt at least one of them has contracted the devil's mark, and they will assist in whatever I ask."

"And what is it you are planning to ask of them."

She looked around to ensure that they were truly alone. She leant forward then and whispered it in the ears of her boss.

His eyes widened in surprise and also a degree of pride.

"My dear," he said as she returned to where she was standing, "I am starting to feel confident again in my decision to hire you."

She hummed in agreement. "Go on, then. I approve. I shall wait on the bench by the front for your return. I'll ensure that the meeting is not interrupted."

"Thank you, m'lord."

She took the dive as soon as he was out of sight. Pulling the two wooden panels open, she heaved herself down the ladder that lead into the church's cellar. Behind her, they seemed to close all on their own and she heard a clunking sound just after as if the chains had refound their physical form.

The actual hallway was much different to its non-subterranean building. Whereas the church was maintained, and any moss or lichen had only come from recent months, the cobbles that held the underground walls up were positively overgrown by wrapping roots and patches of fungus. Even the consecutive wooden plinths that prevented the dirt above from suffocating everyone underneath were splintering, damp and growing patches of mould.

Cast-iron sconces were protruding in intervals but only about a third of them were lit as the space in the cages of the others seemed to be victims of nature's course as well.

At the end of the hallway was a more brightly lit room hidden behind a large wooden door with an iron grate for a window. It had a big, circular handle and an upside down pentagram scratched into the centre of the wood.

"Bit on the nose," she muttered as she approached. Although she did appreciate some other pieces of graffiti scratched into the wood as she walked along. There were far too many pentagrams and pentacles – in both positions – but also there were crude drawings of goat-headed figures. Alongside them, she counted two ouroboroses, five leviathan crosses and a myriad of alchemical symbols of seemingly random variety. She found herself glad that these were amateur occultists because a channel of ether through here would turn this tunnel into a vortex of chaos.

Amateur, but still capable of performing the task she needed, Mary reminded herself.

When she reached the door, she thought a moment on whether she should enter unannounced or simply knock and wait. She imagined what it would be like if she walked in during a ritual and they confused her for something summoned. The thought made her chuckle as she followed through with the decision to just knock.

When she heard strong footsteps approach she stepped backwards to allow the door to swing her way. Holding it open was a rather tall person in a red cloak lined with cream fur and a great aurochs skull on their head. Yellow irised eyes peered through the holes and in their free hand glinted the dark steel of a dagger curved like a reaver's talon.

"Name yourself," the person spoke in a deep voice but it was still clearly a woman's.

"Mary Culver. Magister of worship at The Spire. I am here in Belgrave to perform an experiment and require help from your... organisation."

The woman sighed. She sheathed her dagger and gently lifted the skull from her head. She shook out her hair and looked back at Mary with an expression of disdain.

"You can say cult, you know, it's what we call ourselves."

"Oh. Right. Well, would you help me?"

"The Spire you say? We have a rather large sect in Okhram's university town. Why not ask the Newbridge chapter for help with this work?"

"Because I did not know there was a chapter in Newbridge, never mind that you expanded beyond these sepulchre walls."

The woman's hands tightened on the skull, "so how *did* you come to learn of us?"

"I followed up with a recent acquaintance of yours. William Rushings."

The woman grunted but loosened her grip again, "oh for- does a blood oath mean nothing to people these days! It's like he wants to be cursed."

"You made him take a blood oath?"

"Of course I made him take a blood oath, look at us!" She gestured aggressively at her clothing. "The usual, you know – betray our secret and the blood moon will gleam your soul etcetera, etcetera."

"Oh dear." Mary coughed, "anyhow, would you be interested in hearing me out."

"I may as well," she looked Mary up and down. "Come through and address the council. I am Mother Lianna. Be sure to address *me* as such when you enter." She tilted her stern face into a somehow more serious look before returning the aurochs skull to her head. When it was on, her demeanour seemed to shift to something a degree more elegant as she walked ahead with a smooth gait.

Mary followed and turned a sharp corner into an incredibly large chamber overlit by many, many candles.

Judging by the big, square recesses that could have held great distillation barrels, this room was once a wine cellar for when this church had an Extenic following. These days, the Revolutists did not need so much blood of The Enemy so this cellar must have fallen into disrepair until it was claimed by the Whitley chapter of whatever this larger cult might be.

In total, there were eight members present, Lianna included.

When the Mother stopped she held out an arm and indicated for the Magister to walk and stand in the centre of the perfect circle that everyone else seemed to be stood in. She wondered if they always stood about in geometric shapes or if they had quickly shuffled into one when she'd knocked on the door.

When she looked at them all she saw that they were each wearing unique animal skulls on their heads and the same red and cream cloaks over their shoulders. Mary could only clock that dark, curved dagger on one member other than the mother, though: the thin, muscled man stood beside her. Mary presumed, then, that this might be the Father or some other parentally inclined leader. His skull-helmet-mask was the narrow, pointed skull of a reaver.

The only other feature that marked the group's invasion of this space was that overwhelming mass of candles around the room. The sticks were all either red or white and melting at different degrees. The red theme continued into all their wine glasses that happened to be filled with an uncomfortably crimson liquid.

"State your name and rank for the council." It was the male leader who spoke in a voice that was two-fold deep in tone. It echoed throughout the cellar and threatened to rumble the cobbles out of place.

"Mary Culver," she repeated, "magister of worship at The Spire."

She was starting to get sick of hearing her title, feeling a bit like an imposter each time it was aired out. She also felt like she was spinning as all the yellow eyes around her dug into her soul, each a pinprick on her person.

The Mother spoke next, "what is your purpose here, so far from home?"

"I am on a mission. My work brings me here as I wish to find a cure to ancercy."

Soft gasps came from the onlookers and they all tilted their heads to whisper amongst themselves. The Father held out his hands to silence them and they were indeed silent. He spoke next, "and how would you enlist us in this crusade?"

She swallowed nervously. "I need to study the means by which ancercy is contracted. We know the basics – lay with an infernal creature. But what physically is happening when that occurs? How is the disease transferred from shade to man?"

"And you suppose us experts on the matter, do you?" The Mother asked.

"I suppose you experts on the art of summoning daemons. That is what specifically I need from you." She let her voice rise now as she made her plea with more confidence, "I should like you to summon multiple spirits for me, by whatever means you like, and then send them to share a bed with whores across town. Each would be given instructions to make their circumstance unique. In the morrow I would then survey the prostitutes and see who has and hasn't contracted ancercy. With this data, I should be able to make great leaps into developing a cure."

Mother Lianna turned her head and her eyes met the Father's. They nodded at each other before turning to face forward and joining hands. They also then joined hands with everyone else in the room until a circle of limbs was formed around Mary that made her deeply, deeply uncomfortable.

Her worst fears told her that they were casting some sort of spell or engaging in a ritual. After a few deep breaths she realised that this was simply a means of communication for them and that they were mutually deliberating on an answer for her.

All she could do was pray that they saw the worth of a cure, not just for them but for their entire group, and sign on to help her.

Not that there would ever be one that is.

Finally, their hands fell down to their sides and the cultists all looked at Mary as the Father delivered the verdict:

"We will help you in this endeavour. Let us begin summoning creatures to infect the whores of Whitley Moor!"

A chorus of cheers rose that sent a sinister shiver down Mary's spine.

Abernathy

"Off to the boxing is it," Harlot teased.

The early afternoon sun grazed over the cobbles of Annum's Lane as the mistress of the Happy Huntress made a slow walk back to her place of business. Past the butcher's shop she went, making an effort not to look inside. Then past the grafters in a building site, making every effort to catch someone's eye. And finally, past the house of a dear friend where she made a stop as she happened to catch him on his way out.

"Back from a shag is it," Adam mocked successively.

He turned his key in the lock and shot a cheeky grin her way. While the two had never slept together he had always made a customary gaze up her body as every time they met she happened to be wound up in tight attire. 'A wench's bodice' he called it once, something that Harlot never repeated aloud but always mentally thought off whenever she dressed for a bit of on-site work.

"I can't say. I always respect my client's integrity."

"Come off it. We all know you're doing the boss who sells roots at market. What's-'is-name."

"Gary," she answered, "not that that is confirmation nor denial." She gave him a stern look that sent the two into a quiet giggle.

They both walked around the corner together enjoying the day's nice breeze. Spring was reaching its latter days and the warmth of summer months were beginning to rear. Harlot could not stand the way it made her sweat through a corset but still she much preferred it to freezing her nipples off whenever a client insisted on taking her in the winter time outdoors.

"Go on then. Where are you off to?" she asked. "Surely people aren't buying with so much light out?"

"Nah. No deals until nine of the clock, my lady. But you are going to hate me, I think, for my answer." He chewed on his bottom lip.

She looked at him aghast and thumped his arm, "you are heading for the boxing aren't you? Adam!"

"I know, I know! But the danse-powder has been moving well recently and I'm all clear with the bookies now." He fumbled on his words, "I'm feeling lucky, you know?"

She shook her head disparagingly but made no further comment. The conversations between a whore and a drug dealer were no place for morals so the gambling matter rooted no further. She just happened to worry for him and the way he tended to bet on the losing side.

That didn't stop him from wearing an eager smirk though as they trundled down the road together under the unlit street lamps.

As they went, she took his arm under hers and they chose to remain close. It was a silent agreement they had where his masculine presence might protect her from the sudden approach of clients who weren't willing to pay but still desperate to get off. When that did happen, she just let it run its course before going and finding Adam at his flat and having that extra bottle of gin to wash the memory away.

For now, their hooped arms would do.

"Might I see you on your way back?" She playfully moved her hips in his direction as she disembarked at her own place and moved to unlock the door. The outside of the Happy Huntress was not as much of a sight as the inside; just a blacked out window and a sign dangling from a metal rod that had the name painted in white lettering.

She had spent a lot of her earnings on refurbishing the inside, making it cushy and seductive to give her reputation some sparkle. What she had neglected to invest in was the simple necessity of a picture to represent her place of business – a matter she had sorely learned about after increasingly realising that a lot of her clientele were not exactly literary inclined.

"Let's just say," he spoke slowly in a mock of seduction. His hand wound around her waist and played on her hip, "that you will be the first to know if I'm lucky tonight."

She snorted and pushed him away, "that is an improper way to speak to your lady."

He bowed at the neck and grinned, "if I may be dismissed."

"You may," she grinned back shooing him off. He walked away and around the corner giving Harlot a proper wave as he went.

For a moment, just before stepping over the entrance, she wondered what it might be like to lay with a man like Adam. What it might mean to stay the night with a man who you were so in sync with that your goodbyes were an occasion to smile not frown.

She liked that thought indeed.

Still, she left it at the doorstep and went in to prepare for any clients of the night. Mondays were her quietest, everyone is too tired from returning to work after all. But she still had to be ready, unable to afford turning money away.

So she headed into the back room, into what constituted as her measly kitchen, and pulled a dirty, greyed cloth from a countertop. She went further into the back where a wooden pale of cold water sat and dunked the cloth in.

It came out dripping and gave her hesitation. But she would need it so she went on to peel off her corset and shirt. They came off, sweat ridden but not unclean. While she would decide to keep the corset and her ankle-flashing skirt she would think upon which new undershirt she might wear the evening.

It was a necessary thought, or rather the act of thinking was a necessary distraction, as her body winced while she dabbed at her skin with the icy cloth. She moved to wipe away any sweat she had felt or dirt she might see and even tried her best to erase the eager marks that her previous client had left around her collarbone.

After her best efforts, she hung the damp cloth over one of the rails on her window to dry. She reached for a towel that she had left around here and eagerly pocked at her chest to dry it off and hopefully restore her warmth.

She bent down to pick the corset back up and decided to simply leave her undershirt there to be washed in the morning or whenever she might get around to it. She left her kitchen, pulling the door to a firm close before moving to the only door in her parlour other than the entrance. This was her wardrobe or as much as a wardrobe as an overstocked storage of skirts could be.

With a huff, she dropped the towel and corset on the floor again and tried to rummage deeper into the tarty colours of sluttish fabric and even tighter corsets. She finally managed to salvage something, or at least grab onto a shirt-like fabric, when there came a strong knocking at her front door.

It startled her and she instinctively let go, nearly falling over. The sound was unnerving. Most men who knocked on her door did so with a degree of shame like they were trying to knock quietly. Whoever this man might be was clearly astute enough to let himself be known – and in broad daylight too – as a purveyor of brothels.

Harlot cleared her throat and prepared to yell for the man to wait a moment but then thought better of it. Instead, she pulled that towel off the ground and daintily held one corner just above her bosom so that it covered her chest while still leaving enough available to drive her client crazy.

"Coming!" She cooed.

She padded over to the door, took a deep breath, and turned the key in the lock. She could see an outline through the frost of the arched window on her door that showed he was standing awfully close; eager, she thought. She could shake a lot from his pockets.

When she pulled it to, she expected to see some ruffled vagabond perhaps leaning flirtatiously in the doorway or smirking in a discomforting manner that he might seem to think is hot for some reason.

Instead she saw a gentleman stood upright who was very clean. Cleaner than the mayor's son she had turned away a week or two ago. She shook that memory off and gazed further upon the new client: he was not just clean but groomed to a good standard. And while he had the rough face of a bloke it was not unattractive – she could admire the lines that showed hard work and the creases that betrayed years of smiling. He seemed like a whole man and that made her ovaries weep a lot more than that wretched mayor's son did, however desirable his appearance was.

"You appear to have caught me while I clean," she whispered. It was sultry and inviting.

The man stepped forward and took her hand immediately. She tried not to let her shock be visible as her arm tensed at the sudden grasp. When he pulled away she saw a generous pile of medallions left in her palm.

"You know what you want." She kept her voice at that low, seductive trill and moved backwards to the bed. With the one hand, she tossed the towel over to fall over the gentleman's head and cover his face. With the other, she slid the coins into her purse on the dressing table by the door. After tightening its strings she moved to lay on the bed propped up by her elbows so that when the man removed the towel and shut the door behind him he could bear witness to her form.

She let her eyes go big, soft and begging as she pushed out her chest. The man stalked over to her like a predator, the damp towel still in his hand. He pulled it up to his face as he reached the end of the bed and took a deep, audible inhale of it. He closed his eyes and buried his nose in the creases to lap up any remaining scents of her body left on it, however unhygienic.

She shivered to watch this and suddenly felt the need to cover her breasts. But she had also had worse clients, clients who demanded so much filthier of her, so she suffered the creature before her and allowed him to enjoy his kinks.

Apparently satisfied, he let the towel fall. He didn't drop it so much as any other person might. He just loosened his grip and the fabric slipped down to the floor. In just as fluid a motion he too slipped downwards crouching like a tiger to mount the bed in front of her.

His fingers came up to trace the bare skin of her feet on each side. They slid slowly upwards until his hands came to circle her ankles and soon he was fully gripping her shin. He moved up, his calloused hands covering her like a rough wind as they flowed like a force of nature up her legs. They teased behind her knees and traced around her thighs tickling her into a shiver. It was the kind of shiver that, despite being just a simple tickle, made men think they had some kind of magic pleasure touch over her body.

When he finally reached up to the delicate space between her legs he rose to make eye contact with her. Her thoughts had been distracted so his eye contact snapped her back to reality enough for her to make a begging nod at him. His flat smile widened. He looked down under her skirt with a great hunger in his expression as if he were to dive into a banquet. He readily licked his lips in preparation and Harlot steeled herself for the unwelcome feeling of a wandering tongue that did not know exactly what it was looking for.

'*His tongue,*' she thought. As it traced his lips, time seemed to slow down. A moment of cognition sharpened her senses to really focussing on this client's tongue. She tilted her head and pushed herself up to get a closer look so that she could confirm her disbelief. This man's tongue was forked at the end, lashing in two, wet, red prongs.

This client was no man.

"Daemon," the word came involuntarily out with her next exhale as she scurried backwards from the beast in human skin.

"Daemon!" she shrieked purposefully now, her fear erupting. In an instant, in less than a blink, the creature's face melted into an angry frown. It had an inhuman curve as his eyebrows flared up with grey hairs like an angered owl's.

It leapt upwards to bring its legs onto the bed so that it could make a slow crawl towards her with bowed limbs. Its neck seemed to extend as its tongue flickered out in her direction.

Inevitably she hit the wall behind her and for a second she could bring herself to do nought but stare at the shade's advance. As it came close enough to straddle her its rows of straight but yellowing teeth began to snap with chittering eagerness.

Her head tilted up to observe what she thought might be her death.

It wasn't until her peripheral caught a glimmer of silver that she found strength enough to move; her silver cross had caught her eye. It was a large fixture about the size of a baby. It had four, pale red rhinestones going down the length of it and one again on each arm and the whole thing was outlined in a thin black wiring.

She grunted as she made the effort to vault herself upwards. She did not need to stand to reach it just sit properly up so that she could twist and tear it from the wall. It had only been hung by a hook onto a nail so it slipped into her hands with ease as she cradled it against her chest begging for protection.

She closed her eyes then as the monster's spittle flaked her face. She searched every nook and cranny of her history to find a hedge she could summon, any verse from Sunday mass with her mother or any passage those angry lectures her father would give her when he read of the Bill during a punishment.

In panic, one came to her. It was a passage, just a short one that some other prostitute had shared with her a few months ago. She had dismissed it then out of wild disbelief that she would ever find herself needing it. But on that day, on that very bad day, she was thankful to the Lord that it had not escaped her memory.

It was a passage from the book of Iosefka:

In heart of hearts you know our name,

Our every gold our every shame.

You watch around and round the hour,

Yet still forsake our foe's devour.

Harlot's reciting of it was rushed and broken and stuttering. It came out less like a line of the good book and more like a slew of thrashing resistance.

But it worked. When she opened her eyes, she saw the results that her hedge of protection had borne as the silver cross between her breasts was now filled with a great, golden warmth. Furthermore, the curtains around her bed and even the sheets themselves had wound to tangle around the beast's body. They were chains of silk and bindings of satin that had started to drag the spirit away from Harlot's form and backwards off the bed. It resisted, clawing and screeching as more of its skin melted away to be replaced by scales and rough hide.

To seal her fate and banish the creature, Harlot thrust the crucifix forwards and finished the verse:

I swear my way, a whore no more,

And that I might find heaven's door.

Your light is bright but ours is brighter,

Thank you God for raising us higher.

The shade bellowed out, its head shooting upwards in an attempt to escape the pull back down to hell. Once its body had been slumped off of the bed, the floor where it landed had started rippling in bloody maroons and wicked blacks as the legs and then the waist and torso of the creature seemed to be consumed by the boards themselves. As it transfigured into its full body Harlot saw that it was a pale green with bright yellow eyes and brows that filled the room. Its mouth contorted into a turtle's beak and its desolate screams became ever bestial until at last the head joined its neck in being submersed.

The waves of hellish colour rippled outwards and dissipated as the sheets and coverings lost all stiffness and floated to the ground.

Everything was silent again and still just as before. Everything except her cross which Harlot cradled close as she curled into a ball and silently wept alone.

***

She remained in that place for the rest of the evening.

She prayed again and again and recited that same verse twice as many times. Whenever she dared, she lifted her head to look over at the spot where the spirit had been dragged down for fear that the hole might still be there and for it to come back through.

Eventually she would shake and shunt her head back into the ball tighter than ever before.

It wasn't until the clock struck twenty to midnight that she was moved to pull a limb over the edge of her mattress.

Someone else was knocking on her door.

So close the hunter's hour, she was scared; she unknowingly held the cross so tightly that it bruised the skin of her torso.

She tip-toed over, still topless and clinging to the crucifix, to where the brass key lay atop her dressing table and slid it into the lock. But before she could turn it the voice shouted in.

"Oi oi, you in there or what?"

It was Adam. She groaned and hurled the door open, forgetting her breasts were out.

"What's this? You know how to keep a guest, 'ey." She rolled her eyes and walked over to the wardrobe door to reclaim that shirt she had found earlier on. Adam let himself into the open door and sat on the end of her bed.

"Where's your cross got to?" She ignored that as well.

"What are you doing here, Adam, it's nearly curfew."

His lips pulled up at the ends and he tilted his head playfully, "don't you remember our chat, earlier?"

"Kind of? Oh, you didn't!" After weaving her buttons closed and pushing her plight away she came and sat at his side. She resented his presence at first but was starting to find herself glad for the distraction.

"Well let's just say my ledgers are very happy."

"That's a first. No, I really think that is a first."

"What can I say?"

"Thank God, perhaps."

"Since when were you such a holy roller?"

She looked away from him to hide her shame and thankfully he did not seem to see it from his stupor. He just sat there grinning like an idiot - at her, at the sky, at whatever.

"Are you going to celebrate?"

"Of course. In fact, that is why I came to your doorstep. Would you like to have dinner with me tomorrow? A nice dinner that is?"

She furrowed her brow, "you won that much did you?"

He looked proud, "more than enough for a prime cut from the butchers. Uh, don't worry, I'll buy it before you come over. I know you don't like the raw meat and that on display there, my delicate woman."

"Correct," she lied.

"So how about it?"

"I'll have to think on it."

"Come on. Surely there are worse dates."

"Yeah," she agreed. A flurry of past clients came to mind and the ways they had insisted on emulating romance during their paid time with her. Each one was more sickening than the last and she did her best to forget it.

Except there was one man whose face was stood out to her then in the topic of worse men: the mayor's son. No actually, the mayor himself who had been galivanting around town making a bigger fuss about this whole business with ancercy than the boy who actually had it.

And as his face swirled in her mind suddenly the events of the evening began to make a lot more sense.

"Hold that thought," she commanded. She stood up and neatened her clothes. She made a dash to the door and clutched the key in her hand. "Come on. With me."

"What? Why? I am tired. And it's late, soon enough-"

"I care not for the bloody hunters right at this very moment. Now come with me, I shall need a man's presence to give me authority."

Adam frowned but walked over to her side, "authority on what? Where are we going?"

"To the mayor's office. I had an assailant come to me earlier and I'm starting to suspect who exactly might have been behind it."

Lobelia

It was half past the curfew when Lolita's caravan arrived at the Mayor's offices and she yawned to reflect it. Normally long asleep by that time, she was thankful that her next slumber would not be in a loud inn nor an uncomfortable roll within a tent.

Although she would be lying if she said she wasn't disappointed by the building. On her way she had dreamed of a manor house with a great gate in the entrance way! One rather like Lanship House, the estate her cousin lived in at Summerset. Instead she found some government building with a double doors that connected directly to the same street that the commoners walked on.

It was... undignified to say the least but once again her sleep deprivation allowed for a bit of late night humility.

So while her company worked with the mayor's staff to bring their procession in and establish the rules of hosting a royal visit, the guests and the mayor all entered through the foyer.

Theodore went in first and held one of the doors open for the Lobelias. They simply waited for Manford to catch up and hold the other door open for them. Once inside, Lolita actually began to feel more at home – while it was not like Aunty Daisy's house, where they had stayed in Pool, it was still much grander than the outside had made it appear to be.

There was a great staircase topped by a red carpet and brilliant paintings of various members of the great houses who might have stayed there once before. In the centre of them all stood the largest portrait. It took up most of the wall above the stairway and was illuminated by the chandelier lights. It was a regal image of one of the former Viscount Azaleas in decorative military uniform. He had black hair that went down just over his shoulders and fell in thick waves. In his veined hands he held a silver orb with four sharp crosses linked together around the circumference – an artifact called the heart of Belgrave.

Lolita recognised it for it was currently sitting in a display case back at the palace. It was her favourite piece there, so beautiful without the need for gems or gold.

"If I may give a quick tour," the mayor began before looking over his shoulder to see his son coming down the stairs. He ignored him and gestured to the double doors on either side of the atrium: "here we have the archives, storage, kitchen and the like. And over there are the offices for administration and planning. If you should ever need me you would most likely find me in this area behind a desk or perhaps retreated to the drawing room."

William Rushings joined his father's side and gave a stiff bow at the neck for greeting, "your majesty. Your highness." He didn't seem to smile or have that sparkle of veneration in his eyes. His father looked up at the taller man with concern.

"Greetings," Lolita breathed after William's introduction. Her mother seemed to start talking with Theodore about some specifics of their stay but she simply blocked it all out as her attention had been taken by Will. While he did not seem to be entirely there himself, he was all she could focus on. She did not know why she felt like this, it was new and nerving, but for some reason her cheeks were turning pinker and pinker as she imagined running her fingers through the lad's soft, blond hair.

"And I would like to be put up in the Azalea suite," Katherine finished.

"Of course ma'am."

"Actually," Will interjected, "we already ready have guests in the Azalea suite." He maintained a deadpan frown, innocence in his eyes as he relayed the facts.

"Who?" His dad asked shakily.

"Who?" The queen demanded.

"It was a traveller and his employee. They arrived just this morning. He holds a letter of marque, father, so I gave him our finest room." He seemed to grit his teeth then, "I did not realise you would be bringing *the queen* back with you."

"Marque or not, we will relocate them immediately-"

Katherine stepped forward, silencing the mayor by putting a hand on his shoulder and moving him to the side. She held her chin up and looked down on his indifferent son. She simply repeated her question: "*Who?*"

"Who else?" Another man's voice answered from the landing atop the stairs. He walked down with an incredulous aura that made the mayor step back out of the way of a crossfire between his two houseguests. He pulled his boy by the elbow to stand with him.

"You are still a member of this imperium, whomever you serve. So you will recognise the emerald crown with the proper respect!" Katherine looked at Victor Redding as he made his galling descent into the hall. He had Mary Culver at his side, but she remained obediently quiet. Lolita was quiet too but that's because she couldn't seem to draw her eyes away from quite how round William's behind is – the whole politics of the evening were beyond her one-track mind.

Katherine snapped her to attention though and she eventually rejoined her mother's side. She gave a proper look to the other two for the first time and saw that she remembered the auger's face quite well despite it being three years since their last brief meeting. Except this time his hair had turned a very dark blue that it was almost black. She looked to Mary next and the two women gave each other slight smiles that seemed desperate to escape their handler's issues to go and have tea.

"Of course, your majesty." He craned his neck and then moved a rigid hand to Mary's shoulder, forcing her into a curtsy.

"Your majesty," she echoed in a whisper. She stood up again and locked eyes with the princess once more. She smiled, "your highness."

She could feel the poison look that Victor was giving her now as his facial expressions tried to convey how little he thought of her for undermining him. He continued anyway to make his stake quite clear.

"We will be happy to vacate your rightful choice of rooms, ma'am. But I should like to inform you, so that we are off to no false starts, that me and my ward," Mary crossed her arms, "are here to deal with a recent infestation in one of your towns."

"Now hold on," Theodore walked forward, "is that why you are here?" He turned to Will, "did you know this?" William just nodded. "I suppose that's why you let them stay then, isn't it, well. Well, that is why our majesty is here too I suppose so... it is fine, I daresay, if it is also fine with you, ma'am."

But Katherine had not yet decided. She sized Victor up and then made note of his wild change of hair colour. "When did you leave Newbridge?" she asked him.

"Just yesterday evening."

"And you arrived before us?" Theodore interrupted again.

"Yes, I thought so," the queen was not surprised. "You are still practicing your spells on those poor horses, then."

The auger shot one of his grins that caused Mary to withdraw a couple of steps. "Those poor horses managed to get us here quickly, didn't they?"

Lolita took a turn to frown then, "I remember now. That's why you left, wasn't it. Because we would not patron a man who practiced on living beings."

"Lesser beings," he corrected.

"Beings of the Lord's choir, none the less," Katherine said, pulling her daughter back. She gave her a look that said, 'stay quiet.' Lolita stayed quiet. In trying to cheer her up, though, Mary joined the conversation, "it was actually quite spectacular. Just a few short hours in the carriage, as if all was right, and then suddenly you are halfway across two kingdoms."

"That does sound spectacular," Lolita smiled.

"However cruel the method is," her mother spat. Mary and Lolita returned to their silences.

"Ah, I see." The auger smirked, "and you believe that my methods in finding my ancercy cure are to be cruel as well, do you?"

"Are they?"

Mary tensed and rubbed her arm anxiously.

"They are not," Victor lied.

"Then I suppose," she conceded, "that until I am given proof that you are acting in an underhanded manner, you may remain. After all, our goals are aligned and your purpose is noble."

"A thousand thanks, ma'am," he said, bowing again.

Everyone began to shuffle about then, making for stairs and doors, as the night time seemed to wind down. That was all until a final guest came to barge through the door way, however.

The doors both flung on their hinges as a bombastic woman strode through the entrance with a rather meagre looking man behind her. Harlot Abernethy stood in the home of the Rushings and looked deftly at the auger – who had a judgemental eyebrow raised – before turning her head to see where Theodore was standing.

"You," she growled. She pointed a heated finger and flicked it back and forth between father and son. The mayor looked astonished while Will remained ever pale and slightly nervous. "You both have been plotting, admit it. I-" she grabbed Adam's arm, "we, are here to get the truth."

"What exactly is happening now!" The powerful voice of Katherine silenced the room as Harlot whipped her head around to look at the older woman. She scowled at her for a moment before noticing the large, green gem set into her crown. It had such a pure, deep colour that it could only be *the* emerald and suddenly Harlot was filled with a deep regret for her actions.

"Oh. I- I-" She stumbled and Adam took over while Manford closed the doors behind them.

"We are so terribly sorry miss! Ma'am! Your majesty!" He bowed at the waist with a great reverence that seemed to temper the queen just a bit. "We are here because my... my partner, here, has been deeply wronged by mayor Rushings."

Harlot nodded along with his words liking how the 'partner' touch would strengthen their united front.

The queen breathed deeply through her nose before turning staunchly to the accused. "Is this true?"

"Ma'am! I assure you I have no idea who these two lunatics are!"

"I do," grunted Will. He cautiously lifted a hand in Harlot's direction. "She's the, you know, *the* whore."

"What have you done now, boy," the mayor's low voice grumbled with anger.

"Nothing!"

"Enough." Katherine silenced the room. As the conversation went on she had noticed that her daughter was trying to hide behind her dress as if she were six again. Lolita had taken to clinging to her mother's waist and staring from behind her at Adam. A terrified staring completely unlike the attention she had wanted to give, and receive, from William.

"First of all," the queen continued, "what is the matter with you, daughter dear? Are you well?"

"He's not... he's not real." Lolita remained fixed on Adam.

Adam tilted his head as the queen looked back and forth between the two.

"Whatever do you mean, Lolita?"

"Him. That. I feel sick in his presence. I don't like it, mummy," she pleaded.

Katherine knelt down to put her hands on her daughter's cheeks. "It is rude to talk about common people in such a manner. Even as a princess, remember."

"No," Lolita objected, "it is nothing like that. It is *him* specifically, he is making me feel disturbed."

"You are just tired, honey." She stood back up and signalled for Manford to come. "Take my daughter to her room and ensure she has what she needs."

"Very good, ma'am." Manford's professional disposition shifted as he held out his hand for Lolita to take. "Come on, princess. I should guard the room myself, if that is what you need to sleep."

Lolita took his hand and then desperately pulled herself in to cling to his whole arm. They walked like this as her mother bid her goodnight and she shuffled upstairs to the Azalea suite.

"I, ah, will remove our belongings, m'lord," Mary excused herself from the auger's presence once he nodded to her. She then gave a curtsy to her majesty before tailing after Lolita and Manford.

"What did the princess mean?" Harlot whispered to Adam. He just responded with an incredibly flummoxed shrug.

"Now you two!" The queen boomed regaining their attentions. "Make your case quickly so that we all might retire at some point before the hunt is over."

Harlot took a deep breath, "your majesty!"

"Ma'am," Adam corrected.

"*Ma'am*. As you know, the mayor's son has contracted ancercy at some point. Still he tried to lay with me. After rejecting him from my... parlour, his father went on to raise a fuss all over the kingdom. Earlier this evening, the issue escalated when somebody sent a daemon over to my place of work with the intention of infecting me!" As she finished speaking she turned her head towards the mayor and made a violent expression.

"Is that so?" the queen responded. And although she seemed to believe the whore's story it was the auger who received her accusatory glare instead of the mayor.

Abernathy

"I may have lived a sinful life, your majesty,"

"Ma'am," Adam corrected again.

"*Ma'am*," she hissed, "but that man over there is a true villain. A cultist. An infernal practitioner!"

"Yes. Yes he is," the queen's gaze remained trained on Victor, completely unconvinced that the mayor even knew how to do something like this. The auger just glared seethingly back at her. He went on to walk down from his position halfway up the stairs and interrupt the mayor as he tried to babble out some sort of incohesive defence that was somehow angry at every person in the room.

"Before we take the matter further," the auger said holding out his hands to bring everyone to a quiet, "I should like to ask, what was your name again?" He held his hand out in inviting.

"Harlot Abernathy."

"*Not you,*" he grimaced.

"Uh, Adam Sunvale, my lord."

"Mister Sunvale. Might I ask what proof you bring to us of this attack you claim went down."

His eyes widened. He looked down at Harlot to see that suddenly, all the fire in her eyes and spark in every avid limb had died down. Hope had left her and the excitement that managed to push her to confront the mayor was gone.

She tried to mouth words as she replayed the scene in her head again and again to find something she could pull out into real life but all she achieved was a re-traumatisation that set her breathing off in a panicked rhythm. She clutched Adams's arm and reassessed her situation as her desire for justice became the deep desire to flee. There was an auger there, there was the queen there! Multiple people in the room had the power to kill her for simply giving sex in exchange for money and she had the nerve to *demand*.

"I'm sorry," she says. It was a beg riddled with questions of mercy.

Victor shakes his head in disappointment. He begins to walk over towards her, intention in his step, and shrink her field of panicked vision as he gets closer. It's all Adam can do to cling on to Harlot as well.

But his approach is interrupted. Katherine asserts herself in front of Harlot's eyes and blocks the auger behind her.

This sets her heart to beat even faster until it is quelled by a soft hand on her shoulder as the queen gives comfort rather than cruelty.

"Do not worry. Your word alone is good enough for the crown."

The auger's approach stopped. The queen stood in the middle of the room and addressed everybody present once and for all.

"Until the matter is well and truly resolved," she said, shooting the words at Victor, "these two alleged victims will remain here along with myself and the amethyst auger. Mayor, prepare the Moonflower and Daisy suites for them respectively. I am now going to retire to the Azalea suite opposite my daughter and tomorrow I should like to sleep in, is all of that understood!"

A chorus of 'ma'ams' echoed in the hall as William, Theodore, Adam and Victor bowed their heads and Harlot gave a curtsey.

"Mr Sunvale, you and your partner follow me," the mayor instructed, "William, find Miss Culver and show her and the auger here to the Daisy rooms, will you."

William nodded and led the way up the stairs. Victor waited a moment, scanning Harlot's body for any signs of ancercy, before running after the Rushings boy.

Before the mayor left he addressed the queen a final time, "I can only apologise for all the trouble my offices have brought you, ma'am."

"Seeing as the problems were caused by outsiders I can only say it's fair that you keep your position here. Go to bed, and do not worry," she turns to look at Harlot, "for I believe this young woman's plight is credited to a force entirely unrelated to you."

With that, she left, taking the stairs quickly but elegantly as she ran to her bed.

"Before we go," Theodore began, "I do have to ask... is your name really Harlot?"

Adam smiled. Harlot gave a look of confusion. "I will answer that honestly," she began, "if you were to tell me why there is a son but no Mayoress in these halls."

The short man seemed ready to burst at this point. His red face grew purple and his whole body appeared to shake before he simply took off through the doors that lead to the offices, unable to speak out of turn with people who had the monarch's favour.

She turned to Adam and shrugged, "it appears we are showing ourselves to the Moonflower suite."

Adam held his arm out, "shall we?"

"We shall." She hooked their arms together and they walked up the stairs to explore the first floor in search of their beds.

They found them, eventually, after disturbing more than a handful of the Lobelia staff that were still dragging luggage around into the wee hours. It was two doors at the end of the eastern hallway. The wall in the middle of them had a brilliant painting of a bush of moonflowers. They were a trumpet-like shape and were elegantly white with hints of yellow inside. Some of them even had purple tinted ends to the petals.

Harlot was enjoying staring at the picture until Adam came up to tell her they were incredibly poisonous.

She shoved him away and they each went into their separate rooms to change.

And it was surely the nicest room that Harlot Abernathy had ever, or will ever, have. The bed was big and the windows even bigger. The wood of the floor was actually soft instead of splintered and the bathroom attached had a brilliantly cleaned tub in it. Tentatively, she traced the furniture, feeling the expensive quality of the carpentry that had gone into the dresser, the chairs and the wardrobe. Inside the latter she found a spare set of white night gowns that she laid on the bed ready to change in to. She forwent a second wash out of exhaustion and just moved to sleep as soon as she possibly could.

Unfortunately that would be postponed yet again as she came across an aberration while removing her shirt. The sleeve had snagged on something when she was pulling her arms through so she decided to strip the article off and stand in the flickering light of the lamp on the small coffee table by the window. Once she reached it she held her bare arm close to the flame and saw scales glinting across her wrist.

It was a small patch confined, she'd checked, to one on each wrist. They were a circle of green and silver scales that were starting to protrude from her body. She twisted her arm around to look for more and then blinked and blinked and blinked again until she was certain that what she was seeing was true. And it was.

Her next cause of action was to try and pluck them out as she ignored the obvious implication shouting from her head. But in doing so, she hurt herself greatly as if she was peeling her off own skin. She scratched at them next and even tried to burn them in the lamp's fire but all she kept achieving was self-harm again and again until eventually she sat on the end of the provided bed and accepted the truth of the matter.

She had contracted ancercy after all.

She took deep breaths as she slipped her skirt off before pulling the white night gown over her body and slowly walking over to the full length, oval mirror on the wall. She felt a glimmer of hope for a moment then as she drew up her sleeve and the reflection indicated that her wrists were normal, smooth and pale. Just skin.

But then she physically turned her head to look down at them and the scales had not gone. She came to some disappointing conclusion that the silver in the mirror was hiding her new qualities and returned to misering on the bed. And then, while lying on her back, she made a fist and thumped the mattress. Then she did it again and again before rolling over and punching directly into the mattress repeatedly. She grunted and sweated as she exerted herself into the soft bed, reinvigorated each time her sleeve slipped up and she saw a hint of the scales again.

At some point she shouted and then at a later point she roared.

Eventually she was interrupted when a knock came at her bedroom door and Adam's voice asked to enter. Harlot hurriedly pulled her sleeves down and held them in her hands before shouting that Adam could enter.

He was frowning as he peered through the doorway, "I, um, heard your tantrum. I didn't want to interrupt but you started to sound really... visceral. How are you doing."

She looked at him, still gasping to get her breath back, and then quickly glimpsed herself in the mirror once more. Her hair was dishevelled and sweat was dripping down from her forehead and off of her nose.

She looked back at her friend.

"I'm fine," she lied, "just searching for catharsis. Today has not been kind to me."

"Hey, at least the queen was."

She snorted at that, "for now."

"Do you want me to stay with you tonight?" He was sincere.

She shook her head. Her energy had not returned yet so her words were still rough from the damage to her throat, "you know I charge for that kind of thing."

She knew that humour would satisfy his worrying and gave a breath of relief when he accepted her excuses and they bid each other a final good night.

Once his footsteps had faded, she hooked a finger over the cuff of her left sleeve and took a last cursory glance at the infection. She just shook her head morosely before moving to search for a crucifix in her room. Oddly, there weren't any hung up on walls or tucked away in drawers. She was starting to get worried that she might not be able to sleep without one until she pulled open the bottom drawer of her bedside cabinet and found a crisp copy of the Bill.

It was a standard black, leatherbound copy with gold lettering and a red ribbon to mark your place. She decided that she was too tired to read it but still wished to keep it close in place of a cross while she rested.

So she set it on the countertop, tucked herself into the bed's thick sheets and pulled the text into the blankets with her. She held it close to her, burying it in her chest and curling her body around it as she let herself drift off into the night.

The last thing she remembered thinking before falling unconscious was that this copy of the Bill had felt warm like that silver cross did back home.

Lobelia

Lolita had fallen asleep the moment her head hit the pillow.

Weary traveling, boys both dreamy and disturbing and a heated argument about matters that she didn't really understand had all exhausted her and left her in a state that required twelve hours of sleep to recover.

It was the type of sleep that was so deep it transcended dreams and instead was only an abstract collection of the warmth and texture on an immeasurably comfortable bed. When she finally had woken up, all she could remember was seeing nothing through her misty eyes while still feeling the essence of sleep itself as she stretched her weary muscles in the midday sun.

While her mother had commanded that they be left alone to recover for however long necessary she had in fact given the precautionary command of waking them both by lunch time at the latest so that they might not sleep the entire daylight away after all.

But such a good sleep it was that when Lolita had rubbed the tired out of her eyes she found herself engaging in the most pleasurable of stretches as her muscles rejoined the world around her.

With one last yawn, she sat fully upwards to see that a member of the mayoral staff, in a black and white maid's outfit, was pulling the grand curtains open one by one while another stood at her side with a silver tray. Carried on it was a jug of chilled water which was forming droplets on the glass that called to Lolita's tender throat.

Quickly, forgoing decorum, she pulled a sloshing amount into one of the provided crystal pattern glasses before hungrily lapping it up. Some of it dribbled down her chin while the rest was consecutively swallowed until she drained the glass, returned for air and gave a gentle squeaking hiccup.

Satisfied, she turned to look at the woman standing politely at her side, the maid who had brought the tray, and started to say her thanks.

But the words caught in her throat.

Her pleasant morning was being disrupted by... by some sort of strange feeling that she could not place. While this woman, as well as the other, were both completely ordinary to a superficial standard, they seemed to give off a strange aura that something was deeply and terribly wrong.

"Are you alright, ma'am?" the maid before her asked. She was smiling until the distress contorted Lolita's face and gave her reason for concern.

"Please do not address me," she whispered vehemently. She crawled back into the safety of her covers and sat in the direct centre of the bed as she recalled what this feeling was.

It was the same feeling she had felt the night before when she met the character, whoever he was, that had accompanied that storming woman. The rather common looking woman. But he was common looking too, they both were. Both beings who had come from some drab alleyway, presumably, to pedal their immoral businesses except... he felt wrong.

She did not but he most certainly did. His face was average, weathered by poverty but capable of displaying great emotions. His clothes betrayed a personal history, his hair had seemed like it grew every day like any other persons but for some reason she had said the words: 'he's not real.'

She could not rationalise why exactly she had said those specific words but for some maddening reason, in this vortex of uncanny discomfort that she was feeling right now, those words made a great deal of sense. Those unexplainable words felt more natural to her than both that man and these servants had.

Again, that maid attempted to inquire – she stepped closer to the bed and asked what might be wrong but Lolita lashed out,

"Stay *back*!" She gripped the bedsheets tighter, "please, please do not approach me."

The beguiled maid stepped away and brought her hand up to chew nervously at her nails. She looked gravely at her coworker and the pair's expressions were strained and unsure what to do. Keep serving at a distance? Leave?

Before any of the three women could make a choice, though, a fourth party knocked on the door. Magellan's voice rang through:

"I heard a rather loud voice in there, your highness. Is everything quite alright?"

"No! I mean, yes it is but please, witcher, do enter!"

He tentatively peered around the door although actually seeing the room only confused him further. Three girls all apparently scared of one another and now looking at him with pale faces and wide eyes.

"What exactly is it that I can do for you?"

Lolita put his question away for a moment and addressed the staff, "thank you both for waiting on me. However, from now on, I will only be served by my lady's maid Anna. Please do not ever enter this room again."

They both look at one another. And then at Lolita and then at the witcher.

"Y-yes, of course ma'am," the one by the curtains answered.

"We are deeply sorry, ma'am." The other one lead the quick walk out and soon they were both gone from her sight.

"Please," Lolita returned to Magellan, "come by my side." She was calmer then and colour was returning to her face.

"Harsh words, ma'am," he commented as he approached her bedside. "Might I ask what that was about?"

"You might," she sighed, "but I would not be able to give an answer." She shivered and kept her eyes trained on the distance.

"Hey," he said as comfortingly as he could, "they're gone now. Whatever your gripe, it is dealt with. Relax, and I shall fetch this Anna for you." He turned to leave and make his way to the servant's quarters only to be stopped by the princess' firm grip on his shirt.

"No, please stay," she sobbed. He was shocked to see her suddenly so vulnerable, "please. She will already be on her way up so please do stay until she arrives."

The witcher nodded. He came and sat on the side of her bed and smiled softly at her. "Of course, ma'am." She managed a smile as well and settled to rest on the headboard of her bed. She cuddled her knees and waited as patiently as she could while the room descended into silence. It was nice for a while to be cradled back into comfort but eventually she got sick of watching Cyrus try and find a point to focus on and decided that she was ready to break through the mutual awkwardness.

She cleared her throat as not to startle him, "I see that your hair colour has changed again. I like it."

"It has?" His eyes frowned and he pawed at his head to pull a tuft into vision. His previously bright yellow had become a maroon red overnight. "Yes, it would have wouldn't it."

"Why did you change it, I much preferred the last colour."

"Ah, but I didn't. I was practicing magic last night, just brushing up before the ceremony. The ether does this your hair when you cast, you see."

"Oh wow," she leant forward intrigued. She stared at his hair, her mouth open, before continuing her questioning. "Would you be able to teach me more about ether?"

"Ah, now, I don't think your mother would quite approve of that."

Her face turned sour and after a moments consideration, he conceded.

"But," he reached a hand into his coat, "I will teach you about something that is technically holy, if you're interested?" He winked at her.

She nodded eagerly and watched as he pulled a small, hardbound book from his pocket. It was maroon like his hair but of a pinker shade. Printed on the front was a golden ankh symbol.

"This," he said, tenderly stroking the cover, "is my solemn oath."

"What is that logo?"

"The ankh. It is pagan or at least a middle way between the two worlds. It is considered to be the original cross – the point is that it represents both my pagan practice and the fact that the church is allowing me to practice at all." He shrugged, "there are ancient peoples who also associated it with eternal life, or something of that ilk, but that is a separate matter entirely."

"Wow," she reached out to touch it but Cyrus pulled it back. Her cheeks tinted red with embarrassment. "And, um, what exactly is a solemn oath?"

"All witches and witchers have one. It is what distinguishes us from oath-breakers."

"Oath-breakers?"

"Warlocks." He said the word with a degree of weight. "You see, long ago pagan practices were illegal. Punishable by death in some cases. Obviously this didn't stop people from doing it, it just made them do it more secretively and dangerously. It also didn't stop members of the great houses from employing warlocks for whatever pagan needs they had, they just tried to do it subtly."

"I had no idea," she looked at him in wonder.

"Mmm. Eventually the imperium gave up in their efforts to persecute warlocks and decided that it would be far more beneficial to regulate them instead. So they invented these," he wiggled his solemn oath in the air. "It became law that should a person wish to practice the pagan arts they must head to the church, stand before the clergy and swear on a small book like this. They would swear to only practice as a witch or witcher and never as a warlock. Part of that meant agreeing that God would stand as part of their pantheon, side by side any of the other deities they draw power from."

He opened his book then and flicked quickly through the pages, humming with interest as he picked out the best segments. "What exactly constitutes a witcher and a warlock is defined in here by many, many words. I have read it all, I physically would not be able to swear the oath if I hadn't, but that doesn't mean that it isn't a dreadfully boring business."

"I think it's very interesting," Lolita said. "So what exactly is the difference?"

"Everything written in here can basically be summarised as a list of spells that are either witcher spells or warlock spells. There are also many amendments for different situations where a warlock spell could be used in a witching manner and vice versa. It's a whole ordeal that somehow manages to keep being updated every day. Bleh!" He stuck his tongue out comically and made Lolita laugh.

He knew that she was no longer a child, not in any sense of the word, but that day was the day before her birthday. The day of her baptism, the day she would truly no longer be able to claim her innocence. So just for a few minutes, while they waited for Anna to come up and dress her, he would pull faces and tell her old stories just for the sake of putting tomorrow off for a tiny bit longer.

For both their sakes.

Culver

Mary was tired.

She had spent all morning trying to slyly interview different whores across Whitley in an attempt to gather some sort of practical information about ancercy.

As it turns out, however, every single target had contracted it. Every one!

She had instructed one daemon, one with a bull's head, to ensure that he did not release his seed into her. She had instructed another to only kiss the prostitute but to go no further than that. She had even instructed one of the spirits to simply suckle on their target's tits.

But they all still got it, however direct or indirect the sexual act was. She couldn't understand!

Back at the university, she had thought it would be an easy job: either it is the seed or the saliva or the rubbing of genitals. Once she had narrowed it down she could have made suggestions on how to weaponize that and the whole matter would be over.

But as she pulled back into the mayoral foyer she sighed a cumulative sigh of exhaustion for how much longer she would have to endure this quest... for how much longer it would be until she saw Ahmar again.

She leant against the banister at the bottom of the great staircase and smiled to herself as she imagined him struggling to drag a group of disobedient students through those Spire gardens and on a historical tour. Any other day, the idea would have irked her profusely as the thought of those students ridiculing Ahmar niggled into her brain.

But today she just thought of his reaction instead; how he would smile. That's all, just smile. And he would carry on with a limitless amount of patience that she could never dream to possess.

He is probably smiling in that very moment, she thought to herself.

She was not smiling.

She was stuck carrying a bag with two solitary onions in it up the stairs to her boss to fulfil a miserable promise she had made to him the day before. She groaned as she heaved her tired body to the Daisy suite where said boss awaited.

She walked past the door to her room and knocked on the connected one where she knew he was waiting. He answered immediately.

"Why are you so late?" He did not seem angry just unimpressed. As if he had completely expected this of her but still did not approve.

She bit her tongue. "I'm sorry. It took longer than I had thought to interrogate these women without letting on that I knew something more."

The auger grumbled at her, "you use the word 'woman' very liberally." He snatched the bag from her to inspect the onions she had brought. And in a turn of predictability he did not like them.

"I am most certainly hoping that the results of your primary endeavour do not turn out to be as disappointing as this one, Miss Culver."

He looked at her expectingly. "I will let you know once I have gathered the final result."

"Oh! Because all that time you spent outside today was simply spent on choosing the most unsavoury onions of the bunch, was it?"

"Our unexpected guest!" She quickly dialled back on her terse tone by adding a shrill, "m'lord," to the end of her exasperation. "I still need to interview Harlot."

"Of course. Our eponymous friend in the next suite. And how exactly might you interrogate this one without indicting us, hm? She is suspicious of the fact she has been had."

"My benevolence will mask any suspicious aura I radiate, *m'lord.*"

Victor knew that that one was spiteful but had to make the choice between chasing down the kitchen staff for his tailored lunch or vindicating Mary. In a huff, he walked in the opposite direction to her to make sure his plate had some colour on it other than the beige of meat and potatoes.

The magister instead made her way down the hall to the room with the moonflower painting between the two doors. It was a lucky guess as to who had slept where but fortunately, one of the doors being left carelessly ajar and another being pulled closed had given her intuition a bit of a clue as to which one had a sleeping woman inside.

She knocked on the closed door and hoped that she was not disturbing any sleep. She played with the hem of her sleeve as she wracked her mind for a plan of action for navigating her questioning until at last she realised: whoever was on the other side of the door had ignored her knocking completely.

She knocked again, harder but not insisting. Not only did the right person, thankfully, answer this time but she actually answered quite quickly and she seemed to be rather flushed about it. And then she looked at Mary and deflated completely, all colour draining. In fact, Mary had found herself disappointed... she was looking forward to seeing a busty maiden in her full regalia and not a moping woman in a night gown. It was ruining the amusement she had of the situation that was doubling as her coping mechanism.

"If there were not royalty in residence I would certainly not have answered the door for anyone." But she did not close it either.

"I am so sorry to disturb you. Harlot was it?" she cringed as she said the name aloud for the first time, "my, um, friend told me what happened after I left last night. I wondered if we could chat?"

Harlot gave her a scrutinizing look up and down. "Talk about what exactly?"

"Mary Culver!" She said quickly to stop herself before she said something rude in retaliation to the simmering analysis she just received. "I'm Mary. I wanted to talk about your... relations. The ones you say took place with a shade of some sort."

Harlot shook her head and heated her look even more, "you know, I expected this from that bastard friend of yours but I thought a scholar might be a wee bit more open minded to my situation. The ones 'I say' took place, hah! What are you lot then, lawyers brought in to handle whoever came for the pretty boy's head?"

"Pretty boy?"

"Oh don't act like you don't know. That Victor's an attorney for the mayor's boy ain't he. And you're his assistant!"

Mary tried not to smile. Her thoughts had been too consumed with pining for Ahmar that she hadn't noticed William Rushings at all. She cleared her throat and prayed her cheeks were not too pink. "No, no. I'm not here to discuss the validity of your plight. I would like to discuss the, ah, mechanics of it. What exactly went down, so to say."

Abernathy's face scrunched up into confusion while still maintaining a degree of animosity in her sneering mouth. "You what?"

"That man with me. He is the auger. The auger in Okhram, sorry, and I am the magister of worship at The Spire."

"What's The Spire?"

"A school," Mary clung to her patience like it were a lubricated thread, "I'm a teacher on holy matters."

"And you couldn't just say that could you?"

"Apparently not. Listen, the root of the matter is that we are working together to solve a problem. We're here because cases are rising in this area. Me and mister Redding are working together to find a cure for ancercy."

Harlot's skin seemed to fall a shade paler. She shook her head gently and started to recede back into her room as she spoke with quickness. "Well I can't say I'm familiar with the subject matter, good day Miss Culver."

Mary blocked the closing door with her shoe and pushed her arm through the gap to pry it open. Harlot stared at her with a distraught expression and was taking miniscule shuffles away from the intruder. She was also tetchily pulling at the edge of her sleeves and gripping them in her fists.

"Please, miss. I just want to inquire about the nature of the actual act itself. No accusations about diseases or otherwise. Just talk to me about what happened when you lay with the daemon – however it found its way to you."

The woman seemed to sniffle away an incoming sob. She nodded at Mary but still kept a tight grip on the door ready to push it shut at a moment's notice.

"What do you want to know?"

"How did you meet?"

"He knocked at my place of work. I thought he was a customer, I invited him in."

"Did he force himself on you?"

"No he just... sort of looked at me with hungry eyes until I opened my body to him."

"And what did he do after you permitted his advances?"

"He stuck his tongue out. He hadn't even touched me yet, not properly anyway. He just held my legs and stuck his tongue out."

"What happened afterwards?"

"Well I saw that his tongue was forked so I knew his true form. I pulled my cross from the wall and banished him back to hell."

"You were very brave."

"Thank you... are you done?"

"I just have one more question."

During their interview Harlot's hands had started shaking. It made the wood of the door rattle uncertainly. Mary put her own hand on top of Harlot's and slowly pushed the door open, pulling them closer and closing the gap. Harlot had dewy eyes and Mary's were held open and inviting. She kept bridging that gap until she created a bubble world just inside this doorway. The frame was barrier and all that existed inside was the two of them, their eyes both emotional and their hearts on their sleeves.

"What is it?" Harlot whispered.

"Please. Did you contract ancercy from this interaction?"

Her lip's parted. The words begged to be free but strangled in her throat. A tear slid down the left side of her face as she found herself unable to audibly admit it.

Instead she moved her right hand from where it was leaning on the doorway and pulled up the sleeve of the hand that Mary was holding. She gently pulled it down and revealed a wrist circled by a bracelet of faint, ocean scales.

Mary moved her own right hand from the door frame and up to cradle Harlot's face. She let it rest on the warmth of her cheek as Mary looked her in the eye.

"Do you know why," her voice was choked up. "I did not lie with it at all. I derived no sexual pleasure and did not let it touch me in a place that would."

"You're right," Mary agreed. She lowered her hand and looked away from Abernathy for a few seconds. "Didn't actually have sex," she thought out loud. Harlot tried to lean in and look at the other woman's face until she suddenly turned back to her with a glint of fulfilment in her eyes.

"You didn't physically lie with it!" She exclaimed.

"I'm sorry?"

"The disease. It did not spread because you lay with it, it spread because you let it lay with you at all!"

"But," she started to tear up again, "but I did not know. How could my soul have been damned if I did not know!"

"I'm sorry," Mary sighed. The revelation, taking precedence, seems to have sapped a lot of her emotional attention as she no longer acted with sensitivity. "I just don't think the Lord differentiates between the two. You lay with a spirit of hell... that is a corruptible offence."

"But!"

"Sorry. So, so sorry again but I really have to go and report this." Mary shot one last look of empathy her way before closing the door and making a quick pace across the landing.

Harlot wiped her tears from her face and replaced them with a scared and confused visage. She remained by the door taking only a step backwards. She leant a shoulder on the frame before looking coldly and distantly at the copy of the Bill by her bed. It looked so different to her now.

* * *

Victor had been sat at the head of a lunch table in a rather lavish room for far too long now. Serving dishes were on auxiliary tables all filled with steaming vegetables, cooked meats and smooth sauces just waiting to satiate his irritable hunger.

Instead he had to sit there while the two serving boys mulled in a corner waiting for his employee to arrive so that they could commence with eating.

When she finally entered he growled at her in that low, incinerating tone of his.

"You have delayed our lunch for too long, Miss Culver. Hurry to your spot so we can begin."

She sat at the opposite end of the table to him and furrowed her brow, "are we not engaging in a formal luncheon? With the royal family and the mayor and such?"

The auger ignored that question completely on the basis that it was ridiculous given their stupendous circumstances. Instead he said, "might I ask as to why it took so long to ask a whore whether or not she has a disease, hm?" He chuckled to himself, "I mean surely that question answers itself, does it not?"

She took her own turn to ignore him and instead turned to look at one serving boy and then the other. "Might we have some privacy? We should dine in a moment."

They looked between her and the witcher until, with a deep frown, he flapped his hands at them to wave them away. The room remained uncomfortably silent until the doors had swung to a full close.

Victor rose from his spot then. "I do hope that the next words out of your mouth are very carefully chosen, young lady."

Mary stood up. She wanted to rise up as he did. She wanted to lecture him, to shout at him to go over there, pull one of those wands from its sheath and-

"Of course, my lord." Taming her mind she grovelled instead. "Miss Abernathy was a unique case in this experiment. She contracted the disease but she did not engage in sex with a daemon."

Redding seemed to calm down after hearing this. He did not speak however he just held a hand out to her and she continued to talk. She relayed exactly what Harlot had told her about the encounter and her boss listened patiently as she did so. When she reached the end he shot her a look of uncertainty – uncertain of whether or not this anecdote should please or inflame him.

"Now," he began, "am I correct in assuming that you believe running his hands up the whore's legs like he did was not a sexual act?"

Mary seemed to shrug, "I would consider that a more invasive act."

"Nothing about the way a woman flutters when a man does this is indicative of pleasure to you?"

"I believe the word your looking for is 'shivers' m'lord not flutter."

"Well I know what I know," he leant back and grinned to himself making Mary feel deeply and horribly nauseated. "Remind me of your conclusion again?"

Mary walked eagerly around the table with a degree of pride as she spoke. "That ancercy is not a result of having sex with a daemon. It has nothing to do with the physical act for it is not a physical ailment at all. It is a sickness of the soul. A mark of damnation – a mark of the beast. It is caused when a human allows a daemon into their bed. That is all. Anything that happens after the fact is irrelevant to the singular, indisputable *fact* that the person allowed a daemon into their bed in any way. That acceptance, known or unknown, is a damnable offence that leaves the offender's marked with ancercy. The physical body morphs are just a manifestation of that fact. That is all."

"I am not sure why you are reporting this to me so gleefully," the auger hissed, "it appears that you are simply making a statement to your own inability to weaponize this as contracted."

Mary managed to smile. She was so proud that even in his face she could beam still.

"On the contrary, my lord. This experiment has been a great success. For the data it yields has forced me to seek a new conclusion: a conclusion that has brought me to the first steps of formulating a fantastic plan!"

"What are you saying, miss?"

She stepped closer and brought herself to talk in a low but excitable voice. "I'm saying that I have it. An idea – a plan. I know how to weaponize ancercy." She bit her lip to stop from giggling,

"This is what we are going to do."

Abernathy

"Miss Abernathy, do wait!"

The voice of the Princess Lolita echoed throughout the foyer. Harlot had needed some company to talk openly with so she had made her way to the split in the grand staircase to head to the western wing. In crossing the landing her attention was grabbed by the Lobelia daughter who was just on her way out. The princess promptly hiked up her dress and ran to the top of the stairs to talk to the older woman while a knight in deep green armour and a black tunic waited for her patiently by the door.

"Your highness," Harlot curtseyed as the princess reached her.

"Yes, yes. I need to ask you something. Is it true that you met with Mary Culver, the auger's aide, a few hours ago?"

"Um, yes, ma'am. How did you come to know that?" She looked around her nervously as if she might see a spirit watching over her shoulder or moving eyes in the painting of the Viscount.

"I do well with staff and therefore their gossiping," she said dismissively. "Now I need to ask you. This matter with the cure for ancercy. Do you believe in it?"

Harlot sputtered, her face turning red. "I- I am but a whore, ma'am. Surely my word is of no value to you."

Lolita took harlot's hands in her own and gave her a look of great mettle. "My friend, it does not matter who you are. If you are a citizen of my Belgrave then your word is of great council to me."

She bit her lip and nodded at the girl. "Then if I may... while I have no reason to doubt Miss Culver's intentions she was suspiciously peculiar when last we spoke."

"I see."

"And from what I have heard of this Victor Redding person he is perhaps not a man to lend trust."

"I agree with you there." Lolita chewed on her lip and looked away, lost deep in thought. After a minute she snapped to attention again, looking deeply at the woman opposite her. "And the staff here. The mayor's. What do you think of them?"

"The staff, ma'am?"

"Were they peculiar also?"

"Well they were disgruntled, certainly, to be told to wait on a lady of the night. But that was more amusing than peculiar." Harlot smiled as she said that.

"Right, right. And, ah, do you think that they shared any aspects, any at all, with your friend? The gentleman you came in with?"

"Who, Adam? I don't think they ever met before today and they seemed wholly unrelated to him. Why do you ask?"

"Oh no reason," Lolita drifted into thought again. When she did speak it was distant, "just a girl of the great houses trying to make sense of the common folk, that's all."

But even Harlot could tell that she didn't mean the listed out excuse. Not that it mattered, though, because the girl had run off back to that knight as soon as she had finished her sentence. Before Harlot could even thinking of giving a goodbye curtsey, the royal pair were off into the evening.

She lingered in her spot for a moment and pondered Adam and why the princess might probably be interested in him. Then she snorted to herself as she wrote it off as a young girl crushing. Although that stopped being funny when she realised she might have to tell Adam not to entertain it.

But that didn't matter right then.

She was going somewhere before the princess interrupted her.

She continued on her beaten path and headed into the west wing. She walked past the Azalea suite, doing all her best to ignore the gorgeous painting of an azalea bush, and headed towards the mayoral dwelling.

Like the other three suites, it was compromised of two rooms, presumably the mayor's his self and his son's. Thankfully, she was saved from having to figure out which belonged to whom as the mayor's voice was boisterously shouting through the walls of his at some poor secretary or server. She could practically feel the flying spittle.

Shaking her head of distractions she stepped forth and knocked gently on his son's door instead.

"Enter." Came the voice from inside. It was not bidding nor loud. It was dejected; a flat tone raised just audible enough for someone outside to hear.

When she did enter, she saw him simply laying there on his large bed, bigger than the large one in her room, just staring at the ceiling. He was lying flat with his legs dangling off the edge. He had the same clothes on as yesterday except now they were rumpled and creased from being slept in. His arms were flaccid by his side and his eyes did not move when she entered the room. He lay there and he waited for her to speak.

"Right," she whispered, cutting the silence anxiously. "It's me. Obviously you remember."

His eyes rolled to the left to look at her in the corner of his vision. While it appeared he was trying his best to remain cold and unfeeling, his eyes were round as if he should be frowning. He wasn't - his lips were a loose line on his face. But his eyes were frowning.

"Oh."

She remembered how disconnected and uninterested he was the night before and had expected him to be just as dour. But this state was practically useless. After another minute of waiting in silence for him to speak up she broke the tension again.

"Look, I just wanted to say I'm sorry for... how I reacted to you the other day."

His eyes narrowed. Otherwise he was completely, equally as stationary as before.

"What?"

"You had a problem. A real problem. And I ostracised you, treated you like the daemon... I am sorry."

Harlot jumped then, putting a hand on her chest to still her heart, as Will vaulted to a sitting up position. His blonde hair was soft but damp with sweat. His face was handsome but glistening with the running perspiration. He pulled his knees up to rest his forearms on them but still seemed to be lost in the world of the unliving.

"Why are you apologising to me?"

"I don't understand." She edged closer to him. She came to stand near to the side of his bed and finally he turned his head to her. She could see now that he was not emotionless but rather exhausted. He was pale and drawing close to gaunt. His mouth hung open as if he could never quite breathe in enough air and his emerald eyes were wide with vulnerability. She studied him for a moment, however, as she had to wonder how in this state of fatigue he still managed to look that handsome.

"Neither do I," he replied. "I mean, I was horrible to you in there. I should be apologising... I just don't know what came over me. Well I do. It's ancercy." He chuckled but there was no humour in the noise.

"It is fine," she replied, "I did not even comprehend your threats. I was so terrified of what I saw that my mind had to escape to another realm to cope with it- oh!"

He twisted his body to sit on his side. He had one hand draped over a knee and the other propping him up as he looked up at the woman with such sincere guilt that she swore she had witnessed the picture of masculine beauty right there.

"Did I really do that to you?" His boyish voice dripped with that sincere guilt as it sung through the air.

She swallowed and nodded shakily. "But it's fine."

"I don't think a feeling like that is ever fine."

"Maybe not but... now I get why you acted so angrily with me while I was in that state of utter... rejection. So I just came to say that I shouldn't have reacted as I did."

Will tilted his head, "well that would be the second time you're saying it so congratulations I suppose."

"Sorry, sorry."

"You get it because you have it too, don't you?"

Harlot felt a sudden burst of anger then. She wanted to hit him or she wanted to leave or she wanted to shout but she did not know which. Eventually, the rational part of her mind reminded her that he was right. She did have it. That is the whole reason she is there.

"I do. How did-"

"I see it in your eyes. Don't you see it in mine? The lacklustre. I used to enjoy my life so much. So much that I would try anything, even intercourse with a phantom. And now look at me; withdrawn. Pathetic."

Abernathy tried to lighten the mood. "Are you calling me withdrawn and pathetic, Mr Rushings?"

"No. Not yet anyway."

'Fine, don't play along,' she thought.

"But your eyes are already so, so tired."

'*I get it*,' she thought.

She moved to perch on the edge of his bed. She did it slowly as if to invite his non-consent but he did not give it. He just watched as she fluttered on to his sheets. They did not speak for minutes then. It was a long time where they just existed comfortably together and let their presences, their solidarity, warm one another. When they moved to look at each other's person, up and down, it was not lustful. Just observatory. When their eyes met at certain points, they did not fluster or make excuses. They just stared into them for a second, appreciating it like any other part, before moving on to the next.

The two lost souls found each other in the woods right then.

It was William who ended up breaking that silence.

"Can I see yours?" He asked. When his supple voice cut the air her mind returned to impure thoughts of him. It was as if - in their mutual soul searching - he had seemed like an angel to her with no concept of sexuality. He was just light before her eyes, warming her while being stared at.

But his voice was touched with both charming youth and hitting maturity that it morphed his form back into a human's with all the right parts in all the right places.

Well. Except for one.

She broke her train of thought with another joke then elbowed him in the knee, "I see. I'll show you mine if you show me yours, eh?"

He blinked confusedly at her, "y-you've seen mine?"

She titled her head, "no, I was just- it doesn't matter." She moved so that she was sat fully on the bed. She crossed her legs and he sat up too in a mirror to her. She pulled up the sleeve on her left arm to reveal the band of scales that was slowly climbing up.

He maintained that out-of-it expression as he looked the infected area up and down.

"Is yours spreading like mine is?"

He looked up at her when she spoke. "No," he replied. Harlot rolled her sleeves gently back down while he talked, "it isn't spreading. It isn't growing either. It is just... brooding. I can feel it waiting, eager for something to happen. I feel it, inside of me. Like there is a creature so desperate to burst from my abdomen." He placed a gentle hand on the lower part of his stomach. "Like maybe it is spreading just... inside of me. But yours... yours is so beautiful."

She had never taken a moment to think that they might look pretty. To her they were a symbol of abomination – a blight. But as she thought more on it, and traced the scales through her shirt sleeve, she thought that maybe when it overtook her at least she could cocoon into something wondrously beautiful.

"After consideration, your own is not half bad."

"You flatter me, Miss Abernathy."

"I mean it. I think I would regret a death where I did not give such a unique limb at least one ride."

"And now you try to sell me your craft, Harlot."

The joke sent her into a giggling fit that pushed her to her side.

She leaned into the laughter and enjoyed the way it heated her up especially the way it felt as if her ancercy was sparkling. It was oddly nice.

Through her laughter, she saw such a wide smirk on the man across from her that all it took was one snort to entice him to at least chuckle. The two laughed like that, joy in each other's company, for an hour or two longer as at last the woods no longer seemed quite so lost.

Lobelia

Lolita and her knight had left the halls just an hour ago.

She did not quite realise how late it had been when she awoke until she had had luncheon and then left to prowl the streets only for the horizon to already be turning orange. She sighed deeply for fear of having to give up her search already.

"We should at least be turning back in the right direction, ma'am."

"I fear that I agree, Ser Garland."

She had set out on a trek about town. After recovering from her fear of the two servers and the man, Adam, she had deigned to find someone else who made her feel as eldritch as they had.

But she had turned up nothing. There were no strange feelings of dread, no people who felt as if they should not belong and no reason for general concern at all. She had credited this, of course, to the dwindling street presence. People had closed their stalls by the time she reached Union Square leaving only the punters out for a drink and the women hidden obviously in alleyways. Any minstrels had long stopped playing and all news boys had stopped their 'hear ye's' even longer since. It was barren with no one wanting to risk the dark.

Yes, her search had definitely come to an end.

But she was resolute in finding some cause for her distress so on their way home she was making plans to lurk the streets of Summerset. If it was not too late after her baptism tomorrow than she might just have some luck indeed.

"Perhaps we should take a different path home. Maybe we can salvage the night yet."

"As you wish, ma'am." They had approached directly via the high street that lead to the halls. This time they would hike through the rougher, narrower roads up Hearth Stone and Wembley Lane. There were many names to the many streets in this part of Whitley, it being a spiderweb of more modern housing made in a less modern quality. The buildings were all tall and close together. These streets could not have taken a carriage down them and the smell seemed to compact within the physical space.

But if her subjects could withstand this day to day then so could their princess. For a half an hour of walking, anyway.

But still she did not find anyone to incite her odd reaction. All she saw was a couple of beggars and a woman she swore was a thief because two good-off looking men came by just a minute after her looking rather befuddled.

But while she saw no one to meet her unique criteria, she did happen to come across a man she recognised very well.

Someone she hadn't seen since he was invited to their luncheon earlier. It was the hired pagan, Cyrus Magellan. He had a stoic look about him and the same red hair as earlier. His clothes were a tad dirtied, however, and he seemed to be moving in line with the shadows.

Lolita's first instinct was to wave out to him but then she might not find out what he's up to. So she commanded her guard to stay a few undetectable leagues behind her while she remained that same elusive distance from her target.

As she chased, she recalled how he was at dinner – the way he haggled with her mother about the rising price of divination ingredients. Katherine had made anecdote after anecdote about the prices her father paid and what her own baptism was like as well as Cyrus' own father as the performing witcher.

That man then was both jolly and bashful. He bantered and he minded his manners. And although he graciously tucked in, he asked for no more food than he was offered. He was a delight!

So Lolita really, genuinely was desperate to find out why he appeared as a despot in the evening. Because as he moved he seemed mildly erratic, looking over his shoulder and peering around corners before he darted down them. His face seemed tight like he was managing his awareness and keeping his entire body in a state of preparedness. As he dashed his clothing echoed behind like an after image and at many points Lolita believed herself to have lost him. She even forwent stealth to simply run ahead as she huffed and swore that the man was employing magic to make his escape – although his hair remained crimson right until the end.

Finally her quarry turned a corner into one very long street.

When she turned the same corner he was simply gone.

Seeing no traces she took the opportunity to catch her breath as Mace Garland reached her side.

"He's just... he's just gone!"

"He must be somewhere."

The princess stopped looking down the street for a place he could have ran to and instead started to scan the buildings for somewhere he might have hidden. "Yes, I believe you could be right."

She walked along the buildings dragging her hand across the white and brown walls of houses as she scaled for any discrepancies or alcoves. She analysed any door she came across only to write them all off as lodgings and even made to stare down the only diverging alley on this road. But all she saw down there was refuse and a wiry, ginger cat.

"I know he is here somewhere I can sense it." She made sure to assert herself upon returning to her attendant's side. That did not stop him from protesting.

"The sky grows darker."

"Yet the hunter's hour is still far off. Earn your silver and watch me as I work."

"Yes, ma'am."

She had never felt so emblazoned before but this street was giving her hints of that feeling. She did not feel discomfort but still a similar sense lingered at the fringes of her perception. It is here she would find it and she was resolute in that decision.

She turn back around to stand in the position where she last saw him. She recreated that moment of his disappearance and she leapt around the corner again to only, as expected, see Garland implacably on guard.

She did this again though. And again and again and again with no different results. She tried at different angles with different motions. She even entertained the idea of attempting to channel the ether around her like her mother had told her about until she realised she was far too inept to even begin a career in paganism at that moment. Never mind her status intertwined with the Paradigm Church.

It was all she could do not to give up as the sunlight made its final ebbs over the sky and wrought the street in a minute of darkness. Soon enough the street lamps ignited as the fire runes took their enchantments in stride and set a sombre orange glow on the weathered rocks.

In this glow she finally noticed a new element to the street.

There was a brass hanging, a curled square with an image inside. The whole time of her inspection she had been dismissing it as an ornamental piece put up by some haughty mother – even then she had only brushed it off from the corner of her vision.

The light had changed all that as its orange glow brought the sign into focus with the rest of her vision. The symbol inside it was a brass casting too; two diamonds. One horizontal and the other smaller and vertically placed within the corners of the first. It was a jagged eye.

But what really caught the princess' attention was how, as she slowly moved around the nearest lamp, the centre of this eye seemed to line up with the flame. When they became aligned to her perception – the flame in the iris - she came up to her tip-toes and stared directly at them.

And the eye looked back.

And it blinked.

And she blinked.

And she was elsewhere.

She teetered back as her feet fell on solid ground again. She rubbed at her eyes as they adjusted to the new location she found herself in – while the lighting was the same the space was more cramped somehow that those narrow streets.

Clearing her vision, she took a look around to see that she had entered some sort of dungeon. The walls were stone brick in a very dark grey colour. She seemed to be standing against what looked like the only blank wall. The rest of the space was occupied by a melding of possessions that clearly only meant something to a person who could wield a wand.

The room itself was divided by a large, thick wall that cut down the middle making it into a straight 'U' shape. On this side of the bend Lolita pressed forward. She walked past a series of benches, all made of different colours of wood, to what looked like a coat hung up on a hook. It was blood red and edged with a cream coloured fur. It looked like it was very nice once but now it is moth bitten and catching dust. The benches themselves had myriads of projects on them from charms to runestones to bits of tweed wrapped around each other in intricate patterns. There was a series of small shelves with different gemstones collected on them and a larger shelf above that with geodes cluttered together and threatening to spill over the edge. There were various pieces of thick papyrus with strange shapes and grids scratched onto them. Lighting the whole space up, or at least this side, was a collection of randomly placed and randomly coloured candles. Amongst them there seemed to be a high frequency of red and white ones but they were burning low. The newer ones were blues and yellows and blacks.

But this was just a cursory glance on Lolita's part. There were still so many curiosities to indulge in – the apotropaic scratchings in the stones alone were enough to take a whole day of review.

When she marched on instead and rounded the blunt corner of the dividing wall she found herself in a hall much different to the entrance one. She even made a quick tilt back and forth a few times to ensure that both halves were in fact occupying the same space.

This other room was lit solely by one big torch on the wall at the very end encased in a metal cage. Its light fell on six strange storage tanks – three lining each side of the hall. They were big enough that Lolita might stand upright in one of them but there did not seem to be anyway to open any of them.

They were all made of bronze, or at least a metal that looked like it, and a had a face-sized window near the top. These windows were each a circle lined by a thick silver seal; they showed that inside each one of them was water right to the top. Light blue slightly bubbling water – it was holy water. She stepped closer and stared into the closest tank and put her hand to its cold surface to be sure. She became mesmerised watching it flow like that and glimmer in fractals of cyan.

She could feel its propensity through the palm of her hand – the space it had inside itself for faith to fill; the room it had to channel God.

After resonating with it for a moment she stepped back. And she took a quicker look inside the tank behind her. She did this one by one with the first five tanks until she reached the sixth one in the corner by the torch. When she turned round to look she saw something floating inside and it made her jump. This one was occupied. Still it had holy water but floating in that light blue, ethereal liquid was a small human-like form shrivelled into a ball and bobbing up in down in place.

Lolita did not feel compelled to put her hand on this tank.

It made her heart rate spike as her mind raced to understand what she was looking at but she could not form any rational idea. And then her heart pumped faster as a noise rattled around the bend somewhere and she stepped back against the far wall so she was flat next to the sconce.

There were footsteps and an approaching orange torch that consumed at any remaining darkness as its circle of light grew bigger. And then it cast the shadow of its wielder and Lolita knew before she saw him that Magellan was approaching. She wanted to shout for Garland to come to her side but she had abandoned him out in the street and now she had to face the witcher alone.

He stood at the opposite end of this side of the 'U' with his finger hooked around a chamberstick that held a purple candle. His face was grievous and his voice was very deep.

"What are you doing here, little girl?"

Abernathy

Harlot pulled the door to William's room closed behind her.

She believed that that was the longest she had been in a man's bedroom without taking her clothes off. She had actually connected with him; loved connecting with him.

And any notions of his previous unsavoury demeaner were lost to her. His acceptance of what was happening to him melted his shell down to the real person that was inside. He was emotional with her - honest and loose with her.

And they did all that with their clothes on. A shock to her, to be sure.

But the real treasure that she had found from the interaction, other than an ally with which she could face her plague, was the courage to talk to the one man in her life who actually meant something.

She had resolved originally to waste away until she turned into some sort of mer-creature that would be mercilessly harpooned by the night hunters. She had hoped to spare Adam the grief of watching her slowly contort into something unrecognisable.

But as memories of her sister loosened their control on her she remembered that she was three years younger then and three years more scared. And she realised that she was glad, now, that she at least knew what happened to her sibling rather than just having her disappear without any explanation.

So she would do the courteous thing and allow Adam into the conversation.

She would have wished him to do the same.

She did spend a moment, first, thinking on how she would react if that were the situation. She thought about how she had reacted to Will's aberration and what if it were Adam who showed it to her instead. And she admits she would be terrified. But it's Adam. Adam who invited her on a date before all this happened, Adam who was always there the next street over to inquire about her latest act of debauchery and make it all seem okay.

Adam who loved her.

And while what she felt that that evening with Will was not love she believes that it had opened her heart to the possibility.

That perhaps she might be falling in love with Adam right at the end of her life. As she sees time fleet by and her arm grow ever the more monstrous, suddenly the time she has left with him is compressed into explosive moments of incredible worth! She wants to look at him just to feel how it feels to gaze on him while she still can. She wants to banter and date and walk down Annum's Lane like the world is not turning around them. If only Etherium would halt its march just to let them be for eternity.

It was a rush of feelings that sent her heart atwitter so suddenly - but coming to terms with herself would do that. She not only felt the love to tell him all this but she also felt the love to tell him about the true person who felt it. Harlot Abernathy, as she walked along the landing way to the Daisy suite, was resolute to tell Adam her real name; the name of the woman who loved him.

She just had to tell him about the ancercy first.

"Adam it's... it's me!" She knocked lightly on his door and ignored the fact that it hung slightly open. She knew that meant he had been allowing any matter of staff here have their taste of him but she did not feel jealous in the slightest. After all, the first awkward topic of their relationship would most likely be acknowledging that she would remain sleeping with any man in the nation to earn her keep and he would have to be fine with that. Maybe she would have to keep their relationship a secret to keep customers coming... maybe there is a whole new market of customers that are really into cuckholding...

"Harls!" Her thoughts were interrupted as Adam answered the door. He was grinning ear to ear and had clearly just thrown his clothes back on. His trousers were ruffled and his shirt was only half buttoned up. As they talked she would make the occasional glimpse at the matted sweat of hair on his chest and the slight exposure of his own cleavage. She stopped suddenly when her mind started to drift to William as she suddenly pictured that his pecs would be smooth unlike Adam's.

She cleared her throat, "yes, yes. Can I come in or are you still showing the well-to-do staff what a man of the streets can do?"

He tilted his head and leaned towards her. He didn't say anything as he placed a finger under her chin and pulled her eyes to his. "Are we jealous?" He asked in a teasing sharp. She almost felt her body shudder as his other hand teased its way down her waist and tickled her sides. He poked his finger over the top of her skirt brushing his knuckle against her soft stomach as he trailed along the hem.

She might have let him turn the conversation from one of words to one of action right there had she not suddenly smelt the booze on his breath. Suddenly the way he was hooking her into the room had gone from sexy to just annoying. His other hand was trailing from her chin now as it slid down her neck. It started to be joined one by one by his other fingers as he passed her collarbone before flittering over her chest. He twiddled with the button on the front of her undershirt until Harlot gently tried to push him away.

"Hey, hey. Is this not why you're here? Do you still want to do that dinner thing first, I'm sure theres a good cut of meat in this building somewhere." He burped loudly after that and then looked around the room as if a table with a banquet might suddenly appear from somewhere.

She looked at him sadly and pushed his wandering hands back to his side. "No, I just needed to talk but it appears you're in no state to right now. I will come back in the morning." She smiled politely and hoped that she would not suddenly be transfigured in her sleep.

The rejection just confused Adam. "Wai- wai- wai- wai- wai- wai- ...wait!" He grabbed at her wrist but she slipped out of his grasp. He then came closer and grabbed her by both of the wrists and that time much tighter. "Just tell me whatever it is and then we can return to business, kay?"

"Adam," she spoke lowly, "please let me go."

"Is it that you love me?" He looked at her like she was a child. Suddenly his teasing felt less like it usually did and more humiliating. "Because I love you too! If that's what it takes."

"Okay, you're incredibly intoxicated."

"I usually am," he shrugged, "you didn't mind it when you saw me after work yesterday."

"You were drunk then?" She looked at him incredulously and he just stared back. Still, she shook her discontent off and tried to escape his grip again so that she might just talk when he is sober. Then everything will be fine. Then she can go back to loving him. Not that she doesn't right now, of course. This is Adam! This is Adam.

His reaction to her shock however was a proud smirk. His tongue started to poke out from between his lips as suddenly he moved his hand from her right arm so that both were restraining the left. Instead of fighting or prying she attempted to put her whole body weight into running and pulling herself free but to no avail. His muscles just flexed beneath his shirt as he thumbed up the cuff of hers and dove in to lick the length of what he assumed was her porcelain skin.

It's something he had wanted to do for a while – he was not such a vain man that he told others he had standards. He liked what he called 'roughing' it. Seeing Harlot all hot and struggling excited him into licking every bead of perspiration from her pale arm as he made his way up to her bosom. When his tongue did approach, he saw not what was ahead as he was busy eyeing up the way to her breasts. He enjoyed how they were bouncing in her attempt to break free. When he had finally touched down and the taste of her body hit his buds his brain seemed to focus on nothing but burying his face inside that chest and holding on for dear life to his prize.

This is why he did not seem to notice, for at least three seconds, that his tongue had been trailing up a league of scales. Harlot was shocked to a still as her eyes widened in fear. She kept herself trained on the man's reaction as he slowly pulled away from her while keeping his own vision on the signs of ancercy all up her arm. As his mind processed what it saw he finally seemed to sober up. That's when he flew backwards, nearly falling over himself as he pointed an accusing finger at her disease and cursed profusely.

"Fucking fuck! Are you? Is that? FUCK!" He did not stop until his back hit the far wall and his face switched uncertainly between anger and fear.

"It was an accident..."

"Accident my arse that- that! That is wrong you - need to," as he searched for the word his pointing finger moved to the door, "go. You need to leave just leave for good or something, I don't know."

She winced at his words. For some reason, and she could not possibly quantify why, Harlot apologised. She mouthed the words 'I'm sorry' unable to vocalise anything without a sob escaping.

He guffawed at her, "hah! Fuck that," he pointed at the door poking through the air rapidly. "*Get out*," he insisted again. She was wordless. She did not want it to happen like this.

She took a few apprehensive steps but kept looking at him and pleading with her eyes.

"Has the bastarding disease reached your ears already? Go. I never want to see you again."

His words spurred her to run. She turned and hiked up her skirt and she went. She did not go far, she simply dashed back to her room nearby where she slammed the door behind her. She managed to move herself forward just a bit on the spurs of her energy until she came to a lost stop in the centre of the room. She clutched at her stomach and heaved heavily in an out. As her body shook and her eyes felt both dry and ready to erupt at the same time, she could swear that her heart was climbing up her throat alongside the thin bile. She fell to her knees and pawed pathetically at the floor as if she were trying to clutch to bedsheets.

She remembered her solace then and crawled across the ground to try and find her copy of the Bill. She pulled herself up to the bed to look at it on her side table just as the memory of her conversation with Mary Culver resurfaced.

The book was so cold to her touch now. She held it in her hands and even cradled it to her bosom once more only to feel that it was no longer a warm presence. She held it out to stare at it. She gripped it tighter and tighter and stared at it trying to will it to protect her again but now it just felt empty.

Soon enough she realised the pain it was causing to hold it so tightly and she shouted. She lurched the book across the room and it hit the wall between her chamber and Adam's with a great thud. She hadn't done that on purpose but as the book fluttered to the floor in a pile of peeling pages she turned to look hopefully at her door.

Maybe Adam would react to that bang. Maybe he would come back tamed and apologize to her. Maybe he would be enflamed and in his anger he would take her all night just so that he could express his rage through violent thrusts.

Frankly she didn't care. Harlot stared at that door for an hour hoping that one way or another her man would come back to show her that he felt anything at all.

Culver

Victor Redding had been staring up at the wooden sign for almost a whole minute. It dangled above a storefront from two chains and had a hexagram painted on it with a solid dot between each point. Written above the windowed storefront in bold, yellow lettering was the shop's name; 'Ripley's.'

Finally, a grumbling rose in his throat as he turned to look down on Mary, "what are we doing at an alchemists, exactly?"

"It's a part of my idea," she said astutely.

"And is that idea to transmute a person's soul? Perhaps turn silver into disease?"

She rolled her eyes, "no, m'lord. Let me tell you a story from the Bill."

"I will not be preached to by a woman," he asserted.

It made Mary want to stomp her feet and scream like a child - and she would if it were not exactly how he was treating her. "Of course not," she grunted instead. "In that case, let me share with you a holy writ that I have on many occasions shared with my students as part of my job- and not as any kind of impersonator of the church!"

He bowed his head, with a lot less grace than he thought he had, and bade her continue.

"Now, are you familiar with where the term ancercy comes from?"

His flash of adherence melted as his face contorted into annoyance once more. "Miss Culver, while I subscribe my service to the rightful queen; deeply respect the realm's holy Lord and make every effort to spit on each passing devilist, I still find myself begging the question!"

"And... which question is that?"

"Do I look like a man of the cloth to you?"

"Of course not, auger," she sighed. He stood there waving at the wands on his waist. She swore that if he pulled his bloody solemn oath out she would hit him over the head with it.

"Then please continue your lecture with a bit of consideration for your polytheist audience."

"Of course. Ahem. The term ancercy is first found in the book of Agamemnon. This is the section of the Bill that covers intercourse, fertility, child rearing and sexual diseases."

Mary gritted her teeth as Victor interrupted again, "is that not the book of Iosefka?"

"No, m'lord, the book of Iosefka is dedicated to forgiveness. It just so happens that she is a whore"

"Right."

"Right. Continuing on, at a point in Agamemnon's life he contracts ancercy."

"Did Iosefka not also contract ancercy?"

"YES! Yes, ha-ha, yes she did. But we are on Agamemnon at the moment." The auger just looks at her expectantly. She continues, her head already aching severely. "Humans are born with sin in their hearts. Temptation is natural to us while fear of God and goodness is not. This is why He instils it in us, sometimes harshly even, to keep us from straying."

"To keep us in line," Redding mutters. She ignores him.

"But through Agamemnon's wilful ignorance of the Lord's angels and despite the many ways He attempted to deliver His divine message, Agamemnon still fell. So God curated ancercy to drive the stake further into Agamemnon's heart, even warning him about its existence. But when the final test came up, and the Lord lead a daemon to Agamemnon's door, it was his innate temptation that won over the faith God had tried to give him. Not even the fear of ancercy could ward him. It was on the blade of his temptation that he fell."

"If we take a look at what you just told me," Victor said, his voice haughty and slight humorous, "it does not paint a very good picture for God, does it?"

"And whyever not?"

"Because God gave the poor man ancercy."

"No He didn't, Agamemnon failed his test," she kept talking quicker and louder so that Victor would not speak over her, "the message that this story shows us, and what I am presenting to you, is that sin is in all men's heart. God's test has shown us that it is not morality that we should strive to achieve but temptation we should strive to fight. We should clothe women in more and more coverings as to heel the temptations of men and we should limit the flow of gold to stop the temptation of the greedy poor." She let herself stop frowning as the realisation creeped into Victor's face, "it is the means that we should fight rather than the sin itself... so to spread the sin, we must..."

"Spread the means," he finished in a deep voice "and the humans will sin themselves." The solution made sense; she was sure of it. But Victor, ever the cynic, did not share her confidence. He moved to stand right in front of Mary's face and continued to growl in the same deep tone, "tell me why, right now, it would not be better to simply seek out more wicked cults, cross their palms with gold and simply summon a legion of daemons to sleep with my targets."

"Because," Mary stood up tall, too sick of the man today to back down, "one cultist can summon one daemon at a time. And assuming you want to enact this plan of yours on any kind of scale at all, you will need *thousands* of cultists to bend to your will - a power I do not believe even you possess."

He studied the woman up and down and weighed up the matter in his mind. Then he stepped back, peering between her and the alchemist's shop behind him. "In any case... what is it you are proposing we do with this rock peddler?"

Mary nodded at him. She looked around to see that they were alone and despite seeing that they were, she still she moved closer to whisper her idea in his ear. He nodded as she spoke and explained all the elements of the plan. As she reached the execution element he began to tidily rub his hands together until she pulled away and he gave her his approval. "Lead the way, Mary," he grinned.

She did so, walking into the alchemists and setting off a tiny bell with the swing of the door. She felt a moment of anxiety upon walking in as the room appeared more like a lab to her than a shop but she calmed as Victor strode on ahead to what appeared to be a counter tucked into one corner.

The wall to the east carried a wine-rack-like piece of furniture from end to end. Instead of bottles of alcohol lying on their side in each cubby hole there were jars with various liquids, crystals and powders hidden beneath brown corks. On the tips of each cork was a white label with a black alchemical symbol painted on indicating the contents of the jar. The centre of the room had two islands running perpendicular and each holding different but equally obtuse metal devices. One was slowly dripping a green liquid into a vial while another was emitting small amounts of steam as something red inside heaved and bubbled between a solid and a liquid state.

On the opposite west wall was the brick plastered by scribbling diagrams and messily written paragraphs that seemed to be far beyond the comprehension of Mary's alchemical knowledge. The wall opposite the entrance was simply two doors with a board between them that had pinned up news articles, bounties and job listings.

And to the side of that, in the north western corner, was the curved desk. Upon their approach a stout man with a monocle and brown suspenders huffed his way over to this desk where he lifted up a gate and walked behind. He clapped his hands, pushed his bushy moustache up with a smile and asked, "what can I do you for?"

Victor turned and sent another simmering look of judgement towards Mary before he addressed the shop keep.

"I will be needing a vial of quicksilver and another of brimstone, if you will."

The alchemist looked between his customers over the top of his monocle. "Oh you will, will you? And can I ask what your intentions are with such... reactive components?"

Victor looked as if he were about to lean over the counter and throttle the other man; before he could begin his ranting Mary put a hand on his arm and just nodded at his cape.

He raised a curious eyebrow at her. "Your letter, man," she hissed.

"You should have just said so," he buried his hand inside his pockets and then pulled them out again to present the piece of papyrus. "You would do right to remember that a witcher's pocket is very deep."

Mary turned and snickered quietly, "as is a wizard's sleeve."

"What was that?"

"Nothing! Look, look here," she addressed the man behind the counter and pointed eagerly at the letter of marque that Redding had produced. The man clasped his monocle's lens between two finger tips and leaned in to analyse the paper. Suddenly the red drained from his large cheeks.

"Oh- oh! Deepest and most fervent apologies, my lord."

"Yes, yes."

"I had no idea that the queen had taken a new auger!"

"Oh for," Victor took his own turn to point at the document. He highlighted the area that indicated the emblematic reaver of Charlotte Iris.

"Oh, these are amethyst papers… my most humblest sorries, my lord."

"Now about the procurement of these minerals."

"Of course, of course." He lifted up the gate and hobbled over to a small side table next to the expansive rack of elements and ingredients. He pulled a pestle and mortar off of one of the two large islands and then he located a step ladder from under the shop-front window. He plodded back up to the racks and traced his finger across labels until he managed to locate two specific bottles – one half full of thick, sloshing quicksilver and another rattling with yellow, powdery brimstone crystals.

"Ah, how much of each will you be wanting?" He went and grabbed a tiny metal hammer from another surface that Mary could not see before waiting patiently to hear their request. After the auger blithered about his words trying to come up with some sort of metric – rather than admit that he had no idea – Mary decided to lean in and whisper their plan to the alchemist.

"So," she said, "how much would we need to do... something like that?"

The man blinked. Any pinkness that had returned was now washing even further away. "W-well I should think not too much. You would also need some sort of receptacle for the, ahem, *matter* you are gathering – somewhere for it to linger in a transitionary state until it is compressed into the desired material. Anything that can store a large quantity of ether will do."

"Do you sell anything like that?" the auger asked.

"Worry not," she put a hand up to him, "we have that part covered already. Just these two components please."

"Right. Of course, my lady." And he walked back off to the counter to retrieve some things.

"We have something like that, do we?" Victor hissed.

"Yes! Now trust me, alright."

"Yes, my lady," he mocked seethingly.

The alchemist returned with two small glass vials and a metal funnel. He placed them all on his crowded table before getting to work. He hammered off a shard of the brimstone and placed it into a pestle and mortar where, after a deal of bashing it, it eventually conceded and allowed itself to be ground into a fine yellow powder that looked to be staining the granite device. After, he held the funnel atop one jar and poured some of the liquid quicksilver into it until it was filled two thirds the way. Then he did the same with the brimstone into the other jar before picking them both up between his fingers and waddling over to the desk.

He placed both the containers atop the counter, popped a small cork in each and plastered an adhesive label on them with pre-drawn alchemical symbols: for mercury there was a circle with a cross coming out of the bottom and an upside down semicircle on the top; for brimstone there was a triangle with a cross coming from the bottom.

"Might I also point out," after he was finished packaging their order he pulled out another prepackaged material, "that your plan cannot be completed without a vial of salt. It would give the body you need to your united spirits." The salt vial had a label with a circle drawn on it that had a horizontal line in the centre.

"Oh, really?"

"Fine," Victor stopped Mary before she encouraged the other man to keep speaking. "Just the matter of payment if you will."

"Of course, my lord." The alchemist timidly pulled an accounts book from behind the counter. "Now let us say that will be one gold piece-"

"What!"

"Per jar..." the man seemed to suck in his lips as he stared at the approaching auger who made every effort to worm closely down into the other man's personal space – a talent that he was starting to get very good at when he wanted to make people uncomfortable.

"*Let us say* that it will be the proper price and I might let you keep your head you audacious, avaricious, disgustingly auspicious little imp!"

Mary just remained in her place nervously biting her nails and thanking God for the fact that it was happening to someone else for once.

"My- my lord!" the man stuttered. "If I dare say, you would be very hard pressed to find such quality materials in Whitley at all, never mind at this particular hour."

Victor reeled back and scowled at the short man. But he knew better than to barter with a merchant that knew his product's worth. He tossed three medallions onto the counter, snatched the vials and swept out before his cape had settled.

The bell of the shop door rang as they listed off into the night.

"I suppose," he grumbled to his companion, "that we had best head off to the next part of our little operation." He handed her the three vials and she kept a tight grip on them. After scanning her dress and remembering that God had apparently told all the tailors in the land that woman shalt not haveth pockets, she slid the vials of brimstone and salt between spaces in her bra and kept a tight clutch on the quicksilver.

"I hope you can handle your task, illustrious auger of the amethyst crown."

"Of course I can, Worry about yourself, miss Culver," he said with pomp. "It is just their... very presence that I am not looking forward to."

The man shivered as he spoke.

Mary just smiled, "I don't know. For devil worshippers, I thought they were alright."

Abernathy

William Rushings had an idea. He had not had one of those in a few days – a misfortune that can only be attributed to a rampant of ancercy that had rendered him catatonically depressed. It wasn't until he had properly met Miss Abernathy that his mood had changed from dangerously fatalist to deeply guilty to... hope?

Well, a fatalist kind of hope, anyhow.

This idea of his had been that he would spend his last days doing something, something indulgent. And to begin he would thank Harlot by letting her pick the first hedonistic activity. In fact, he had one in mind that he thought she might be interested in.

Unfortunately, his enthusiasm was curbed when he came to knock on her door about an hour later only to hear her ask, "is that you, Adam?"

He cleared his throat, set aback. "No, no. It's William."

He could hear her sighing through the door. "Please, leave me alone."

He frowned through the wall. He turned his head to look and saw that the other Moonflower door had been shut for what he heard was the first time since Adam arrived.

He knocked on Harlot's door again concerned something had taken place.

"You know you can talk to me."

She ignored him.

"I mean, literally, you do know that. We did it just earlier."

Although it was much quieter than her sigh he did hear a very low snort of laughter from inside. He took that as an invite and tentatively pushed the door forward while edging inside. With no arguments, he stepped confidently on and shut the door softly behind him. He looked around the room to see it largely untouched. Other than the pile of pages that he assumed was once this room's copy of the Bill, everything remained as it normally always was.

"How does it feel being the one not wanting to talk this time?"

"It makes me feel like I owe you an apology for interrupting your previous wallowing," she spoke with discontent but did not aim it at him. "Wallowing is important and I strongly believe we should both be doing that until we are invariably consumed..." Her bed sheets were a tangled mess of blue silks and her body was sprawled across them. She only shifted to one side when he came to join her by sitting atop the duvet. She sighed as he did and pushed herself up on to her forearms as he sat with his legs off the side.

"I'm actually here to make a case for the contrary," he explained. "I wanted to invite you on an evening of hedonism."

"I've had a lifetime of that, ta."

Will didn't bother pushing. He knew that he would have ignored her if she invited him to do the same thing. So he remembered instead how she grounded him and thought to return the favour.

"That's okay. Why don't you tell me what happened then?"

"Nothing happened... you don't know that something happened."

"You don't hurl the word of God like that for an everyday inconvenience," he noted as he thumbed at the book on the floor.

She sat up and turned to look at his face. She prepared herself with a laser look that would display quite how immeasurably much she disliked that observation. That's when his crooked and unsure, but wholeheartedly well-meaning, smile melted her intentions away. His emerald eyes seemed to look right through her and she felt like baring herself might be the right thing to do after all. So she pulled her body across the bed to sit side by side with Will as both their legs hung off the side.

"I told Adam, my friend, about my ancercy."

"How'd it go?"

"As well as one might think. I was going to his room to tell him... to tell him how I really feel about him. But he was drunk and I wanted to leave and wait until tomorrow but then he grabbed my wrists and- and when I tried to leave my sleeves pulled up and he... he saw. And he cast me out never to see him again. I don't even know if he is still here in this building. He may have even fled the kingdom..."

William felt that that precise moment would not have been appropriate to point out that her final assessment might be a little over the edge. So instead he just asked her, "and how does that make you feel?"

She turned to look at him a sneer on her lip, "how do you think it makes me feel?"

"I wasn't asking you to tell *me*."

"Oh."

His soft words and softer expression calmed her down once again. She looked down at her feet and let herself fiddle with her hands in her lap.

"It made me feel... he made me feel... I feel... I feel like I have always known that I am pretty," she started. "While I may never delude myself into thinking that I am beautiful I certainly know that I have everything in the right place – I can charge a lot for looks like these. And I do. Because I am pretty. I thought I was, anyway. Now I feel something else." She hugged herself, "I feel like I am ugly. So, so ugly."

"Is it the ancercy?"

"I want to say yes. I want to throw the truth at the wall and say yes this ancercy has ground my perception of myself to dust but I can't. It's him. I spoke to him and then I reclused back into my chamber because I finally realised how ugly I am." She pulled her legs up so that her feet were teetering on the edge of the bed. She hugged her knees into the embrace with her chest.

"Do you want to know how I got ancercy?" Will offered.

"You slept with a daemon."

"Do you want to know why?" He kept looking at her with those soft eyes and that tilted smirk.

She just shrugged at him. So he pulled his own legs up and sat cross-legged at the edge of the bed. He looked at the floor this time.

"I have been sleeping with girls for a long time. Like, yeah obviously," Harlot scoffed at that, "but I mean a long time. Since I was eleven years old." And then it was her turn to look at him. She gave an appalled frown as he talked. She remembered being forced into her line of work by her father, desperate for cash, at a similar age and looked on Will with both morbid sympathy and a desperate feeling of wanting to help the child he had been.

He continued, "the first was a maid. She was nearly thirty. She had always been playful with me which is why my dad trusted her to look after me when he was out or working or whatever. But her playfulness came from somewhere else. And one night a few weeks before my twelfth birthday she... hah, well she slept with me didn't she. She held me down and licked me all over as if she had finally got her hands on the finest dish in the lands and... I let her. And then she properly took me and I let her and I did it because I am a man. I acted like I was proud of it, like it was something spectacular but it really was not. But because I had let it happen once I had no right to say no the next time. Or the time after that all the way until I was sixteen and I finally had her fired for some inconsequential reason. I don't remember the excuse but I know that I slept with a lot of people after that and that I was very rough with them. Really rough. They didn't deserve that... but for the next seven years of my life I spent every day trying to regain control to take back the power she took from me by being more and more... assertive. With women who didn't deserve it. And I was never violent, never ever. But I still pushed and one night when I had pushed too far I decided I had to sort myself out. I took to the streets for weeks asking around about cultists and devil worshippers until one of them grabbed wind of the fact and took me to their hideout on Rewbridge Road."

"Will," Harlot whispered his name and ached to put a hand on his shoulder. Suddenly Adam was gone from her mind and all she wanted was to wrap this man up in her arms.

"I told them exactly what I wanted – a daemon who would shift into the form of my old maid. And they gave that to me. And that is the first time that I was violent with a woman. Not pushy or demanding. I think I killed that daemon. I thrust myself inside it and saw the face of *her* and then I thrust harder. I held her down and I bit her and I pulled her hair and I hit her and I twisted her limbs and when she tried to crawl back into hell, I grabbed a knife from one of the people who summoned it and stabbed and stabbed and stabbed until it was unrecognisable."

His hands were clasped together in his lap and they were shaking. Harlot told herself that this story should be scaring her but it wasn't. She realised that she would do the same if she were him. She realised, that after an hour of wallowing over a man who would have had her without her consent and without her love, she would spend her life desperate to regain what he took from her. In William's position she would have reclaimed that power. She was not scared of him. She felt only kinship.

"I want to think that it was wrong of me," he carried on, "but I think the only thing wrong about it all is that it worked. I feel better after doing that. And while I know that the real her is still out there, she still suffered my vengeance in here," he tapped a finger to his head. "For the morning after my dad told me that I looked incredibly well. Healthier than he had ever seen me in his life. I felt it, too. Obviously that all went away when, you know," he gestured his hands to his crotch. "So that's when I came to your parlour. To find another person whose control I could take because I had lost mine once more... uh, sorry about that again- oof."

Harlot jumped over to wrap her arms around his neck. She held tighter until he finally hugged her back and she could tell him, "never, ever apologize to me. Never apologize to anyone ever again, okay. I don't care what happens. You're good in my eyes."

When she pulled back he could see her finally smiling again.

"You know I think most other people might disagree with that sentiment."

"I do not care. Would you like to know why?"

She stood up from the bed and walked over the wardrobe. She started flitting through the three spare dresses that were inside and trying to pick something actually nice to wear for once.

"Why is that?" Will asked standing up and joining her. He walked over and leant back on the wall next to the wardrobe looking at Harlot.

"Because that whole story of yours was of great interest to me," she hummed. She pulled out a sky blue frock with some very comely frills and started holding it against her body to mentally measure it against herself.

"The whole story?" he asked, "or the part where you can fuck the brains out of a daemon that looks exactly like the person you hate most in the world." He crossed his arms and tilted his chin up. He looked at her with a macabre approval that finished the conversation for them.

"Now, now Mr Rushings. That is no proper way to speak to a lady."

He grinned, "a lady of the night, perhaps."

She giggled before pushing him to wait outside her door as she prepared herself for that night of hedonism he had promised.

Culver

Mary watched impatiently as her boss studied the symbols in the cultist's corridor and appraised them with increasing noises of disregard

"I did tell you that they were inept," she pointed out.

"Yes, but you see, I simply didn't believe that you knew what you were talking about," he walked past her still fixated on the scrawlings in the stone.

"I'm starting to believe you hired me simply to hide your morality behind my credentials," she muttered. Victor ignored her. When he finally reached the door at the other end he gave it a galling thump that set Mary on edge. She had been confident in her plan until that moment when it would seem she actually had to enact it.

This time it was not Lianna who answered the knock but instead the man with the reaver skull. Like the others, he wore the red and cream robe and like the Mother he bore a curved talon-like knife tucked into his belt. He stared at victor tipping his head down to look clearly at him over the beak. His yellow irised glare seemed to be the first thing Victor had ever seen that made him realise quite how uncomfortable his own gazes had made other people. He seemed to make a precarious step backwards from the Father.

And then the cultist turned to Mary. He lifted his head back up but did not removed the skull; "Miss Culver, was it? You are returning with good news of our little experiment, I hope."

"Extraordinarily good news, in fact. This here is my friend – an alchemist – and he helped me fashion my results into this," she flashed the vial of quicksilver at him, now with the label peeled off. "A prototype for a cure. I was hoping you might offer your services once more so that we may test it."

He continued staring at her as if he were a real reaver stalking prey in the shroud of night. He turned to look at Victor once more before returning to her and inviting them in, "come. Kit, one of the Children, will be more than enthusiastic to lend his body."

He promptly turned down the corridor to the main room of the cellar without waiting to see if they followed.

When they did, Victor looked down at Mary and mouthed, 'children?' concerningly. She stopped them again, turned him around and lowered their heads so that they might converse privately.

"Yes, m'lord, Children. The two leaders are called the Mother and the Father while the standard rank for the other members appears to be 'Children.'"

He frowned, "how desperate."

They turned back around to make a hurried walk in the Father's footsteps. Upon entering the room they quickly realised that they might have been interrupting something; all eight members, except the Father who stood in the entryway, were standing equidistant from one another around a large red circle. Inside the circle was the pattern of an eye drawn by two diamonds, one horizontal and another smaller, vertical one in the centre for an iris.

Mary noticed Lianna stood nearby and gave her a nod of acknowledgement. It was not returned.

"Children," the Father said, his voice rumbling, "this is Mary Culver and the alchemist who is assisting her." One man in the crowd seemed to perk up at her name. "Kit, my son, if you would approach." The Father waved for that man to come over.

"It's only a first draft," Mary said as she held out the quicksilver, "but I hope it can help." When Kit got closer she could tell his skull was that of a cow's. It looked like a diminutive version of Lianna's aurochs fixing. He reached out to take the proffered vial only for the Father to suddenly snatch it from her hand. She let out a shocked breath and stepped nervously backwards. Victor followed in similar quiet and they both found themselves backed into the doorway.

"Now hold on a moment, young lady," he growled. As he spoke, the Mother was unsheathing her dagger behind him and glaring through her skull at the pair. She protectively moved Kit to stand behind her.

The Father inspected the vial and then gripped it tightly, "did you genuinely believe that a member of our organization would not recognise the unique shade of quicksilver when it is presented right before their eyes!" He did not need to shout; his voice was intimidating enough as is.

But Mary was not scared. All she felt for him was pity.

"Actually," she asserted, "we were counting on it."

She took a quick step to ensure that she was behind the auger when he drew one of his wands and pointed it at the Father, before the Father could even draw his own knife. From the tip of the pagan instrument came a wave that rippled through the air – a boom of power in invisible rings. It was small and contained but it was aimed just so that it would pass over the Father's hand and shatter the vial in it.

"What witchery is this!" He shouted then as the glass cut open his hand and a few globules of quicksilver dropped to the floor. The majority of the pseudo liquid, however, seemed to decide it did not obey gravity as it clung to his palm for a few seconds instead. It wormed its way into his cuts then. Blood and silver mixed as the material seemingly climbed its way under the Father's skin.

The only thing he did after was shout. He raised his curved blade as if to stab down on the witcher and ran at him with a fury that could have moved a whole herd of aurochs. But not Victor Redding – he stood his ground as arrogantly as he always had and simply waited for the ritual to begin.

And it did, allowing Mary to breathe out again, as the body of the Father slowed down until it froze in place and the man was stopped in time. Victor smiled at that.

He pushed past the frozen form of the cultist and allowed himself into the centre of the eye pattern on the floor. The others all stepped away from him for fear of what spell he might throw next. Instead he chose his most potent tool – boasting.

"One of the very first lines in every witch and witcher's solemn oath is 'Suffer not the infernal to live. For their mark is as the oath-breakers; black and irredeemable.'" Some of the Children were cowering. Some others were crouched as if to pounce on the auger. The Mother remained stood upright with knife in hand staring down their group's assailant. "Which is why, under imperial law and through the authority granted by the amethyst crown, I declare this gathering to be infernal. And I am sentencing each person present to death on the basis of devilism, debauchery, deviance and deconsecration of holy grounds."

He pulled out a different wand from his waist holster and then a small glass cap from inside his cape. It was a focus lens that he attached to the end of his wand to concentrate his attacks into the ritual that Mary would initiate.

"I am also executing you," he pointed the wand invitingly around the circle of his audience, "on the grounds that you disgust me."

It was the Mother who took the bait. She swung the knife at him like a swiping claw and he dodged with great deftness.

Taking her cue, Mary ran forward and placed both her hands around the reaver skull on the frozen Father's head. When she did she closed her eyes and focused on what exactly it was she needed from the leader. She let her mind wander to the many rituals she did with the group the night before and focused all her will on that aspect of this man; on his ability to summon daemons. She squeezed her eyes tighter and groaned as if she were pushing the very concept of this man summoning a daemon out of him and into the skull. And to her shaking surprise, it was working, she could feel it. She had never once engaged in the effort of channelling ether before for it was nothing that a purveyor of the holy arts would need to do, but today she found proof that necessity could push people to do all kinds of new things.

When she finally released her efforts and opened her eyes she found that the body of the Father was missing. She was panting and doing her best not to drop the reaver skull in between her hands – the last physical trace of Father... oh God, she had never even learned his name. But she could still feel him dwindling. His soul was a part of this skull now – not all of it, not even necessity could push Mary to engage in a degree of magic like that, but just the part familiar with summoning spirits from hell; the part that Mary needed.

After all, animal skulls once belonged to a living being and would have needed to channel that being's energy. Therefore the cultists had already provided them with the ethereal battery they required to begin the ritual.

Mary took it and walked further into the room. Everyone stayed focused on Victor, which she liked very much, so she was free to hold the skull out, the beak still facing her, and wait to collect the remaining souls of the Children and Mother Lianna.

Souls which Victor began sending her way upon seeing her step into place and nod at him. He ended his dodging dance with the Mother in a way that positioned her between himself and Mary. She raised her arm, just like the Father did, ready to slice down on Victor's body when finally he retaliated. He shot his wand out directly forward freezing her in place across the room. Her knife clattered to the floor from her locked hand and she gave a soft gasp as the witcher began to twist his wand around like a knife buried in the air. He slowly turned his forearm around until the spell had finished and he had blasted her soul backwards from her body. Nobody could see it; they could only tell it had happened by the way the woman had given a silent groan before her aurochs skull thumped to the ground atop a pile of her empty clothes.

Mary looked behind her to see that the Father had left red robes behind also. She turned to look down at the skull in her hand and could feel the weight of two segmented souls dwelling inside waiting to be configured for her means. Thanks to Redding's focus lens, whenever he would send a soul her way, the skull would only receive the part of it that it needed, i.e. the part familiar with devil summoning.

The rest of the soul would wash over it, sending a chill up Mary's spine as it passed on to the afterlife where it would wait bitterly for its missing parts to be used up.

She nodded at him to continue.

He scoured the room looking for his next victim and found that even the ones ready to pounce had been reared into fear. When his eyes landed on Kit again he smiled at him widely and with great pleasure. Kit tried to run forward and grab the knife of the Mother only for Redding to lunge and haul the boy up by his collar. The red cloak slipped off as he was lifted upright. His hands moved to guard his masked face as he wept and begged for the auger not to kill him too. Victor just jabbed his wand into the boy's stomach and twisted until his soul relented. He was a much easier victim than the resisting Mother Lianna and it made the auger hope that the others would fail to defend themselves in quite the same way as he had.

One of the children, the only female member other than Lianna, suddenly remembered the organisation that she belonged to and reached to grab two melting candles, one red and one white. She hissed as the wax dripped onto her fists but did not let the pain dissuade her as she made an 'X' with the two items. She held them out and threw her head back – a symbol of opening the body for habitation – as she shouted, *"in absence of Mother, Father and Other I beg your audience: Grandparent to the family and leader of the kingdom-* AGH!" She screamed as Victor gripped her shoulder blade and threw her closer to the middle of the room so that he could shoot her soul out as well.

He had killed her too late, though, as she had galvanised the other Children to continue her chant, all four of them saying the words in eerie unison:

"In absence of Mother, Father and Other, I beg your audience: Grandparent to the family and leader of the kingdom true. In absence of..."

And they continued repeating the chant linking their minds and souls so that some sort of new form could begin to apparate in the centre of the room. Redding cursed as this new form became more physical in an increasingly bright, white light until he realised that they had not saved themselves but actually just handed him his victory.

He moved once more to position this new light, which was beginning to take a humanoid form, in between himself and Mary. These cultists had conveniently linked their souls and while the effort would be strenuous this would allow the auger to banish them all to the skull simultaneously. In ignorance they kept chanting, each with a candlestick in both hands and their heads thrown back.

"Prepare yourself Miss Culver," he shouted over the maelstrom of noise. He saw her nod strongly with a look of determination from across the room. "These devilists are about to learn why Victor Redding was handed a letter of marque!" He held his wand proudly up at the centre of the apparition and hissed a last clarification, "twice!" His mouth opened and unleashed a deep shout. He shouted as he pointed his wand at the luminous figure and put great effort into twisting the device. It resisted like a tortured, rusted screw but Victor still fought on.

Mary, too, had begun the final acts of the ritual. She pulled the brimstone out, still holding the skull from underneath with one hand, and uncorked the vial with her teeth. She spat it out and held the yellow powder at an angle above the skull so that she could dust it all over.

It was also her turn to chant now – to use her words to focus the collection of eight soul-segments into one physical object, unified by the quicksilver as spirits through the brimstone and physical form through the salt.

"*One becomes two,*" she began as the yellow coated the skull.

Victor began adding laughter to his roar as his twisting not only robbed the apparating light of any human-like form but also caused the Children around him to start dropping dead.

"*Two becomes three,*" as each of the Children's robes and skull-masks all clunked to the floor, the white form in the centre of the room disappeared completely. Victor had not only done his part but also prevented whoever was attempting to pass through from doing so.

"*And out of the third,*" once the vial was empty the powder seemed to set into the bone of the skull and warm it into a yellowing colour. Soon it lifted itself out of Mary's hand and began to crack and creak as it levitated into the centre of the room.

Mary watched in awe as she continued the ritual. She pulled the third vial out, the white salt crystals.

"*Comes the one,*" the skull seemed to rear back and the beak of it opened wide. It peeled further, unnaturally far, until Mary threw the vial of salt into it like it were a ball into a hoop.

"As the fourth," she finished.

While one might expect the salt vial to simply fall through the back of the floating skull it instead disappeared as if it had been swallowed. The skull shook and from the beak came a tearing squawk that ripped through the room. It echoed, slowly ebbing quieter as the skull began to gently float down from its place in the sky. As it came closer to the ground it left a piece of vermillion rock, a jagged triangle of cinnabar, floating where it once was in the air.

The wobbling and profusely sweating auger reached up to claim it. Once his fingers wrapped around it the bird-call came to an abrupt halt. The reaver skull shattered in place leaving cream fragments spread across the ground.

Mary allowed herself to breathe out again.

Victor eyed the red stone suspiciously. All it seemed to him was a particularly arcane rock. "And this is it, is it?"

"Yes, m'lord," she sighed. "That is an alchemist's stone."

She held her hand out and he reluctantly let it go to her. As soon as it pressed to her skin she could feel that their plan had worked – this was exactly what they needed.

Before she could rest she had to explain this fact to her boss before he threw her ability under scrutiny yet again. "You are aware of the philosopher's stone," she chose to make that a statement to avoid a repeat of the whole Agamemnon conversation. "An alchemist's stone is like a simpler version – it is like mobile knowledge at your fingertips. While it is commonly used to quickly perform reactions without the need of a piece of equipment it can sometimes be used how we have used it today – to store the knowledge of a person or group of peoples so that we may employ it at our discretion. In this case, the knowledge – and ability – to summon daemons. This stone," she waved it at him, "can summon eight spirits with no need to bleed yourself or draw a circle or light a candle. You just hold it, wish for the spirit to come and the rock will do it for you."

Victor seemed to nod approvingly at this, although it lasted for less than three seconds. "While that is an impressive achievement, might I ask what the next step is?"

"Yes, m'lord. The ultimate plan is to distribute these around, well, wherever you wish, via dealers or other incongruous methods. With an economy of daemon-summoning-alchemist's-stones flowing, soon enough ancercy will be rampant and your goal will have been achieved. For, as we have established, temptation will do all the heavy lifting."

"Excellent!"

"However," she held a finger up to pause him. "There is still the matter of replication. We only have one of these and this can only summon eight daemons before it loses its potency."

"And I am presuming you do not possess the knowledge on how to do that," he sniffled. "Although, I feel duty-bound to ask how you learned of the alchemists stone in the first place, hm?"

"Right." She smiled as she answered, "it was actually, once again, from the book of Agamemnon. To illustrate his deviance from God the book describes his many dealings with devilists, pagans and alchemists. One such ritual was the binding of an alchemists stone."

Victor harumphed at her explanation, "you would think that in dissuading certain activities, God would then not illustrate them in his holy texts."

Mary bit her lip to stop her smile growing, "and that concept is the basis of my 'give them the means and they shall sin' plan. So thank God!" She smiled at him so brightly it made him frown, "literally."

Abernathy

Harlot and William perused their way down Rewbridge road, him with a generous bottle of gin in his hand. It was half empty by the time they'd made their way to the church as the two had already giggled, hiccupped and stumbled their way through it.

"And then he just never showed up again! Can you believe it," Harlot chortled her way to the end of an anecdote. The two had spent the walk there not only drinking a spirit as if it were water but regaling in her tales of the most memorable clients.

"And you live on the same street as him, yeah? This is the butcher on Annum's Lane?"

"He is now," she slurred. She walked up to Will and flopped an arm over his shoulder as she got far too close to his face, "but he was just a boy when I got my hands on him." She slinked away laughing. He chuckled too, already forgiving her for when she would apologize in the morning about the comment.

"Come on, pretty lady, the den... lair... place is over yonder," he said waggling his finger over at the church on the street corner. She looked over to where he was stood on the opposite side of the road, all illuminated by the street lights, and squinted as if she had forgotten why they were there at all.

He laughed at her and shook the bottle to lure her over to his side. She followed like a moth to a flame and he rewarded by lifting the bottle up until she opened her mouth. He tipped the gin, a little loosely, so that it poured down her throat and slightly down her chin. When he finally pulled back and she wiped her mouth off, she looked him up and down and said, "you look sort of like an angel in the firelight like that." And then she laughed as she walked off once more.

William felt a moment of warmth in his cheeks and then his head started to ache. So he downed another gulp of gin until it all went away before he rejoined Harlot.

"Come on. 'S round here," he lead the way to the back of the church where the cellar door sat. When Harlot approached she saw him squatting in front of it and poking at the chains while mumbling something.

"What's that? Is that Bill-speak?"

"Calariarian... Calareen... It's Calarian!"

She snorted, "that's what I said."

"Other things were written in that language you know." He hiccupped and lost his balance falling back on his arse. Harlot snorted again. "I think that I should sober up a li'l bit before I try any daemon words," Will conceded. He crawled across the floor and sat on the right side of the entrance leaning over the top of the wooden panels. Harlot sat on the other side doing the same.

He looked at the bottle, the neck of which he had been tightly gripping for a while now and decided that the last few swigs at the bottom weren't worth it. He offered it to Harlot who shrugged and accepted it. She had enjoyed being able to drink clean water during her stay with the mayor but she may as well get used to drinking whatever she can afford before she returns to her own bed.

When she had finished it off she threw the bottle into a nearby bush and smiled delightfully at the sound it make as it smashed against the ground.

A little calmer now, Will said, "that was bad someone could cut themselves."

Harlot didn't stop smiling. She shrugged, "I might die tomorrow I do not care."

He laughed at that, "oh yeah, I nearly forgot." He twisted around to face her, both his shoulders resting on the entrance. "Is there anything you want to do before you die? Something entirely selfish or just evil because, you know, you won't care about it soon enough? Other than the whole thing were about to do, yeah."

She pursed her lips and thought about it. She mimicked his position again and looked up as if ideas would appear from the sky. Honestly, there was not anything. She even felt bad about leaving shards of glass in a public space – she only threw that bottle in a moment of thoughtlessness. But then something did want to come to mind.

"Well, I had always wanted to tell someone my name. My real name."

William squinted at her; his face twisted in disbelief. "That's a sad final request." He blinked a few times and then leant back, "also, is Harlot not your real name?"

She snorted loudly that time and fell into a tiny fit of giggles.

"Of course not!"

"Oh."

"I picked it when I was young, far too young to remember. My dad had died and my mum had fallen sick so I had no choice but to work the corner," she tilted her body so that she could point around the side of the church, "specifically that corner. Ever since then I was Harlot Abernathy."

"And no one knows your real name? Is it not even in the doomsday book?"

"What would the emperor want with a whore's name?" She sneered, "I haven't money enough to fund some foreign war."

"But everyone's name was written in it, was it not?"

"Yeah. Everyone important."

"Oh..." he bit back a smile, "my name's in it."

She smiled at that too, "fine. Perhaps if I am to die then I should tell you that my real name is-"

"Hey!" he stopped her. By now the cold night air and grim discussion had returned them to some of their senses and the world stopped seeming so soft to them. "I don't think that I'd like to know."

"Why not? Everyone else does. And this time I actually want to tell."

"Because I don't think it matters. You are Harlot Abernathy. I don't care for the girl you were before."

"How sweet. But I would not like to be remembered as such." She sighed and rested her head in her folded arms. She looked up at the stars and seven planets far in the sky and Will did the same. "You know I always had this sort of... fantasy. That one of my clients would like me so much he would scoop me up and marry me just to keep me for himself. I wasn't so foolish to believe that someone might love me but I did hope that something like that may happen. And then I would bear his kids and when I did that my job would then be to be a wife and mother and not... you know. And then, just maybe, I could change my name again. Not return to the lonely little girl or remain as a Harlot, although I admit I am fond of Abernathy, but instead be someone new."

"I imagine you would have taken your husband's name," Will muttered.

She ignored him. "Maybe if I am to be remembered, by even just you, it should still be under a new name after all. I may not have become a full woman yet but in death I will still have my fantasy."

"Harlot," William turned back to her and was speaking frankly then, "this day has been a bit of a wild chariot ride. But a good one. My last days are better because of it. And that's not because I had a mother nurturing me or because I had a wife to cater to me... but because I had a father who, in his own way, has nurtured me. And a friend who... has been a friend. What I'm trying to say is that it baffles me that you can't consider yourself a 'full woman' or what have it despite the fact that you can uplift people just by being as you are.

She looked back at him, "what are you saying?"

"That it matters not that you aren't a full woman. Nor that I am not a full man. Because here, under the starlight and planetsight... were just two people. You can be independent,"

"And you can be pretty," she added.

"Yes," he chuckled, "And we can just be us. I think that as you consider your new name, that is what should be on your mind. Not ideas of being a proper woman."

"I am still sad to lose my fantasy." She cupped the air in front of her as if it were the rosy cheek of a bouncing baby boy.

"Yes, well that is a matter of your untimely fate not your character. There are no phords in the world I can say to ever make that okay. I am sorry."

"What did I say about apologising," she grinned.

"Yeah, yeah. Just pick a new name," he commanded. He rolled over so that he was kneeling on the cold dirt directly in front of the cellar entrance, "and be quick about it because I think I'm about sober enough to remember the pass phrase."

"And what? You're in a hurry to stick that thing somewhere?"

He looked down to his crotch and snickered, "hey if 'that thing' is going to kill me then it can at least have the good faith to send me out on a high note."

"Alright, alright." She stood up and dusted as much mud and gravel as she could off of her borrowed dress. "How about Cassandra?"

Will thought about it and hummed, "it's a bit, um,"

"Tarty." She finished.

"A bit."

"Lenore?"

"Slightly poncy."

"Felicity."

"Felicity Abernathy doesn't really work."

"Oh then why don't we keep it simple!" She clapped her hands together as the idea formed. "Harley Abernathy!"

"Because... you're not a man?"

She hit him on the shoulder as she walked around to stand behind him, "just open the door, Rushings. I think Harley is a very comely name."

He held two fingers out ready to begin the unlocking cant. Before he started he turned around to look up at her. He smiled in that crooked way that made her want to run her hands through his soft blond hair.

"It's nice to meet you, Harley Abernathy."

The door popped unlocked. Harley put a startled hand over her quickly beating heart as the ringing metal sound sent her reeling backwards a few steps. A shocked Will joined her crawling back up to his feet and holding her protectively.

Out of nowhere, the padlock had burst and the linking chains – whose ends were blackened now – had begun to slink and slide off the edges of the entrance. And then the doors finally flung themselves open.

"Wow that was... I didn't even see you do it."

"That wasn't me," Will explained gravely.

Harlot took another frightful step back, "then is someone coming out? Are they going home, were we too late for the devil summoning?"

"No, no one's coming. That lock broke, Harley. It just shattered."

"Yes, I am here too."

"No, you don't get it." He turned his head to look her in the eyes, "something has happened to the person that made the lock."

"Oh."

"Come on, let's go look." The pair stalked over to the cellar and peered over the edge. After ascertaining the ladder's safety, William moved down it and Harley followed. He moved ahead, taking a slow step at a time towards the ajar door on the other side while she made awing faces at the engraved symbols all over the place.

He held a finger to his lip as he peered through the gap in the door. He pulled it open just slightly so that he might hear what was happening inside. Harley joined him, crawling underneath his body slightly to get her own ear in the widening gap.

"Excellent!" Came a man's voice from inside.

"However," came another – a woman's. "There is still the matter of replication. We only have one of these and this can only summon eight daemons before it loses its potency."

"And I am presuming you do not possess the knowledge on how to do that," the man sniffled. "Although, I feel duty-bound to ask how you learned of the alchemists stone in the first place, hm?"

"Right." The two voices continued on to discuss portions of the Bill.

"I think... I recognise those voices." Will whispered to her.

"Yes. No. His is uncertain but that lady's voice... I think that might be Mary Culver's voice."

Will pulled back, "then the man's is that horrid auger's voice."

"Yes!" Harley whispered a bit too loudly. William leant in to place a finger on her lip and they both cringed as suddenly all the voices in the cellar had gone quiet.

From far off they heard Mary whisper something followed by the commanding voice of Victor, "who is there!"

"Run," William insisted.

"What?"

"Run, now!" he pushed Harley in front of him by the shoulders and they quickly paced back to the ladder. They heard the door creak quickly open behind them by the time she had her hands on the first rung.

"What are you two doing here?" demanded the spitting voice of Mr Redding.

Mary gasped by his side and put a hand to her mouth as Will and Harley kept bounding up the ladder. Mary tugged at Victor's sleeve, "they might have heard everything, m'lord."

"Hm?"

She looked him in the eye, "*everything.*"

His eyes widened. As Harley pulled up from the cellar and William followed, the auger pulled out a new wand and passed the alchemist's stone to Mary. "I command you to stop!" He shouted after them. He ran down the corridor with Mary in tow.

Back outside, Harley lead the escape down the streets as she knew them far better than he did. She also let out curse after curse as she hiked up her dress and made the other man blush with her exposedness. They dashed turn after turn after twist, so much so that Will might have thought they'd lost them by now but Harley was not so convinced. She kept going no matter how much her throat burned with the exertion. Finally, she did allow them to turn to a jog rather than a sprint as they reached the north-eastern crowded streets of thin walk-ways and tall buildings.

They decided to make one last turn into a dark alleyway to catch their breath. They leant against opposite walls and huffed and puffed as their chests rose and fell. Their faces were red and hair all over the place but they had at least believed they had escaped.

It was then that a rustling came from the dark in the alleyway, the deep inky dark that the streetlights could not reach. Like a doorway to another world, it melded into pure black like it might stretch on forever. And from that pure black came the stomp of a man's bare foot at the end of a deeply muscled leg. The skin was fire red and the veins pulsed orange and each toe wiggled individually as if having just been formed in the flames of hell.

That powerful calf then pulled the rest of its body from the dark, black depths – equally red and orange with mighty horns protruding from a shock of midnight hair. It seemed like the form of a naked man but it was nine foot tall and grinning with all the spite of a devil.

"Run," Will repeated.

He pushed Harley ahead of him and let her lead the way again as they dashed between the intricate streets of Whitley. At one point they came to an abrupt stop when, at the end of the street, the glimmering mirage image of Victor seemed to appear. They turned a different corner only to see him there as well before the same thing happened a third time.

Forced to turn back, they inevitably ended up being cut off by the daemon who waggled his clawed fingers at them. They turned back down the last available street and found that it was empty and they could keep going. Unfortunately that is also when Will had an idea of his own.

"Hold, hold, hold." He grasped her arm and pulled her to a stop.

"What! Come on we need to go; I think I can-"

"We can't escape this," William huffed, "we just can't." He pulled her close, grasping each of her shoulders and bumping their foreheads together.

"Look. I'm going to stay behind. You didn't get infected till a bit later than me so you have few extra days."

"Don't be so stupid, William Rushings, we can outrun them."

He let their sweaty, red, heaving faces prove her wrong. That and the memory of the red devil paired with Victor's pursuant mirages.

"If this is the last thing I do," he whispered, "then I want it to be saving you."

"You fool don't you dare!" She was cut off when he pushed her away from him. She caught herself on the walls of some house and watched as he waved at her from the end of the street.

"Go and be Harley, I beg you... and," he swallowed dryly, "forget all about me."

He ran backwards to where the auger had cut them off threefold. She wanted to chase after him but knew it would be stupid to do so. So she just ran into the night her tears staining her face as she searched for a place of refuge.

A fugitive and all on her own, she realised, with no place to belong.

Lobelia

"I asked you what you're doing here?"

Magellan seemed like he was still trying to decide how he felt about the princess' presence here in his lab. She, on the other hand, knew that she had been caught and was processing her fear. She had never felt fear before, not really, and now she was battling between her God-given claim to superiority and the fact that she technically was trespassing.

"I am wanting to know..." she slowly spoke her words as they had formed at the same time as her lagging trail of thought, "what exactly that is." She pointed at the tank in the corner. She stood up taller and spoke with more confidence for her next assertation, "and what exactly that thing inside it is."

Cyrus walked over to her side and looked through the window of the tank. "Ah."

His face still danced with indecision as he looked at her and studied her. Then he decided that he ought to break into a smile, one of the same melted subservience he usually displayed her as an employee of the crown.

"My deepest apologies, your highness, for not giving you the welcome tour." He spread his arms out in showmanship, a change that jarred Lolita for a few moments as he explained himself. "You are currently in my bottle."

"Your bottle?"

"My bottle."

He pushed his arm deep into his coat until he pulled out a glass milk bottle with a cork plugged tightly in the hole. Inside she could see a floating, disc-shaped black light with flecks of white. It shimmered while slowly rotating and spiking outwards.

She reached out to touch it but he pulled away from her. "Careful. Anything happens to the bottle then everything inside, including us, goes splat."

She pulled her hands back quickly.

"How, might I ask, is the bottle in here with us if we are in the bottle?"

Absently, Magellan stuffed it back into the depths of his coat somewhere. "Oh, because I carried it in with me. It's safer on my persons than anywhere else."

"But... it's inside itself?"

"No, it's inside my coat."

"Of course." She stopped questioning him for fear of appearing lame.

"Right, the elephant in the room."

"What's an elephant?"

"Nothing to concern yourself with, ma'am." He moved to stand by that tank in the corner of the room. "This is a bronze growth tank"

"And that thing inside?" she repeated.

"Well that," he stroked his chin and measured his words. "That is what a baby looks like when it is growing from a seed to a person inside a mother's womb. I call it a foetus."

"And why, dare I ask, is this process occurring in a vat of holy water and not in a mother's womb," Cyrus tried to answer but Lolita kept going, "as God intended it to be."

He really struggled to find words then. The right ones, anyway. He knew the answer just not how to articulate, not to a fourteen year old girl, anyhow. He just ummed and awed at her, nibbling on his nails and starting some noises that were meant to be words while she stood there growing increasingly impatient.

Eventually he came to one knee to be at eye level with her. He softened his face and tried to talk to her with a low and serious voice that still carried warmth.

"Now, I will be honest with you, but I would like you to remain... mature about it. It is a delicate situation, one that I am trusting you to hear with an open mind."

She nodded to him keeping her mouth shut and turning from impatient to excited as she waited to be clued in on Magellan's secret.

"Good. Now, as you may know there are some women out there who... can't have babies of their own. They just have something wrong with their bodies where it won't cultivate the man's seed. So, after stumbling upon a specific spell in some... unsavoury company, I came up with the idea on how I could adapt that spell into one where I channel ether into life itself."

When Lolita heard this, her perception was completely tilted. She moved back over to that corner tank once more and placed her hand on it. Her mouth was open in a small 'o' of surprise but now it was pulling at the corners into the slightest of smiles.

"Wow," she slowly stroked the bronze and stared at the growing foetus, "I can't wait to see who you're going to be."

She whipped round to look at the witcher then, fully beaming, "can you show me how it works? Can you do it now?"

He chuckled at that, "I'm sorry ma'am," he stood back up, "but life is precious. You shouldn't make it unless you're ready to take responsibility for it."

"Oh, I see. No of course. Very wise." She put her hand on the tank again, "and the holy water is to channel the ether through, I presume? And even sustain the growing babe?"

"Very astute, ma'am," he came to lean on the side of the tank, "although it is wych water not holy water."

"What's the difference?"

"Nothing, other than the fact it was made by a pagan. So it would not work for holy ceremonies like exorcisms or your baptism."

"I see."

He cleared his throat, "speaking of holy, there is one more thing I must trust you to do, ma'am."

"Yes?"

He did not mince his words then, "you cannot tell anyone in the church about this. Anyone. That includes your mother."

She blinked, naively confused. "Whyever not? Surely this is a brilliant endeavour!"

"Because," he replied, "the spell I use is still relatively modern. This whole thing is. I've only been doing it for about two decades or so. And because of that it has yet to be declared to the church. It's not in the solemn oath yet." He tapped the breast of his coat.

"It's not... warlock magic is it?"

"No, no. Well, that's an arbitrary term anyway. It's not defined in the solemn oath at all and I would like to keep it that way for fear of them making it a warlock spell."

"But why would they. Even if it is bad, you said that your oath illustrates extenuating circumstances where a warlock spell may be used in a witch or witcher fashion!"

"Aha, you did pay attention didn't you. See, I just don't want to take the risk and ruin this whole operation. Especially not if they learn where exactly I got the spell from."

"I see," she said. His eyes wandered across the room to the corner where that red robe hung on a hook. She wondered what he was looking at but couldn't remember what was on that side of the wall and so thought nothing of it. "Seeing as I approve of this venture," she said so regally, "then I shall not ask where you received this power."

"Truly kind, ma'am."

"Although I do have one final question."

"Anything."

"Those two serving girls. And Adam. Are they...?"

"Another sharp observation." He stepped cautiously, "I am not sure why but your body is having an adverse reaction to my creations. You can tell that they were not born of natural means."

She frowned, "that's a shame. I think what you're doing is noble."

He smiled in contrast to her, "however can I thank you for such kind words?"

"By keeping on," she answered, letting herself brighten up a bit with him, "keep on contributing to your community. That's what it's all about, is it not? However my body may seem to react."

He nodded his head and bowed his upper body to her.

"Right then, I should like to be shown how to exit this bottle of yours."

"Yes, of course," he led the way back around to the other side of the 'U' where they came to stand in front of the blank wall that she had appeared next to. It was still blank, as blank as it was when she arrived, but Cyrus seemed to think otherwise.

"Just exit the same way you entered." He gestured to the centre of the wall.

"With the eye pattern? Is there one around here?" She looked at where he was pointing but saw nothing.

He smiled at that and tilted his head, "yes, ma'am. There is one here, you just have to focus to see it. I presume that you couldn't see the entrance before until the street lamps flickered on?"

"Correct."

"That is because it is hidden by an arcane filter. Stops most people from seeing it. Unfortunately, that illusion is broken at night because runelight shatters it."

"I see. And do you have runelight here to help me?"

"No, ma'am. But now that you know what it looks like I believe that you have the propensity to seek it out for yourself."

She nodded at him, afraid to be proven incapable. She focused on the spot, in the centre and a little bit above, where the eye might be. She relaxed herself and remembered what the other one looked like bathed in the warm glow of the runelight and soon enough her mind was allowed into seeing what was always there.

Just like outside: a brass square with those two diamond shapes had been nailed to the wall and when she looked at it she could feel it looking back. Except she was less uncomfortable and more celebratory this time as she turned to look for Magellan to tell him.

But he was there no longer.

Once she looked away from the eye, he had gone and so had the room. The desks and crystals were all replaced by the dour, windy streets of Whitley Moor. And the only person in her company was a very, very panicked Ser Garland.

"My knight! Rest easy!" She called after witnessing him attempting to turn up the path in search of a hidden tunnel that she might have fallen down.

"Your highness, thank the Lord for your safe return." He ran over and both parties resisted the dreadfully informal and overly emotional urge to embrace one another.

A third voice joined them then, as Magellan had suddenly appeared at her side with a perfectly calm demeanour. "Worry not, honourable ser, she had simply stumbled upon my place of work. I saw that no harm came to her." And he craned his neck at the knight as well.

* * *

With both a knight and a loyal witcher at her side, Lolita worried not for the impending night hunt even though she had made it home still with thirty minutes to spare.

As soon as they entered the mayor's foyer she spotted Manford scrabbling up the left stairway and scoffed, "well that's my mother incoming." She pulled off her cloak and handed it to a nearby servant who took it off to a coat rack. She hesitated a moment in doing this but the man was one of the members of staff who hadn't elicited that uncomfortable sensation in her so she would be fine.

"And what time precisely do you call this?" Katherine's voice could be heard filling the room before she even hit the top step. As she marched down them towards her daughter her face grew increasingly annoyed, although it did not shift too far from her default regal look.

Lolita pursed her lips and looked away from the oncoming storm, "I call it eleven thirty-five."

Once the queen had come to stand directly in front of the princess, she growled at her deeply, "do not play rhetorics with me. And you two, why is my daughter in the street at night?"

"I take full responsibility, your majesty. I should have taken her home before the night had fallen."

"Yes, well, I can believe entirely that it was Lolita who commanded you to stay out. But you," she pointed a sharp finger at the witcher, "what is your excuse?"

"Mother," Lolita put her hand on top of her mum's arm and lowered it. "I only caught him on my way home, you know for certain he had nothing to do with this. It was all me."

Katherine considered for a few seconds. "Fine. My apologies, Cyrus. Are you prepared for the baptism tomorrow?"

"I was just out procuring the final ingredient, your majesty," he rummaged into that bottomless coat of his again and revealed a small, silver knob of some sort. "Wychroot," he explained, "divination reveals the future, but there are many futures to be seen. A sprinkling of powder from this would focus any revealed futures into the most likely one. This is customary for any royal baptism."

"How interesting," the queen fibbed. "Come on, sweetheart. Off to bed with you, we have another long trip to Summerset tomorrow."

"Yes, mother," she turned and waved to her two companions as she followed her mum to the Azalea suite.

"Goodnight, Ser Garland. Goodnight, Magellan!"

They both waved to her and Cyrus shot her a wink that made her giggle as she carried it with her to bed.

Culver

"Do all witchers have one of those?"

"The good ones do."

Mary's last conversation with Victor rung in her head as she walked around the strange new room that seemed to have formed around her. It was quite large, very high ceiling, but was completely empty except for its three fixtures. The first being a line of thick bars that divided one third of the room from the rest of it; the second being a window on the opposite wall to the prison that looked out into a sea of stars; the third being a bell hung on the eastern wall.

Everything else was plain. The walls were made of a glaring yellow brick and all the light seemed to ominously pour from a spot in the centre of the ceiling despite there being no observable source. Inside the cordoned off area sat a rather starstruck looking William who was being guarded by the devil that Mary had summoned with the alchemist's stone.

"Does that have to be here," he complained with a frown. He seemed to be unable to take his eyes off the fact that the devil was both completely naked and grinning wildly at him.

"It won't hurt you," Mary responded absently.

"Then why did you summon it?"

"It was a bluff," she groaned. She had been trying not to look at him for fear of bringing the subject topic into her peripheral vision. "I can only summon... courtesan daemons.

"Oh. Because that's all you needed, right?"

"Ugh," she returned to facing away from him and staring out the window. She sighed as she admired the cosmos unfolding before her. After long enough, she attempted to locate and trace any of the few constellations she knew but couldn't seem to find any of them. She didn't even see any of the seven planets which confused her.

She was brought back from her pondering, though, by another unwelcome interjection from her prisoner.

"This devil is a male," he said, rather loudly.

Mary looked at him with astonishment, "what exactly was your first clue?"

"The horse-like appendage-"

"Make your point!"

"Well, I am also male."

"Now that one was hard to figure out."

"How droll. My point is that... he lusts for me. Another male." William attempted to cringe further into the wall behind him as he said that and away from the daemonic warden.

Mary just sent him a very scalding look loaded with all her discontent for the well-off and their lack of awareness of the real world. She returned to her place by the window. To save her sanity she decided it was best not to keep pondering over whoever's stars she saw out there and instead just stand with her back against that wall. She kept looking between the uniquely arcane bell – brass and dressed with a red tassel – and the captive who, despite his complaints, could physically not stop looking at the devil in great discomfort.

The silence managed to ring true for just about another five minutes of the devil's tail lashing back and forth until eventually Will spoke up again.

"So."

"For God's sake," Mary hissed immediately. The daemon hissed louder at her for that, though, and she took a precautionary step away.

"...So," Will started again. "Where is the other one? Tall, dark and miserable?"

"Getting his lens fixed."

"Is that a euphemism?"

She sighed and prayed, mentally this time, for strength. "Lens. Like a wand cap – it cracked a bit under the pressure he put it through during our encounter with the cultists."

William frowned, "did you know their names?"

"Oh they were the Whitley chapter or something. Called themselves the Family of Mara."

"No, I know what their band was called. I'm asking if you knew their individual names."

Mary didn't answer that. She just stared at him like he was a thousand miles away. And she kept staring as if that could push him further. Images appeared of Mother Lianna in her mind. And then that scared girl with the candlesticks... the Father disappearing in her hands as she spirited his soul away.

"You don't get to ask me that," she whispered.

"Why? Because I'm diseased?"

"Yes!"

"Well so is that poor woman you and your mate are about to go chasing across the kingdom."

"She's a whore," Mary scoffed, "nothing poor about her but her purse." She spat her words and began pacing in her rising vitriol, "in fact it's women like her who are making it hard for women like me! I have no sympathy for someone who continues to sell out her body like... like a whore!"

William stood up and walked to the bars, eyeing the devil wearily as he did so. He didn't rise to her anger he just kept talking, "really? Because it seems to me that it's that auger fellow who is making your life harder right now, not her."

She stopped pacing about to clutch her arms around herself. She turned to look wildly at the man and returned her voice to the husky tone of accusation, "it doesn't matter. What you two know can't be left out there."

"I promise you; we don't even know what it is we know."

"Regardless. Information like that could jeopardize our work if it gets to the wrong ears."

"Whose ears are the wrong ones?"

"It's not my business."

"I see." William returned to sitting against the back wall of his cell and letting the silence return to the room. The devil's tail kept swinging back and forth like the pointed pendulum of a grandfather clock for ten more minutes.

When Mary dared to peak out the window briefly she had noted that the stars had moved slightly in the sky. She tilted her head and wondered if perhaps it was in fact the room that had moved instead.

Her meandering had been interrupted when a sudden voice spoke out asking how everything is. She whipped around to scathe at the prisoner again only to see that he was just looking blankly at the actual speaker. Victor was there, stood by the bell, and looking at Mary impatiently.

"Well?"

"All is fine, my lord," she coughed, "yes, it has been quiet."

"Good," he crooned. He walked over to stand in front of their captive who stared back at him indifferently.

"Uh, my lord." Mary walked over to his side raising a finger of inquiry. "I know you showed me that bottle full of the unknown. But where exactly are we?"

"Were inside it."

"Right but... how? Are we smaller now?"

"Size is relative, miss Culver, were the same size inside the bottle as we are outside it," he then reached into his cape and pulled the bottle out, "for it is always smaller than us."

William leaned forward to get a closer look at it.

Mary pointed at the sharp, amorphous, black light, specifically the white flecks. "Are they the stars that I see outside?"

"No, those are the same stars that hang over Etherium. We are merely occupying an alternative pocket of space in the realm which I have condensed into this bottle." He tapped the top of it, "for convenience."

William whispered to Mary, "does that make sense?"

"Pipe down, you," commanded the auger.

"Actually," Will groaned, rising to his feet again, "I may just pipe up instead. You know that house Iris has no authority to arrest citezens of Belgrave, especially not people of the upper class."

"Yes," Victor hissed, baring his teeth, "you are right. Which is why I am acting on a different authority; my authority. i.e. better judgement!"

William narrowed his eyes, "I dare you to say that to queen Charlotte."

"My lord, if you please," Mary interjected before he got too angry. "Tomorrow we must begin an arduous search across Whitley for the whore. We desperately need to rest."

Victor harumphed at that but still walked away from the bars and over to the bell. "Quite. I made sure to stop at the Happy Huntress on my way here,"

"Wehey!" Will cheered.

Victor ignored him, "and made sure that she had not gone home. We will search the mayoral hall tonight and then sweep the city in the morning."

"Very good, m'lord."

He clung on to the red hanging from the bottom of the bell. Before he rung it, he turned to look at William one last time, "and you. You had better hope that disease of yours finishes its course soon. Those bars can't keep this devil at bay forever." He rung the cord.

Will looked nervously at the guard who was licking a forked tongue across his midnight black lips. He turned back to the ringing bell to see that it had transported the auger away and back to into the realm. Mary followed, leaving him alone in the light with a creature whose pointed nails were starting to graft away at the prison bars.

Lobelia

Lolita was glad to wake up that morning to the sight of Anna pulling her curtains open rather one of Magellan's contributions to alchemy.

As much as she wished to encourage his work, she still could not stand to be around the fruits of it. She was reminded sorely of this fact while being hurried out the door by her pushy mother wherein she was jolted by one of those maids again. She rushed to the royal carriage right away and found her solace in their plump benches and the caring gaze of ancestors.

Also accompanying them on the trip to Summerset was the mayor himself.

William had not returned home last night and people were starting to suspect the worst so Katherine had graciously allowed Theodore to attend the baptism ceremony as thanks for his hospitality. She had whispered in her daughter's ear right after that the man would need some fancy distraction as his mind was most likely running rampant with worst case scenarios.

On the other hand, she had also informed Lolita that the Viscount Azalea will be attending the ceremony – a matter that had not been in debate seeing as their house resided in Summerset but still a delightful turn of conversation as she deeply looked forward to seeing her cousin Thomas again. A boy that Katherine simply loathed.

"Of course, the Archbishop of Stourford will be presiding."

"I don't really like him," Lolita pouted as the carriage kicked into a start. "He always looks like he's glaring at me."

"Yes, well try attending a privy council meeting where the man stands there in all his white and gold finery glaring daggers at me whenever I speak my mind."

Her mother's gossipy complaints about royal affairs always cheered the princess up. She enjoyed listening to them like they were just another story being told to comfort her. It also helped that she would never have to experience such plights; Aaron would take the throne leaving her free to disconnect from the seriousness of it all.

"It is a shame, though, that the mayor's son is not coming. I rather fancied him."

"Are you sure he would not have averted your gaze from the baptism ceremony?"

Lolita grinned, "not if he's in it, he wouldn't have."

Katherine just sighed at that, "you know you cannot marry beneath you, dear. He will not show up in the witcher's divination."

"Is a mayor's son really so below me?"

"Yes," she insisted, "you will marry from one of the high houses. Noone beyond that."

"Fine. I'm still not marrying Thomas, though."

Katherine scoffed, "good. I should like you to take a proper man."

"He is a proper man!"

"I thought you weren't marrying him?"

"I'm not," she argued. She hated when her mother talked about her friend like this. "But you should not be so disrespectful to him."

"You wish to hear of disrespect," her mother chided, "then hear this." Lolita knew she was about to experience one of those rare moments where she regretted to support her mother's gossiping habit. "Your friend, Thomas Azalea, was found with his mother's lady's maid in his bed. Not a single garment between them."

"Surely that's not true?" Lolita asked, genuinely confused. And slightly concerned too.

"It is. She was fired on the spot and sent back into the streets without a single penny!"

"And Tommy?"

"Oh he had his access to the servants quarter's taken away until the day he ascended as viscount."

"What a dreadful tale," she muttered.

The queen gave a slight nod, "maybe. But both me and his mother would be lying if we said we weren't a little relieved by the news..."

"Oh, let us not!"

"You're right, even these closed doors aren't suitable for such vulgarity."

"Mmm," Lolita murmured a quiet agreement.

And the carriage continued to trundle on through the latter streets of Whitley Moor as they moved back on the northern trail.

Soon enough houses were getting shorter as stone paths were replaced by dirt ones. Bricked walls became wooden fences and eventually streets became fields as farms overtook any urban landscape. The royal procession continued upwards and witnessed the grey skies turn slightly lighter as its horses trundled from muddy ground to a slightly more solid foundation of earth.

The sheep further up the road seemed less likely to be caked by a layer of brown on the lower portions of their bodies; the flowers that grew became more colourful and the shoots of wheat and barley became more plentiful.

In all of the eight hour trip they ended up making very little talk. Each trundle forward brought the cathedral, and Lolita's anxiety, even closer to mind. Whenever her mum might make inquiries or share a tidbit she had overheard while they stayed in

Whitley, the princess would nod or grunt in response or simply smile and turn her gaze out the window.

Katherine understood though and just harboured a wistful expression at each dismissal. When she was of the same age, and rocking herself down the southern roads, she had shown her own father and mother a degree of nervous ignorance. She had tried to think what had soothed her, what made her ready, and she realised that she didn't know. Katherine had spent that entire journey in terrified silence letting the unknown factors bear down upon her until she reached her destination.

Once there, while the now deceased Viscount and Viscountess Azalea bowed and curtseyed and everyone else was smiling and staring, she had marched stiffly to the pool opposite her witcher – the senior Magellan.

What ensued was a very disgraceful display of shaking as she bore witness to a future where she stood alone atop the palace and stared over Belgrave as it burned... it was the very next day that her parents introduced her to the son of the Duke Moonflower. That boy would grow up to be Aaron and Lolita's father. He would sire two Lobelia heirs, argue dramatically with the queen about raising them Extenic, refuse to share a bed with her other than to procreate and stew in his insecurity at only being the prince to Belgrave and never king. She never liked him, no, but the kids did. He had ended up dying when they were each twelve and eight. He had taken off with the boats, awarding himself some dressy naval title despite his lack of seafaring experience – an action that inevitably killed him. Of course Katherine felt that this news was a mere inconvenience but she wished not to mar his children's perceptions of him so she wept when she was in their presences and made sure all the appropriate funeral measures were taken.

To this day, his son and daughter honour his empty seat at the dinner table. And their mother has not the heart to tell them that he probably left it empty on purpose...

But there was one matter in the whole farce that she could never forget even to that day in the carriage – she could never forget the day that the letter of his death had arrived. It made her mind flash with such vivid imagery of that blazing vision from her baptism. She hated it and cemented her hate for him by telling herself that if that future ever did come to pass it would be due to her husband's wilful absence.

She sighed with melancholy and Lolita turned to her and joined in her frowning.

"You know it is I heading to the slaughter, not you?"

"Oh, yes? And what would you know of slaughter, sweetheart?"

Lolita frowned deeper, "I don't. That is what irks me so."

Katherine became thankful for her recollections as she realised that that is exactly what had scared her too.

"Well, I have done this before. You could ask me what it was like. The actual ceremony, that is."

Lolita considered this for a moment, "I suppose that might help." She pivoted in place to fully face her mother again. Her hands sat restlessly on her lap as she fiddled with the frills of her dress. It was a white and green garment imbued with all the vibrant emerald of their house and the purity of a girl becoming a woman.

"I would like to know what exactly the whisps are."

Katherine tried to maintain her composure, "that... that is not a question about the ceremony, is it?"

"It wasn't a question at all, actually."

"Then perhaps I shan't answer you."

Lolita stared defiantly at her mother and gritted her teeth. She had hoped that the two could at least bond a bit in their time together during the ride but all Katherine had done was grind her down to her thinnest patience which, for a fifteen year old girl, was very thin as is.

"Please," she finally managed to grunt out through her clenched mouth, "please could you tell me about the whisps?"

Katherine sighed, "I am not sure I should. They are *ethereal* beings."

Lolita pouted, "but you do know about them."

"Yes, well, when you have to raise kids of your own you might find yourself doing research into even the nichest of subjects to ensure that they are safe."

"How sweet, mummy," she commented deadpan, "but I would still like to know now. It really would make me feel better."

"Oh, fine. But if you are kept up at night with terrible dreams about beings from a higher plane, I warn you not to dare wake me up for help."

"Of course not!"

"Fine." The queen looked for a moment at the ancestral miniatures on the wall and mentally begged them for assistance to find the right words. When her eyes fell on the visage of the previous king – her own father who had forced her to marry that deplorable Moonflower boy – she remembered that perhaps these people were not the right place to find familial advice after all.

So she mimicked her daughter's sitting position and spoke confidently, trusting said daughter to be mature, intelligent and most importantly, clandestine with the details.

"When the witcher begins a baptism ceremony, they will add their divination ingredients into the holy water where they will be dissolved as they begin the process. You see, ether has a unique signature, let's say, depending on where it came from. On the whole, ether can be universally used for lots of things, but for deeper, more intricate spells you might need to get it from a specific source. Such is the case with divination. The practitioner needs to be well handed in scrying to channel the ingredient's ether properly and keep the window stable."

Lolita moved to speak but her mother put a hand out. She sat in silence and Katherine continued, "this window is a window to the future. The reason that you submerge your forehead and eyes under the same water is because this is a simple way to channel ether that even a mundane like us can do. It will concentrate in that area as you tip yourself back and lean into the water where the window will then focus on your future alone."

"And the whisps?" the princess leant forward eagerly, drunk on her mother's fantastical explanation. She didn't get her answer, though, until she quietened up and sat back straight while her mother stared implacably.

"The whisps," she answered, "are a bit more complex. Imagine time itself to be an everlasting line, stretching into the horizon forever. Now imagine this line, this perception of time, to be the trunk of a thick tree lying flat across the realm. Time is like that trunk. Except time is on fire. It burns at one end. This end is the present. End every second that the end is burning and therefore moving its position to further up the log is another second of the present that passes by."

"What's left behind is the ashes, that is the past already burned away, unchangeable and definite. What is yet to burn is the future and how it burns, how bright and how hot and what kind of ashes it leaves, is yet to be determined."

"Does time branch off like a tree?"

Her mother allowed her the question, "no, dear. One might think it to, but no. It is simply one line. It is the fire that changes and the potential ash that is malleable, but not the trunk itself."

"And the whisps?"

"What you will see curling up towards your future when you dunk your head in the pool is the whisps of the smoke of the fire that burns time away from one moment to the next. Picture divination as grabbing a section of bark from further up the tree and peeling it down and around until eventually it is next to the present. There we can view it through a window – we can observe it through divination."

"But then it would be next to the fire..."

"Exactly, sweetheart. With divination always come the risk that the whisps might rise, curl around the viewed future and burn it like the present. And if that were to happen, if you were to completely lose your nerve and allow the whisps to burn through that window then they would eat backwards, consuming that entire section of bark and destroying that one individual aspect of the future until the fire returned to the present."

Lolita was no longer entertained. "Mummy?" she asked.

"Yes?"

"What happens to a person whose future is burned away by the whisps."

Katherine regretted letting herself get carried away then. She realised that perhaps she might have made the situation worse instead of helping her daughter. But she could not ignore her now or her wide, begging eyes, as she awaited an answer.

"It won't happen to you, because we will all be there to protect you."

"Mother, what happens!"

"You would die," she snapped. "A person without a future to go to would simply die."

Abernathy

"Get out."

Cyrus Magellan had not been very impressed when, after settling into his carriage for the long journey to Summerset, the doors suddenly swung open. From her place hidden in the nearby bushes, Harley had leapt suddenly into the witcher's personal transport and sat herself opposite to him where she was trying to get her breath back.

"No wait, please!"

"Do it, or I'll have you arrested."

"Magellan, please just hear me out."

He raised an eyebrow at her. He did not know who she was by the look of her but something had clicked once she indicated that she knew of him. He looked down at her dirtied, sky blue dress – far too luxurious for a street woman – and scrutinized the desperation on her face.

"Now, hold on a minute. Tell me your name?" He was suspicious but none the less curious as to if she might be who he thought.

"I'm Harley Abernathy," she explained. "I mean, we never met but I did stay in the mayor's place with you. As Harlot."

The witcher smiled widely, "well that is fantastic news! And you say you need my help with something?"

"I really do, sir," she begged.

Just then the carriage kicked into gear. Harley felt guilt and gave a panicked look but her apparent travelling companion just bid her sit down and get comfortable. She nodded.

"Now this has really, really made my day."

"Why exactly is that?"

"Because that windbag auger came storming in last night turning the place upside down looking for 'the wretched, daemon-fucker whore.' He made sure to knock down every door and bother every person, except the queen and princess of course, to ask if they had seen you. He turned yours and Mr Sunvale's rooms inside out looking for clues as to where you might have gone only to turn in defeated."

"That's... unfortunate." Cyrus assumed it was fear that brought on her sallow frown. It was actually his mention of Adam that dragged her further into despair. While Victor had been looking for her, she had been sleeping in the alley with one eye open. She was mortally tired then in the carriage because the fear of Adam suddenly bumping into her in the night was a more terrifying encounter than whatever the night hunters might have been fighting.

"On the contrary," he still seemed delighted in this little story. "It brings me no greater pleasure than to act in discordance with that high-on-himself little bootlicker."

"W-what do you mean?"

"I mean that his work and mine have a sort of clash of ideals. Don't worry about it."

"Alright," she said apprehensively. She was starting to think that maybe swapping one eccentric witcher for another would only make things worse but she still had to try – for Will's sake anyway. She would hate for him to spend his last days in a cell like that.

"So tell me what I can do for you to stab into the heart of that auger. Why's he after you?"

"I kind of heard something I shouldn't have. He found out and locked my friend away."

"Adam?"

She grunted, "no, no. William. Uh, Rushings."

Cyrus widened his eyes, "of course! I knew that wicked devil had to have been omitting something from his story, oh how the queen would love to hear this!"

"No!" Harley begged, "hold on. I don't want to... prolong this. I want to do whatever I can right now to get Will back from him. Then you can throw him in front of the aurochs' horns."

Magellan responded to that by cocking an eyebrow and smirking at his fellow passenger. "'Will' eh? You two sound friendly."

"Just friends," she sighed, "I mean I have only technically just known him for over a day now. Wow. It feels like he's always been there," she chuckled. "He's always been there for 'Harley,' I suppose."

"But you are Harley, no?"

She forgot she was speaking her thoughts aloud and opted to just move on, "so will you help?"

"Fine, fine. What exactly is it you overheard?"

"Right. Well..." she tried to consider what it was she saw, troughing through the hazy memories of semi-drunkenness. She had drank a lot more than that on much worse nights, of course, it was just the time with Will that she had been choosing to get high on. She repressed a smile then as she remembered seeing him spill a lot more of his share than she did and realising that it might have been the first time he had drunk so much, even if it was largely down his top.

"Yes, stone, of course. Sorry. Um, they were standing in the lair of these cult worship people. I won't lie to you; my friend was taking me there to experience what it was like laying with one. A daemon, not a cult worship person. Of course we couldn't because when we got there it was just Mary Culver and the auger standing in the room. I'm not too sure what happened to the cultists themselves, though."

"Very nice," Cyrus interrupted with dripping sarcasm, "now would you mind telling me what you heard them say?"

"Yes. Right. Sorry. You see, he had this stone, this reddish stone. It was all jagged and was what they had gone down there to get, I think. They called it an alchemist's stone."

Magellan leaned forwards, his eyes widening, "do go on."

"W-well. They said, she said, that the problem they have now is replicating it. The problem being that neither of them know how to do it."

"And do you know what this particular alchemist's stone can do?"

"They said something about summoning daemons with it?"

"Hm," Cyrus leant back against the chair again, "that explains where the cultists went."

"What do you mean?"

"It doesn't matter. Look, I know how to replicate an alchemist's stone. They don't because one of them only knows alchemy from the Bill and the other would rather spit on the craft then admit any respect for it."

"And how do *you* know?" she asked with a degree of caution. He grinned at that making her even more uncomfortable. To her, Cyrus was one of those people whose head was so abundant with knowledge that it intimidated her. Not so much because he was smarter than her but because he was smarter than *everyone*. To be so well versed in the world made her believe that he only has the intention to change it and people who wish to do that rarely do it for the right reasons. Or so she thought, anyway.

"I know because I'm clever. And because it's a simple piece of alchemical knowledge: we know how to duplicate the philosopher's stone so we simply apply that to an alchemist's stone."

She blinked at him, "what's a philosopher's stone?"

"It's this nifty little thing that grants eternal life and transmutes base metals into precious ones etcetera, etcetera."

"Oh my... is that, um, real?"

"No. Yes. Maybe. It is a legend as far as I'm concerned. Although sone alchemists are still dedicating their lives to harnessing the prima materia – and all the power to them – but I quite frankly think it's a waste of time. None the less, we can still apply the theory here."

"What's prima material?" She waved her hands in front of her, "actually never mind, I don't care. Can you just give me an answer without all the dressing up? Please?"

"Yes, I can help you," he sighed. "And you're lucky I'm getting spite out of this because all the dressing up of stuff is what makes being a 'Godless paganist' fun!"

She stayed silent for a minute sucking her teeth loudly until she finally decided to comment on his sentiments, "I thought you pagans had your own gods-"

"Yes, yes, thank you. I meant capital 'G' Godless. It was a joke."

She smiled, "I know."

He just shook his head and pulled out a blue, leatherbound book from inside his coat. He then moved his hand to the other side and pulled out two red ones and a blank piece of parchment.

"Hold this, will you." He then pulled out a capped vial of ink and a feather both of which Harley held on to with a noise of surprise. "Gets awfully bumpy on the road," was his explanation as to why she had become his desk.

He went on to prop one book open on his knee and balance another one closed on top of the other. He held the parchment on top of that to use as a flat surface and then reclaimed the feather from Harley. He waved it at her for an impatient moment until she realized that he needed her to open the ink and she did so.

They spent most of the ride like this, him dipping the quill in ink and asking her to hold both items while he flicked through books and jotted something down on the parchment.

After apparently finishing on one side, he left it to dry for a couple of hours as not to smudge the lettering before he eventually turned it over to write on the back. Whenever Harley tried to make small talk or ask about his writing he simply would shush her or make a face of great pain until she shut up of her own volition.

It wasn't until they were an hour out from Summerset that he finally tucked all his instruments back somewhere into his coat and addressed the other woman again.

"This," he declared handing her the scroll he had been working on, "is the both the list of ingredients you need and the instructions on how to use them. Go into town to a shop called Ripley's and show him the list."

Harley took it and peered at the instructions, hoping they would make more sense once she got her hands on the ingredients. It was not reassuring then that she could not understand a thing on the other side.

"What are all these pictures?"

"Those *symbols* are the ingredients."

"Oh."

"Like I say, just hand the list to the clerk."

"And this will work will it?"

"Sure!" And he was telling the truth. After all, he was more than happy to come in the way of a man he so despised. Whether or not it actually would help Harley.

Lobelia

When the procession arrived at Summerset it saw the royal carriage split off from the trunk with a group of knights. The rest went ahead to their dwelling allowing only the witcher's and mayor's carriages to also split away and follow the princess up to the cathedral.

While it was no seaside vacation with her aunt, Lolita was happy to feel the breeze on her face as she stepped into the soft grass atop the hill. She much preferred urban living after all but she still found it in herself to appreciate that an isolated location, like this one on the hilltop, would feel a lot less suffocating.

The cathedral sat on the outskirts of the town in its lavish fields of dark green grass. The hill it stood on was said to have been from where the third emperor stood and defended the boarders of Belgrave from the Wey's Rebellion and establish the new border. It stood as a testament to that act by shining proudly in the sunlight and bearing a fortress like quality. It had all the protrusions and spikes of gothic decoration with a few too many chambers and towers. It always intimidated Lolita in that sense — made her feel small. It was another reminder that she should be grateful not to inherit the burden of defending the kingdom for she would need a spirit capable of filling halls like that one.

As she looked up at it for another one of the many times she had and would in her life, she ascertained that she would *definitely* never have such a spirit.

As everyone dismounted around her and took in the scenery or stretched their legs, she remained affixed on the looming architecture; the subtle ways you could tell it was made later than most cathedrals, the intricate stained glass windows depicting the births and deaths of people from the Bill; the statue of the two aurochs above the door who were being led by the dark rider.

Now there was an image that made princess Lobelia shiver where she stood – the dark rider appeared on the arms of the imperial house. It was a man atop a great black stallion with a mane of brilliant orange. The statue only depicted it in limestone of course, but the coat of arms always ensured that you knew of its fiery hairs. And the rider himself wore armour as black as his steed but covered by a white tunic bearing the ancient Templar's cross. On his head he wore the crown of the five kingdoms, for he was the Old King, and in his hand he carried no sword; just a torch befitting the man who united the island and brought light to its cultures.

Until that damned-be third emperor lost everyone outside of Engelland to those revolutions...

She was only brought out of her stomach-turning rapture by the cutting voice of her approaching cousin. He ran at her with his arms open. The sight and sound made Lolita smile wider than she had in a long time as she opened her own arms to receive him, as much as it made her mother cringe.

"LOLLY!" the boy shouted in camp tones as he ran up and embraced the princess.

"Oh, Thomas!" She said just as relieved to be in his company. He picked her up in the embrace and swung her around until they looked into each other's eyes and laughed together. Their fun was interrupted when the queen cleared her throat.

Thomas looked up at her and forced his face into a serious line. He bowed his neck, "your majesty." He tried to make his voice deep and serious thanks to hours of lessons by his parents to stop him from sounding, as they accused, curt.

Still, he opened one eye and looked to Lolita. The pair broke out into grins as he turned to her and repeated his action, "your highness."

He took her hand and kissed the top. Through giggles she thanked him, "positively enchanting to see you again."

"I beg you," her mother whispered huskily in her ear, "go and do that elsewhere while we prepare."

"Of course," she grasped Thomas' hand and dragged him out eagerly to the fields of flowers surrounding Cathedral Hill.

Ser Garland approached her then, "should I chaperone them, ma'am?"

Katherine watched the two bound off and then turned back to her knight, "you might as well." She walked off to the building, completely indifferent to whether he actually did or not.

* * *

Once in the field, Lolita took the shawl she had wrapped around her shoulders and placed it on the grass for them to sit. She would not be wearing it in the ceremony so it did not matter how dirtied it became.

"Happiest of birthdays to you, cousin!" she said as they settled down. By then, Garland had caught up and was stood a metre away on guard.

"Thank you, thank you. But today is all about you!" Thomas replied as graciously.

The two had first met on their eighth and ninth birthday's – him being the senior – when their parents were attempting to arrange their engagement to one another to be wed once they came of appropriate age.

Unfortunately, all that came from it was a bitter rivalry as the two children bemoaned having to share in their celebrations. They saw it as half a party, half the presents and, heaven forbid it, half the cake.

When the ninth and tenth birthdays came, a miserable Lolita came to her mother's chambers to beg her not to make her share it with the Azalea boy again. At first she was delighted to find out that she should never even have to see him again if she wished not to. She only felt guilty, though, when Katherine started to rave about how Thomas Azalea took no interest in any women and how disappointed his 'poor' mother was that her son acted more the peacock than the bull.

So while her mother's love in giving her everything she wanted was filling her, she could only possibly think about how hard it must be for Tommy, that his own mother would not do the same...

They met again about three months after that at some ball or other. When they did, she had asked him all about it. They both snuck out to the kitchen then where he bared everything and cried and ate so much food. And she listened and she hugged him. And she promised that even if no one else did, she would love him.

He thanked her and they were cojoined ever since.

"If today really is all about me..." she bit her lip, trying not to sound too mocking, "then why are you wearing that garish outfit?"

Thomas looked down at his suit, frowned and then threw his head back to groan loudly. He was in a completely white formal piece that made him look like a bride.

"I know, I know. It's devilish, is it not? I mean, with this milky skin and near platinum hair you would think it obvious that such a garment would wash me out entirely but no! The Azaleas must uphold their rich tradition, and all that hokum." He huffed and crossed his arms.

Lolita patted his shoulder, "come now... an outfit can be both garish and comely."

"I don't want to be comely," he hissed, "I want to be gorgeous!" He raised his hands to the sky like he was giving a church ceremony and it made his cousin laugh.

"Speaking of gorgeous, tell me about this lady's maid you slept with, hm?"

"Ah, you heard that little tale did you? You see, I framed the whole thing to make my parents believe I could fancy women. After she was thrown out, I met her in the dark of night, handed her a handsome purse of gold and now I hear rumours that she is making a nice homestead in Gallarie. Can you believe it!"

Lolita chuckled at his story, "do you think that they do believe it now? That you like women?"

"For now," he shrugged, "they will start to spite me after long enough again, although my dad did drink with me for the first time that night. How dreadfully awkward." Before Lolita could respond or react to that, Thomas made a cautious glance up at Ser Garland and leant in towards the princess to whisper. "He, um, isn't going to spread any nasty rumours, is he?"

Lolita looked at the knight and then waved her hand dismissively to Thomas. "Oh, no. Do not worry. *The queen* rarely lets *the heir to her kingdom* go out unobserved. It just so happened that Ser Garland here was the one who had escorted Aaron to a 'tavern' only to find out it was a brothel that kept man-whores. A lucky matter, because Garland was one of the few knights all too happy to keep his secret for him."

Thomas gave a sigh of relief. "And how is your brother doing in... that regard. Is he happy? Is he safe?"

Lolita looked down and lost her smile. "I love him but... he is adamant in bringing boys back to the palace. He even has a favourite servant who he takes when the mood strikes him. He should be thankful that our mother is not so wise to figure out why he always asks for the clumsiest of the footmen to bring him his whiskey at night."

"But she suspects nothing?"

"Not yet. But I fear that he will place his trust in the wrong person someday. He grew lucky that Garland is kind and lucky that I found out when I was too young to know that your two's shared quality is apparently not well liked."

Thomas patted her leg sympathetically, "now, now. He will be fine. Tell him, from me, that if he ever needs someone to talk about this with, if the isolation gets too much and he may feel the need to let free his secret, that he is always welcome with the Azaleas. I lend my ear dutifully."

That reassured her. "Thank you, Tommy." She smiled slightly and looked off at the late-afternoon sun, rippling away into the latter half of its journey. It illuminated the grass so that the dark green had a vibrant edge of yellow to it that lit the field up more than any flowers could.

She turned back to look at her cousin then and sucked her lips in, "our, um, parents hadn't set you up with the wrong Lobelia... had they?" Her voice was suggestive as she tried and failed to sit still.

Thomas just laughed her away, though. "Aaron? Of course not. He is not my type after all. He's too... plain. Much more of a 'man' than I'd like."

The response confused her, "surely that's exactly what you like?"

"Oh maybe when I feel down and I crave the arms of a fellow who can make me feel protected. But if I were to wed – or as close to wed as two men can be these days – it should be to someone more of my own ilk."

She snickered, "perhaps a more closely related cousin then?"

He smacked her lightly on the arm, "don't be so naughty, princess! I just mean that I would rather strut for a peacock rather like myself."

"Than an aurochs like my brother," she finished for him.

"Precisely."

She nodded at that, "I see."

He tilted his head at her, "and is there a man you're hoping to see in your vision today, Lolly?" he teased. When she tried to turn her head away, he smiled wider and poked at her sides to try and tickle the answer from her.

They squirmed together, too afraid to stain their clothes that they were confined to the small shroud. Eventually, unable to escape, she relented under his hail of 'tell me, tell me!'

"There is no one serious if you must know," she straightened out her dress and patted her hair down as she spoke. "Just a man I rather liked the look of back in Whitley."

"Ah, but he has no blood of the Old king, I presume?"

"Yes, so my mother forbade me form even thinking about him... him and his lovely bottom," she blushed to speak like this, but it was nothing she and Thomas had not discussed before.

In the early days of their friendship, he had tried to veer away from crude conversation, still dazzled by her royal status. It wasn't until he could see Lolita being increasingly frustrated that he relented. Only another reason for Katherine to disapprove of their friendship; she would talk to him about men in no way any of his male friends would and he would do the same for her, as no woman dared to comment on a man's body rather than his honour. Or his money. It was usually one of the two.

"Is this man in your company?" Thomas asked, gazing back up the hill to where the royal and witcher carriages stood. "I might like to appraise this fancy of yours," she hit him on the shoulder then.

"Although... you might have more of a chance than I. He slept with a daemon after all."

"Oh dear me. Ancercy, is it?"

She nodded. "Terrible case... even whores are turning him out."

"Well, now I just feel sorry for the man," he frowned.

"His dad is he-"

"Whose that?" Tommy interrupted her to point to a woman who had emerged seemingly from nowhere and was searching the area near Cathedral Hill.

She was wearing a lovely red dress – nothing quite so extravagant as a member of a great house might wear but definitely something more middle class. It had black ruffles but beyond that it was simple, in a beautiful and intimidating way.

Lolita leant forwards and squinted, "why... why I believe that is Miss Mary Culver!"

She deftly stood up, hiking her own dark green, and much more lavish, dress up so that she could jog over to the woman while lightly calling her name.

Thomas just sighed as he stood up. He bundled the muddied shawl up and stared at it with an arching frown for a second. Then he held it out to Garland. Reluctantly, the knight took it in one hand. Thomas' frown turned into a grin of wide thanks before he ran to catch up with Lolita and this Culver woman.

Abernathy

It was a good thing that the witcher's carriage had two doors.

When he had pulled up on Cathedral Hill, behind the royal carriage, he quickly ushered Harley out of the one facing away from the holy building.

She thanked him as she did this and saw him smile in return before pulling the door closed. She presumed that he then went to walk out the other side and greet the queen with stories of an uneventful journey.

Meanwhile she was tucking herself into as small a figure as she could, hoping that the horses would block any downhill view that anyone might have of herself.

Once she reached the flat fields she decided it better to run. After kicking her shoes off she made for the nearby cottages that marked the road to the centre of Summerset. As she went, she caught a glimpse of two figures running in the opposite direction of her, followed by a large lumbering knight. She could not tell who they were as they disappeared into the distance. She allowed herself to slow down then, realising she must be far enough that even the queen would assume she's just the blurry image of a local resident wandering close enough to see the royals.

Once her bare feet reached pebbled pathways and was close enough to smell the stench of civilisation again, she pulled her shoes back on and made way to where the witcher had told her.

He hadn't used any street names so she avoided looking at signs to keep herself on track. She had only been told landmarks; 'once you see the first church, the small one with the green windows, turn left until you find The Rose and Hound.' Once she reached it she saw a rather run down public house with an old woman shooing off some young lads. They had a half bottle of muddy wine between them and were hollering the afternoon away.

'Then head right until you see the broken street lamp... no, it hasn't been fixed yet, I saw it when I last left and our Viscount's city council is by no means that fast to fix it.' She remembered his command and headed onwards. She hugged herself in an attempt to feel small. She slinked from wall to wall on her way through a city where she was a stranger. It would have made her laugh, had it not brought so much anxiety, to think that not a soul around would have heard of the Happy Huntress.

Cyrus had not explained how exactly that post was broken, but after twenty minutes of assuming she'd gone the wrong way, eventually Harley found what she was looking for. The broken lamp post in question had a large, round dent in the side causing the top to be bent over itself and the glass sides to be smashed open. Inside, it looked like birds had attempted to nest but all they had to show for it was some precariously balanced twigs and a pile on the ground below it of the ones that hadn't found a perch. Below those twigs was a large, black burn mark.

She went closer to the pole itself, curious as to what could have done this. Her curiosity died when she saw brown specks around the dent that eerily reminisced of long dried blood.

'From there, face the street with the tailor's workshop and walk dead ahead until you reach the fountain.' She nodded to herself, affirming her memory and shaking away thoughts of the broken lamp post.

This instruction had taken another thirty minutes of walking. As she got closer to the centre, the population grew more dense and there were more pairs of eyes to stare at her marred blue dress. While their whispers might have shaken her confidence, she did not stop until she reached Saint Mungo's square.

She took a sigh of relief and moved to sit at the marble edge of the circular fountain in the centre of the square. There was a statue standing in the pool – she assumed it was Saint Mungo – of a bare chested man pulling an arrow back tightly in a bow and pointing it at the sky. While she could not express the reason, it deeply unnerved her to see that Mungo's arrow, at this time of day, was centred so squarely on the lowering sun.

A shudder brought her back to her feet as she moved on to the final instruction. 'Turn in the square and look down each street you see. You should find the alchemist's sign from there.'

Eventually, after three turns off each avenue, she spied the wooden hanging that displayed a telltale hexagram with a dot between each point.

'Ripley's' the shop was called. A little bell rang as she walked through the door. Inside, it appeared to be identical to the Ripley's alchemist shop in Whitley. Having been a regular there for all manner of pills and potions, Harley was jarred to see the almost identical decoration. It shared the vast wall-shelf of stoppered jars containing materials; it had the two islands with brass machines; the wall plastered with writing and even the humble desk in the corner.

The main difference was the man who ran the place. He was of his forties, muscled but wiry – strong looking but hunched. A man beyond his prime. He had hair that was mostly grey but still speckled with the odd black strands of his youth and a smile that had not yet seen its wrinkles in the mirror.

"What can I do you for?" he greeted cheerfully as Harley made her way to his station. She cautiously eyed everything as she went, terrified that she might set something out of place and disrupt delicate work.

She smiled at the man uncomfortably. She thrust the papyrus that Magellan had scribbled on over to him and pointed at it wearily, "can you please provide me with these items?" He looked the list over once and then twice and then a third time.

Then he looked back up at her with a silent raised eyebrow. "Worry not, I can pay for it!" She assured him. She was ever thankful that she had snatched her purse from her parlour before Victor, right on her heels, had come and ransacked the place.

"Ma'am... it's not a matter of money it's... well, why exactly do you want these?"

She cleared her throat and spoke assuredly of herself, "I need them to replicate an alchemist's stone."

"You can't replicate an alchemist's stone."

"Well," she flapped her arms at him, "transmute a part of slate into a copy of an existing one! I don't know how you chemists work just please do this for me!"

He sighed his sympathy at her. He turned the paper around to glaze over the instructions that Cyrus had given her. Then he lay it town and plucked a feathered pen of his own out from behind his desk. He dipped it in a vial of red ink and began making notes.

"Excuse me," she put her hands on the edge of the counter to lean over and see what he was doing, although she did not interfere. "Why are you... annotating my guide?"

"I'm correcting," he said. "If you had followed this, especially the third step, not only would you have split your stone you would have also started a rather large fire around yourself."

"Oh."

"Indeed," he handed it back to her. "For a few extra crows, I would perform the process for you?"

She took the paper from him and shook her head, "thank you but the alchemist's stone is not mine... this is a favour of sorts."

He shrugged and walked off to pick bits and pieces out from across his shop. As she waited, he ground some elements with a pestle and mortar and fired others to change their form. He combined certain things in and separated others out and finally packaged them all in appropriately sized jars. When he was done, he returned to her, placed them all on the counter and asked for four silver wolfs and a medallion.

"Before I pay," she said, her eyes dragging back and forth across the basket of odd materials she now possessed, "I need to know which is which..."

"Here," he said taking the papyrus from her again. He began to write words above each symbol so that she knew what she was dealing with. She took it back from him with thanks. Thanks especially for that fact that he did not seem too impatient with her. He provided his service, with however many indifferent sighs, and looked not to be overcharging her.

"You are an honourable businessman," she commented as she held out a palm with the five coins. For the first time, he smiled.

"My father would be disappointed otherwise; God rest his soul."

Harley took the basket of product and hooped it under her elbow. She moved slowly, for fear that whatever's inside could start that rather large fire she had been warned about.

"A family business, then?" she asked the man.

He nodded, "Ripley's. I'm John Ripley, my father was Richard Ripley and my brother Derek."

"Was he a Ripley too?"

"Of course," John kept smiling as he talked about his family. "When we came of age, me and Derek agreed that instead of squabbling day in day out about the running of the shop, I would give him my half of the inheritance so that he could start a shop, just like the family one, in Whitley Moor. I kept his half of the original shop and now we're both happy for it."

"Oh. I did think the association with my Ripley's was..." she gave the room another judgemental scan and tried her best to smile, "eerie."

"You from Whitley?"

She nodded, "Annum's lane."

"Right, right. Last year I went to a butchers there getting a nice meal to share with my brother... that was a good visit." Harley cringed at the mention of the butcher and just shot a nervous laugh in response. "Bear you, if you ever do visit Derek's shop, he will tell you the exact same story I did, claiming that our family started out there and not here."

"Why would he do that? I mean, normally he just huffs at me for all the IOUs..."

"It drums up more business that you have an established history." He answered. The fact of his brother's fibs did not seem to annoy him, he just shared the story as an exciting means of conversation.

So Harley played along, "and how do I know you've not made the story up all together to, as you say, drum up business?"

That made him frown, "well... you don't, I suppose."

She giggled at that and started off out of the shop, "thank you for your work, Mr Ripley."

He waved back at her as the ringing bell signalled her departure, "... come again."

Lobelia

Mary stopped and stooped into a venerating curtsy as soon as she heard the approaching voice of Lolita. She remained there until the princess arrived to hear her say 'your highness' before rising again.

"I did not know that you were a part of our caravan?" Her smile was one of surprise as she caught her breath.

"I wasn't, ma'am," Mary answered with trepidation, "Me and the auger followed - or rather we would have had we not gotten here much faster - because we believed that Harlot Abernathy was in your party?"

Thomas caught up then and grinned at the magister. He did not say anything, just hoping to listen, but it caused Mary to be deeply uncomfortable as she did not know whether she was meant to curtsy for him too or not.

"No, she was not with us," Lolita answered, "do you require her assistance for your research?"

"Yes! Yes, she was a vital part of our work to find the cure but she seemed to have disappeared from Whitley. So we trailed, if that is quite alright with you ma'am."

"It is fine," she said, no longer caring too much about the details, "although while you're here, could I trouble your mind for some... holy information?"

Mary looked around her nervously, wishing to flee and pursue Harlot. But between the princess and Victor, she decided that it would be the best decision to just lie and say that Harlot is nowhere to be seen. It was most likely true anyhow.

So she just relaxed and faced the emerald royal, "there is no better person in the imperium to ask, ma'am."

That seemed to please her, "excellent!" Her hands fiddled in front of her with the pure white gloves covering her skin, "so, I have been told about the whisps. And before that, about the act of dunking my eyes. I was wondering about one more matter of my baptism, however."

"Ah," Mary chewed her tongue nervously, "you see, that is a pagan matter, not a holy one. I can only help you as much as I know, I'm afraid."

"That is fine," Lolita sighed. "If you could... do you know if the future shown there is a certain one? As much as I would like to peer through that window, I believe it would be maddening to go through life knowing where it ends. It makes me ever so reluctant to spoil all the fun!"

"Ooo, good question, dear cousin!" Thomas placed a hand on each of her shoulders from behind and peered over the left one to eagerly await Mary's answer. Lolita placed one of her own gloved hands on top of his for comfort.

Mary cleared her throat. "As far as I am aware, scrying does not show a definite future. Even instances in the Bill where a warlock might do such a thing, it never plays out as predicted. It is more like... a possible future. Our lives change at every decision we make as does the time yet to come. It only becomes definite the moment it becomes ash under the heat of the whisp's flame."

"So the future I see in the pool is just a possibility... but it could still change?" Lolita asked, too afraid to celebrate yet.

"Sort of. It is not just a random possibility. Assuming you have a talented witcher presiding, the future you are shown would be the most likely future. But yes, even that is still malleable. There is a tell, you see. The likelihood that the future you see in that pool will come to pass is shown in how solid the image is. Most are distant; hazy. These ones are a glimpse into a good idea of what will happen but will probably not happen in that way, if at all."

"And the clearer ones? The more solid visions?"

"These would be the kind that any observing house members might report back to the emperor..." her eyes flittered briefly to Thomas for a moment.

He stuck his tongue out at her, "that is my father's business, not mine. I am only here to support Lolita!"

"Of course, sir," she muttered.

"So I should pray for a transparent sight," Lolita responded, ignoring the both of them.

Mary shook her head at that. "Your highness, your future is yours, no matter what you see. It has been known that even the sharpest image has been defied and the future of that person turned upside down despite even the emperor making plans based on how concrete the image was."

Lolita frowned at that, "then what is the point of it all?" She realised she was being capricious in suddenly disliking that her foresight would mean nothing at all.

"The point is that you are an important person. What you do with your life could change the realm. This matter of scrying... it is because you are powerful, Princess Lolita. I urge you not to run from it, but to take it in stride." She blushed, realising she had ran away with herself. "I-if it please you, of course."

Thomas seemed to have stars in his eyes. He clapped his hands at Mary for her little speech and would later tell his cousin that Mary had empowered him. Right then, Lolita had smiled with genuine for the first time in the conversation.

"Thank you, magister. Your council has truly brought me to my senses. At last, I find myself ready to enter the cathedral."

Mary curtseyed again, "it is only my duty, your highness."

"Come, Tommy!" The princess took his hand and made back for the hill, "we ought not keep everyone waiting."

"Ma'am," Ser Garland interrupted. Everyone stopped to look at him. "Before you return, might you think of a story for this?" he held out the muddy shawl in its crumpled form.

Lolita pondered it. Then her mind turned to Mary who still remained.

She took the fabric; it was an intricate black and grey pattern of fine cashmere. She shook it out and analysed the state of it before folding it into a neat square and handing it over to Mary Culver. "Here. I need rid of this and I should also like to thank you for your kind words." She smiled as Mary slowly pulled it into her grip, afraid it might be some sort of plot.

"It is in a bit of a state," she continued, "but after you clean it, it should make a fine centrepiece for your wardrobe!"

"Th-thank you, ma'am," she stuttered, truly in awe as the fifteen year old giggled and ran off once more with her hand in Thomas'.

The pair of cousins made for the top of Cathedral hill, where it appeared that everyone bar the two carriage guards were waiting inside.

As it was, they were just behind the rest of the Azaleas and in time for everyone's introductions. When they came in, Thomas shot a bright pair of thumbs up to Lolita as he took his father's side.

Just past the large, pointed archway of the entrance, Katherine stood facing away from it. To her left was Cyrus and now to her right was Lolita. Once she found her place, her mother had smiled and put a warm hand on her shoulder as a means of hello.

The Viscount Azalea had just ignored the arrival of Thomas, most likely indifferent to whether he was there or not. On his side of the greeting was his son and his wife. Next to that group was the Bishop of Summerset besides the Archbishop of Stourford and an acolyte girl of a similar age to the princess. She had fair skin and seemed to be doing her best to keep the reins on her slowly widening smile. She had a simple white robe tied with a black rope high at the waist.

The archbishop and bishop both were wearing mitres, although the former's was more a solid gold colouring with a white lining whereas the latter's was smaller and mostly white with a simple gold pattern embroidered. The archbishop was an older man with a stout face like an aging dog. He looked over his sallow cheeks with an eye of superiority, even in the face of his queen, and his mouth was always upturned in a small arching frown of disapproval. His robes were also a holy white colour with even holier gold accentuations. The bishop's outfit was, again, a much simpler version being a white rochet with a black covering chimere – a chimere being the, usually, colourful part that goes over the top, as Lolita had been informed when her mother's own anxiety about the situation had started to manifest in useless lessons about pointless church trivia.

She also learned that the staff which the older clergyman had in his hands was the crozier; his was gold of course and curved into a circle at the end. Surrounding the curl was a round of elegant petal shapes meant to mimic a rose. On the inside, rather counter to the intricate flower design, was simply a cross.

And contrary to the sterling look of this superior, the bishop appeared to be quite young. A similar age to Magellan except less handsome. He looked more the part as if when he was younger he could have been anyone's husband but instead chose to have his personality ironed out by a life of hard, hard service to the Holy Paradigm. Lolita decided she liked him most of the three church residents for this fact - she thought him admirable. He reminded her of her father.

"If we may get on," the archbishop cut through the silence that followed after everyone took a turn to greet each other with all the proper formalities, titles and gestures that took an eternity to rattle out.

"Of course, your excellence," Magellan agreed, only slightly mocking. "Allow me to gather my ingredients and we can begin the ritual with your discretion." His lip curled up in the corner as he took his leave.

The archbishop shuddered; the loose skin sagging on his face wobbled with the reaction. "Suffer not the pagan to run his mouth around me," he grumbled, "come now, your highness. Your majesty. I shall bless the water." He turned to Lolita, "once it has space for God's love it will stand the brunt of the witcher's spell to reveal your forecomings."

"Yes," Lolita shot a dry expression back at the man, "I know how ether works."

"S-sorry?" His voice wobbled as much as his face did as he leant down to hear her better making a cup around his ear.

She opened her mouth to repeat herself but her mother had given her a light kick on the ankle. *Ether and casting is not a topic for a young lady to discuss so you will leave this conversation in the carriage.* She looked up at the queen to see that she was still looking at the archbishop but her jaws were clenched.

"Nothing, your excellency," Lolita mumbled. Her mother seemed satisfied by that and untensed her face.

The archbishop waved the conversation away as he would rather dismiss notions entirely than admit his age was catching up to him and his hearing.

As he went on, allowing them past the entrance and through into the brunt of the building, the princess began to marvel at the sight of it all. She was being trailed by the bishop and one of the cathedral's acolytes. While he was walking on with as placid an expression as ever, the girl was nervously eying the princess trying to capture her reactions to the beautiful building around them.

While the outside might have been intimidating, a reminder of power and fortitude, the inside had more of a celebratory feeling to it. There were the largest rows of pews that Lolita had ever seen all stacked against the tallest stained glass windows in the kingdom. One illustrated the fall of Agamemnon. Another displayed the blessing of Iosefka. One that particularly caught Lolita's eye was the window made nearly entirely of reds and browns – it was the window depicting the First Feast; men, women and children were all drinking and eating of the blood and flesh that came pouring off of the body of a crucified giant.

It made her stop and contemplate what she was doing, seeing that figure. She had never finished the story on The Enemy. Knowing that it was a gruesome one she had always asked her brother to skip it during their readings together. But there it stood, as average as any other tale of rise or fall in the Bill. It made her think of every mass where she had eaten the blood and body of The Enemy herself, transubstantiated by the priest at cathedral back in Stourford.

The acolyte had turned back to come and retrieve her only to end up joining when she saw what she was looking at.

"Beautiful, isn't it?"

"Not really," Lolita replied. "It makes all that bread and wine that I have consumed in my life feel... stale."

The two continued to admire it for a moment until the acolyte spoke up once more, "seeing this... it's what inspired me to dedicate my life to the church, you know. Just one Sunday with my mum and a glance at the sun's rays through that beauty... I was hooked."

She spoke solemnly and with gentile grace. It unnerved the princess.

"What about it?"

"The peace," she answered, neither of them looking away.

"The peace?"

"Of course. Have you read the book of Anaximander?"

Lolita shook her head.

"The enemy crops up throughout the Bill but is not defeated until the end wherein Anaximander, hero of God, rises his templar army to crucify their emblem."

"But why? Who could do something so bad that they deserve... that?"

The acolyte nodded as she gave a new glance to the illustration and realised that normal girls might have construed it as gory rather than epic. "It's not because they're bad," she explained. "The Enemy was punished because they could not keep the peace. They took threats of war with a response of war, took their issues in stride to resolve them violently, chose not to step in to stop when others fought and deigned to take what they wanted by force. Their souls weren't blackened by a devil's temptation or human sin but by animosity itself. They just find reasons to fight. So they had to be killed to teach peace. That's why we eat their body and blood at mass. To remind us that peace is always right. Always God's message."

Lolita sighed, "I suppose I had better read it then."

"Is there something you didn't understand, ma'am?" The girl looked to her princess now and tilted her head, beguiled by a person who did not instantly fall in love with the tale she had just spun.

"It just all feels a bit inconsistent. The Old King... Anaximander and his Templars. They covered the length of the island until they had taken all the other territories by force making one nation. One empire. Is that not in the spirit of The Enemy?"

"Ohhh," the girl shook her head. "It is always an act of peace to spread the Lord's work for under his teachings we become a peaceful society. It only becomes animosity when this is rejected, which unfortunately happened, forcing the Old King to take all of their states by force. It is just a shame that the nine kingdoms is now only five. I pray that perhaps one day, a new emperor will renew the order of templars to reclaim the island in God's name..."

Lolita nodded. "Do you know what?" She turned now so that they both met eye to eye. She was smiling, happy to have had this chat, "so do I." And she meant that.

Because that was the feeling this building rose inside her. In between the chambers, where the pews sat and the space where the golden, reaver shaped lectern faced them, was two branching corridors making the entire cathedral cross shaped. Down each was rows of armour, swords, paintings, records, and the plaques that labelled them all showing the history of the Great Crusade. It inspired awe in her, reverence and rapture. It made her think of how mighty her culture was that this building was the bastion upon which they defended themselves from heathenish rebels.

The centrepiece to it all was the large alcove in the floor with a golden trim that depicted a circle of angels flying amongst clouds. Inside the concave formation was the clearest blue water awaiting a blessing from the Archbishop so that it may become holy water.

She had pictured approaching it all this time and thought herself anxious or unprepared.

As it turns out, all the princess could claim to be was ready. Ready to see her destiny. Ready to see how she would shape Belgrave. She was ready to serve the emperor and she was ready to serve God.

Culver

Mary skulked down the road away from Cathedral Hill. She stepped uneagerly towards a small cropping of woods beside the entrance to Summerset.

To some, it was a grove; it had connotations of light and associations with the 'fortress' it stood by. But to most, non-starry eyed folk, it was just some woods. It had never even seen battle before, always being a part of what would peacefully end up as Belgrave and never being taken by the Wey rebels.

At this particular moment, however, it served as the cover for Victor's carriage and his two odd horses. Once Mary reached him she took notice that the animal's bones were starting to show through their bodies and that they were panting. She had never witnessed a panting horse before. It made her feel a gnawing pity.

"Do you have her?" Redding said when he heard her footsteps and turned to greet. "Did you find the fugitive?"

"Yes, m'lord." She replied, "Harlot Abernathy is hidden beneath my dress."

He narrowed his eyes and let his raspy voice fall again, "as much as I admire the tenacity of your wit, miss Culver," his words were sharp, "I am inclined to remind you that if what we have done is let out to the wrong ears, to *royal* ears, then everything we have worked to do will be for nought."

She paused for a moment, pontificating her wording, before answering with a question. "Dare I ask, what exactly is this all for in the first place?"

A third voice came astutely from a nearby tree, "yes, I would rather like to know that myself."

Victor and Mary turned rapidly to see the waggling fingers of Cyrus Magellan. He got up from where he was leaning against the trunk of a tree and strode over to be dangerously close to Victor. Mary stepped back, quite unsure on who would come out on top if the runestones and wands broke out.

"Your hair is still that horrid crimson colour," Victor noted as he tried to make himself appear taller.

"And yours is a sickly, dark green now. Surely, a reflection of the way you beat the life from your steeds?"

He hissed back at that, "you have no right! You've been helping that whore, haven't you?"

Cyrus lazily lifted his hands in the air in response to the accusation and answered, "guilty." His complete disregard for the auger's power and increasing anger made Mary take a further step back. She had no interest in being in between them when they started... throwing crystal balls at each other? This was not really her area of expertise.

"Why?" Victor's words tended to curl out of his mouth like thick smoke - now more than ever as he glared at his contemporary.

Magellan just shrugged in another blasé response, "because. Well, she came to me with a sudden interest in alchemical stones and I thought 'that's funny!'"

"She told you?" Mary asked, walking back towards them, her words coming out breathlessly. When Magellan raised an eyebrow of surprise, she found herself cowering slightly behind Victor for protection.

"And what is funny about that?" the auger asked as if Mary were not there.

"Well I thought that her interest happened to coincide with what you were doing at that chapter house of The family."

Mary gripped Victor's sleeve suddenly for support as she realised that Magellan could be acting to arrest them. Of course! He was serving the emerald crown; he would have told Katherine Lobelia. And she would have sent him into these woods to exterminate them. In that moment, as her boss reached for a wand on his waist, she begun to recount her life. In a fraction of a millisecond, she experienced happiness, sadness, love, nostalgia and regret all at once. And as she closed her eyes to brace for a burning fireball all she could see was Ahmar's face. 'You're the magister now,' she thought. 'You deserve it."

"Put the wand down, I don't actually care how many cultists you kill," Cyrus scoffed. Victor, who had half unsheathed a rather gangly looking wand, had begun to slide his weapon back into the holster. Feeling the fool, Mary opened her eyes, let go and straightened out her dress. She also blinked away the early dews of tears while feeling very silly.

She spoke this time in an attempt to draw attention from her cowering. "And how do you know what went down under Rewbridge Road if all the whore asked you about was alchemical matters?"

The witcher simply smirked and tapped the top of his cheek three times pointing at his eyeball.

"I doubt that any chapter of The Family of Mara approves of you using their infernal network to spy on them," Victor scolded. "Very unprofessional thing for an ex-colleague to do, I would say."

Magellan sighed, "would you like to know where Abernathy is or not?"

Victor looked ready to scathe him again, but Mary interjected, "Please, yes."

He nodded at her. "She will be waiting for you by the fountain in Saint Mungo's square. I believe she has something you want, so hold back before you suck her into that piddly bottle prison of yours."

Victor's eyes went wide, bulging as he stomped uncomfortably close to the other pagan. "I most certainly hope that you are not helping her evade us?"

"All I'm saying is give her a chance. She might have the solution to whatever damned artifact you're trying to harness."

Mary gnawed on her lip, terrified by how much Harlot might have let slip. As the two men talked, constant images ran through her mind of the city guards arresting her the moment she stepped across the threshold of Summerset. Even more terrifying was the idea that Victor would command her to meet up with Abernathy at night and instead the pair would be chased down by the night hunters like they themselves had done to the whore and the mayor's boy. It was the first time in her operations with Redding that she actually felt regret.

Then she experienced an even more biting emotion as guilt followed to remind her that in all the horrid things she had done, she had only regretted facing the consequences and not... not killing eight people or infecting eight others or arresting William Rushings.

It was a spark that made her clutch her stomach as the feeling seemed to burn her insides and bring bile up her throat. The guilt and regret battled one another in a dance that stoked the painful flames and left her with a final decision to make.

She could go. Make an excuse and cower and beg fealty to Queen Katherine. Maybe Magellan alone could not take him, but the archbishop would surely have no trouble of burning away Victor. Yes... she could even rat out Magellan's former associations with The Family for extra points... just maybe they would show her mercy.

She turned and looked through the gaps in the trees and past the beams of late-day sunlight. She pondered the outline of the church remembering the multiple times she had visited and studied its contents, how safe and patriotic it had made her feel. She remembered the swords that had defended Belgrave's borders, held high not only by templars or knights, but by city guards, farmers and ministers too.

She remembered each stained window, how it is the only cathedral in the empire that has one for each book of the Bill, and all the memories that each one taught.

Her hope died when she remembered the mural of the book of Anaximander.

She had broken the peace... and she had been helping Victor develop a weapon.

If she walked into that church and ratted out the auger she would only be confessing to crimes of The Enemy. She would be crucified. The bread that she had eaten, the wine that she had drank... they would be her body and blood.

She moved her hands from her stomach and straightened up as she snuffed out the fire in her belly. There was no room for regret and no room for guilt. Just dedication. Her ideas came from a good place. Because she is a good person! She has to be, it's herself. She knows she is... the work done with Victor is better than if it were done by a worse person. This reminder kept her strong, emblazoning her core with cold, solid iron as she remembered Ahmar's face again. He would approve.

"Damned?" Victor responded, "you call my work damned? How dare you."

"The rest of your work is damned; I can only presume that this latest operation of yours is too." Magellan somehow managed to hold his head higher than Redding's, a humorous sight to Mary. She had resolved to stand next to, rather than behind, her boss now.

"What you do is not so pure either."

Magellan's superiority was short lasted as he craned his neck and finally showed a degree of harshness, "you know nothing of my work."

"Quite so," Victor returned to his usual cockiness. "But I am aware that is macabre in nature. I could feel it ever since I entered that hall. I could see that even the princess felt it." This made Cyrus wince. "I would watch my back if I were you. Remember that the church does not make allies of witchers... it merely permits them."

Lobelia

Cyrus Magellan returned to the cathedral with a stern look on his face. Nobody seemed to notice except Lolita who turned to face him. She was sat on the front pew by her mother and he came to sit by them. He melted into his kind smile when he looked back at the princess and any wondering thoughts she had melted away with it.

On the pew to the right of them was the Azaleas. And, as it is not for a bishop to help out, he was sat distanced from them on that same bench while the acolyte had taken to lighting candles and opening up the thick volume of scripture on the lectern's back. Once she was done, she took a small bag of salt over to the archbishop who took a pinch and sprinkled it into the pool. Then he walked around the perimeter of it, acolyte in tow, taking and spreading pinches of salt until he had finished the lap.

Once done, she ran off into the expansive rear chamber to leave behind the matches and salt before rejoining Lolita on the bench. She sat between her and Magellan. Lolita had learned that her name was Alex and after their little talk before she agreed to become friends with the princess even inviting her to sit beside her as they watched the archbishop consecrate the pool.

He started by taking his place, standing above the water on the platform where the lectern stood.

Behind him, high on the wall, was the only non-stained window: a large circular opening of glass that provided a beam of light to perfectly encircle the pool. It cut a shadow of a cross onto the water as the window was spotless except for the two bars that cut across it in the shape of a regular, horizontally symmetrical cross.

It shone bright and white with the middling sun of the early evening and illuminated his back like a portrait of a haloed angel.

After re-familiarising himself with the exact passage, the man cleared his throat, held his arms outstretched and began to recite from the book of Anaximander. These lines were early on and depicting the story of the Old King's encounter with a giant ocean serpent. When the archbishop read it, he did so with a deep, but sultry voice that filled every corner of the holy site with mellow words:

"'Purge the beast with green eyes.

Bring my crusade from the shores inward.

Close in on my rightful kingdom, avatar of light,

And judge those who resist my peace.'"

Two hills began to rise from the surface of the pool with curved tops. They grew wider as they raised high into the air before joining at the bottom. Lolita realised – as scales shimmered in and out of view across the surface of the apparition – that it was the maw of Leviathan.

"As the august beast wants land's domain,

He too attacks from outwards in.

The island made from titan's envy,

Must shore its shore from eating waves."

The echo of it slithered upwards in a cascade of brilliant blues and whites. The higher it rose, the more its faux scales refracted the light from the circular window and illuminated the room with brilliant rays.

"With templars abroad the beach,

The torch was lit in the land of Weys.

'Nax came to their hail and witnessed the writhing fins.

Alas light could not permeate the domain of the sea."

Upon reaching its zenith the echo unlocked its maw wider and the frills that climbed its back shook in eagerness. It peaked with the crest of the window on the far wall appearing to be inside its mouth like a glimmering silver ball. Like a bright planet in the sky.

"'Expose thyself,' Nax did command,

Not in haught, but cunning.

'The Lord has land far wider than mine,

See the planets that hang above and rapture.'"

The image of Leviathan curled then as its mouth clamped shut on the visage of the moon. The second it did so the entire form rippled into blue sparklets that twinkled out into the light and left not a splash in the body below.

"The beast did as was bade.

The beast liked not to see another's domain.

The beast wanted only the sea.

And when scales erupted towards the second planet,

The body became light in the king's smiting."

The archbishop lowered his arms after the final sentence, finished with the ritual. The water was now holy. The princess, finally tearing her mind from the memory of the sight, looked down to see that the water glowed with the same bright, sky blue essence that the wych water had in Magellan's bronze tanks.

The archbishop then took his turn to sit, swapping with Magellan as he moved to the far end of the circular pool. He knelt down and unfurled a brown bundle, letting various ingredients spill out in front of him as well as the tools to properly apply them.

"You're up, sweetheart," Katherine whispered to her daughter. She gave her an encouraging but gentle push on the back that forced Lolita to stand. When she looked back at her she saw that her mother was smiling and nodding. She nodded back and padded nervously over to closer side of the pool and knelt with her back to the pews. She looked at her warbling reflection on the surface of the glowing holy water and saw only the present looking back. She had told everyone she was ready. She had told herself she was ready. But looking in her own eyes as the witcher added ingredients to the stew, she felt like she was only saying goodbye to herself.

She looked right over her shoulder to see the bishop and the Viscountess Azalea making indifferent smiles at the display. The Viscount was frowning, not out of displeasure but as if he were holding his face in a void waiting to be filled with information. When Thomas saw her turn he grinned and held a sly thumbs up to his side where his father wouldn't see. She liked that.

She turned back and decided to focus on what Cyrus was doing to keep her mind occupied. He noticed that and talked as he worked to focus her as much as himself.

"Traditionally, scrying is done with an obsidian mirror. Or any reflective surface, if necessary. It requires no ingredients and is based on interpretations of the images you see manifesting in the reflection or the ripples of waves." He had removed two things, a small silver grater and the knob of wychroot he had presented last night. He moved them to one side while he took the rest and placed them in the centre of the thick parchment he had rolled out. Lolita couldn't quite tell what they all were; there was some sort of red powder, a claw of some small bird, a range of herbs and another strange silver shaped object in the centre of it all. Magellan removed one last thing, a brown ball of thick string, and began to close the parchment around the ingredients. He finished by tying it together with the twine and creating a neat package.

"Traditional scrying, in that sense," he continued, "is more of a symbolic form of divination. All about interpreting what the reflections are trying to tell you about the future. Like reading meaning from an upturned major arcana, it is all about an arbitrary interpretation of the same situation." He stood up again and held the package flat on his held-out palms. He looked intently at the pool, lowered his arms slightly and gently lifted the package through the air to land softly in the centre of the water. Lolita recoiled, prepared for a splash that never came. Instead it just passed through as if the water weren't there. When she looked down to see it sink to the bottom she found that the package was nowhere to be seen. And neither was the bottom of the pool. What had once been a distorted view of the granite curve of the shallow dip was then a deep, inky void.

"The royal baptism is a whole other matter entirely," Cyrus moved to sit cross legged. He held the wychroot over the water and began grating silver flecks of it onto the surface. "It is as much a holy practice and alchemical practice as it is a pagan one. The combination of tireless work form the highest offices of the imperial palace. The work was commissioned so that the Old King could keep the peace by ensuring the futures of his great houses were aligned."

When he finished talking he gestured an open hand to Lolita and then down to the pool. She looked and saw that the shavings from the wychroot had spread equally across the open waters like stars in the night sky – small flecks across the infinite void.

She swallowed her fear and repeated all her talks, all the preparations, in her mind as she forced herself to turn around. She didn't look at anyone this time, not even her mother. She had to focus on getting through this despite the fact that her heart wanted to strangle its way out of her throat. She scooted forward and awkwardly lowered herself backwards on wobbling arms. She gave a soft gasp as she felt her hair begin to float atop the water's surface knowing that it would be ruined now as it became wetter and wetter. She kept on, though. She pushed lower until another slightly harder gasp was elicited by the cold sensation on the back of her skull as she began to tilt her head backwards into the pool. She was laying down flatly then and tilting back further, submerging her scalp and then her forehead.

She paused once her eyebrows had been smattered by droplets. She closed her eyes and made one last reassurance before pushing her body back just that last bit for her eyes to be fully submerged. She did well not to go too deep, not letting her head go in further than the bridge of her nose.

The hardest bit was opening her eyes. She was terrified that suddenly water would rush into her sockets and blind her. But as her eyelids gently flickered, as if in gentle waking, she could sense that no such thing would happen. She opened one cautiously to see that while she was certainly underwater it felt different to any kind of bath or basin she had experienced. She opened the other and rolled them left to right to survey the dark expanse around her. It didn't sting or feel wet. It was just cold.

When she looked down – or up, as it was to everyone else – she could see above the water, the circular edge where Magellan was sat cross legged. The surface, as if it were a film dividing two words, was gently rippling but she could still tell that the witcher was smiling at her through it. Then he moved to hold his two hands out just above this surface and finalise the ritual.

Lolita could feel this as much as she saw it. It was like a sudden tug downwards as the ether from her body was mingled into the water through the top of her head. Shapes began to form then from the silver stars that surrounded her. They danced and swirled and formed patterns in the abyss that slowly moved closer to one another by an unseen force of attraction.

The only other light in the dark was her caramel hair floating around her head like a halo as she looked in awe at the unfolding vision.

By now, everyone else had risen from the pews to observe the images in the water; Alex and Thomas looked with glee and open mouths; the Viscount's frown did not shift but his eyes did widen as his brows furrowed; the two ministers turned and looked at each other quite unsure what to make of the sight. Her mother was the only one who did not betray an emotion. She simply watched with the mind of someone ready to accept what she was seeing. She had come here resolute to fight her way out if necessary in support of her daughter's predicted future. What she saw did not change that.

Magellan was the only one who made a look of visible animosity. He didn't stare at the vision itself; he stared through it – his glare permeating to the princess.

But for the moment, she was too enthralled to notice him as she watched her future unravel to reveal herself stood in the cathedral back home at Stourford. She was wearing large, flowing, white robes with exquisite gold designs all over. She had a mitre on, gold and edged with white, and in her hand was the most illustrious crozier that one might call it a sceptre. She stood in a room that was dark but for the multi-coloured illuminations of the towering stained glass window behind her.

She was witnessing her enthronement as the future archbishop of Stourford and a head of the church of the Holy Paradigm.

And the prospect excited her greatly. She loved hearing her brother read, loved hearing the way the Bill inspired people like Alex and the way peace was brought by a universal following of the laws of God. She accepted this future.

She then attempted to narrow her eyes and focus on what was behind, to try and see what the stained glass window was depicting. The colours and blurred lines were all wrong to be the window that currently stood in the building. But in trying to see past her future self she managed to look too far and only bore witness to Magellan on the outer lip of the basin.

She tried to make out his expression between the water and the far sight as she pondered what he may think of it all. Surely a pagan like himself would not mind to see a woman in a position like that so why did he appear to be so sour?

"You cannot tell anyone in the church about this. Anyone."

Her ears began to burn then as she realised the malice he must be feeling. The one thing he had told her not to do with the information about his project was not tell the church. She could only imagine how he felt seeing that she would not only join the church in more than just a figurehead position but as one of its most senior members.

She panicked. Her fingers fidgeted for something to hold on to but she was laying on the flat ground of the cathedral floor. There was not even a carpet to crumple up this close to the pool. Everyone else was too excited by the vision to notice that her limbs were cloying for help.

Her ears burned hotter then as the image began to lose its colour. It was not losing clarity but just colour as it greyed away like ash.

The whisps.

She remembered the fate she had been warned of and moved her eyes quickly upward to see that intermingling with her hair was tendrils of grey smoke erupting from some far off place in the pit. The more she squirmed, the more she feared them, the more she was worried about Cyrus, the more those tendrils rose higher and increased in volume. She even whimpered as the point of one started to tickle the bottom of her future-vision like it were trying to catch a portrait alight.

The nervousness of losing that vision took priority to her. Yes, she may be burned away by the whisps but she had to know the rest of the matter. She gritted her teeth and focused her mind on the black and white display so that she could truly look at the stained window behind to see what it depicted. She ignored any hard looks from the witcher above and let her care for her future self as the archbishop fade away as she grounded herself in that window.

It was easier to tell what shape it cut without the myriad shards of colour hazing her eyes. She could see that it depicted a regal man with a head of brown hair and a great crown inset with a brilliant green gem. He was wearing a fine green outfit with a brilliant cape and held a gilded sword in his hand, the point facing the ground. She wondered who it might be for just a second until a grin broke out when she realised that that was the future king of Belgrave! That was her brother, Aaron Lobelia as ruler of the land.

Suddenly colour returned to the image as she thought of the implications. She thought on her prosperity as a woman in such a position and then of her brother's prosperity to be so proudly where he is. Perhaps in the future as king he can rule as himself.

All the attacking whisps recoiled back down into the depths as she joyed in seeing herself and Aaron being themselves and doing greatness as themselves – uninhibited by other's disregard for them. She thought that they would do that together that they *were* together even though not literally in the vision. She thought of Thomas and her mother and suddenly she erupted from the pool in a fit of giggles as she thought about all the people she loved standing true in a future of their own design.

Her mother knelt down beside her and tentatively draped her arms around her shoulders - shoulders which were becoming increasingly wet with the tendrils of hair. She whispered cautiously to ask if she was quite alright, but Lolita just continued to snicker quietly as the prospect of such a time to come lit her heart with so much joy.

She only moved when she turned to look over her shoulder at the hard, steely gaze of Cyrus Magellan and his unfortunate secret. She did not panic this time, she only smiled back at him. Widely. Proudly.

The archbishop was the first to break the silence.

Katherine was pleased by this because she was now one of the rare few who had gotten to see the man truly astounded. For he looked upon the remnants of the vision and declared, "this is the most solid a royal baptism has been! This future... it surely will come to pass... surely." Although he declared this boisterously, his reluctance betrayed his opinion on the matter.

But as Thomas and Alex crowded around to congratulate her, she simply looked up at the high ceiling of the building and promised herself that yes: that future would come to pass.

No whisp and certainly no witcher would get in the way of that.

Culver

"Victor."

The closer the pair got to Saint Mungo's square the faster the auger walked.

"Victor!"

Mary hurried after him, trying her best to slow him down as he seemed to grow more infuriated with each step.

"Victor!"

"What?" He snapped, turning to face her, his mouth contorted into the most vicious of snarls.

Mary stumbled on her words for a moment, afraid to speak. Then she shook her head and got on with it anyway, "my lord... I believe you should calm down a degree before we meet with the whore."

"Hah!" his condescension trumped his anger, "and why is that, hm? Are you thinking that we should head into that square and do anything other than immediately arrest the woman? Well?"

"You heard what..." Mary searched for a name until she realised that she wasn't entirely sure who Cyrus was, "...what that other witcher said! She could have the solution to our duplication problem. At least hear her out first."

"Oh, you trust Magellan do you? Has my company really made you so favourable to pagans? My, my I had not thought myself so beloved."

Mary rolled her eyes at that comment and shook her head, "just, listen to me, man. No, I do not trust this Magellan person. But I certainly do trust that he hates you enough to reveal the secrets of alchemy to a whore!"

Victor seemed proud of that, "now there, you see. I do know that I am hated. It is a sign of betterance."

"Yes," Mary spoke with a blank expression and still voice, "you are necessary force of nature, m'lord."

The auger strode over and leaned down into her face, although this time she had learned to stop reacting to him when he did so. "And don't you forget it."

He pulled up and began walking ahead again but in a less frantic pace. She hoped that was a sign he was ready to hear Harlot out before jailing her and followed silently behind him. As the sun began to wane in the sky and the light blues became dark ones mingled with orange rather than yellow, the two finally made their way to the open area with the fountain. It was quite busy as people were closing up shop with the darkening sky or just heading out to get a few rounds in before curfew. There were people going all over the square that initially made it hard for Victor and Mary to spy their target until they thought to look directly in the centre. And that's exactly where she was, sat in her messed, blue dress and fiddling with a basket of mismatched jars while looking anxiously from left to right.

It was Mary who saw her and tugged at her boss' sleeve to point the other woman out. As they approached, she stood up quickly and held a firm grasp on the handle of the basket. She was both anxious and steeled in a moment.

"Please, just hear me out, my lord. I-"

"Calm down, woman," Victor hissed. He looked around himself and saw that everyone passing by seemed to have no interest whatsoever in what they were doing or who they were. He simply sat himself on the fountain's edge and ushered for the other woman to join him. Mary chose to stand instead, not wanting to get too involved. When their fugitive looked at her she gave a tentative wave.

"Hi, Harlot," she said awkwardly.

"Actually, it's Harley now." She moved to sit on the other side of the basket to Victor who was already poking his nose into the collection of ingredients despite clearly not having any idea what they were for.

"So," he mumbled, "you've finally left your debauchery behind, eh?" He kept focussed on the basket as he jibed her chosen name.

"I didn't say that..." she muttered back. He looked up at her over his nose and gave a very judgemental glare before turning back down to inspect her collection again. After a minute of pulling out jars and pretending to understand what the symbols on their labels meant Harley finally cleared her throat and offered to begin their negotiations.

"Negotiations?" the auger said the word like he had never heard it before, like the woman was speaking a foreign language. "Madam, I will tell you what's going to happen here. You are going to show us how to use all this and then thank us for not arresting in you in turn, should I even decide to be so kind!"

"Actually," Harley stood up and put her hands on her hips. Mary could see fear in her wide eyes, it was the diminutive fear that the auger made everyone feel, as she chose to stand up to him anyway. "What's going to happen, is I will give you the recipe only after you sign a contract ensuring both mine and William Rushing's freedoms!"

Her voice faltered slightly when she said her friend's name but powered up again at the word 'freedoms' as she finished on a strong albeit wavy footing.

Mary admired her for that, especially seeing as when Victor rose to match Harley, he found no words of rebuttal. Harley had them, they each needed something that the other wanted and this way it would only cost the freedom of a prisoner rather than another generous handful of gold to a particularly avaricious alchemist. So instead of arguing, he grinned and pulled a curled piece of parchment from his jacket.

"In that case, how about I suggest a blood contract?"

"W-what's a blood contract?"

Victor was ready to answer with a malign grin. Mary noticed that Harley's bravery was running out so she stepped in with a soft hand on Victor's arm to quiet him so she could explain in a way that didn't sound... psychotic.

"It is just a quicker way of going about this agreement business without waiting for notaries public to open. We can decide the terms, sign and ethereally bind both parties to it in about five minutes instead of involving solicitors."

"I rather think that I might have been a lawyer had I not subscribed myself to the pagan arts," Victor commented.

"You would have been good at it too," Mary grumbled to herself. She moved to put her hands on Harley's shoulders now and seat her back down on the fountain. Victor followed suit and rolled up the blank parchment in his hand to begin the agreement procedure.

"Here," he held it out, "take the other end."

Mary stepped back from the signing. Harley and Redding each held half of the rolled up parchment and looked into one another's eyes. She started to ask, 'what do I do,' only to be interrupted by Victor's talking.

"*With the moon as our witness...*" When he spoke the colour of his eyes turned a deep crimson. The roots of his hair started to transform to the same colour and his voice became distorted by echoes. It went on for a wholly creepy five seconds until the whole thing was abruptly cancelled off with Harley's interruptions.

"Sorry, sorry," she said cringing at herself for stopping him, "but – and I cannot stress this enough – the moon isn't out right now..." she looked up at the sky to confirm her assertation and then looked at the auger with pursed lips.

He blinked and when his eyes opened they were back to their normal colour. The red roots remained in his hair though.

Instead of answering her he just glowered and nodded his head at the fountain besides them. Harley looked into it and then back at the man, blinking cluelessly. "The... water?"

"No, the reflection!"

She looked back into the rippling pool once more but saw nothing except the image of the sky above. "It's just a reflection of the sun," she said, uncertain.

"And what is the moon but a reflection of the sun?"

Harley chuckled nervously and looked between Victor and Mary, "d-does that count?"

Victor grunted and turned to the magister this time inviting her to explain in lieu of his frustration. Mary did, although she raised her voice just a bit as she did not want to step closer until they had finished the ritual.

"Actually, yes it does! You would be surprised by how many pagan spells, alchemical practices and miracles of faith use clever wordplay to get around inconvenient circumstances!"

"Right... cheers," she responded. Harley turned and faced the other man again and nodded at him to get it over with.

He sighed, closed his eyes and opened them again to reveal the blood colour in them. As he spoke his hair slowly became enveloped by the dripping crimson; his voice curling with thick fog.

"With the moon as our witness I press my terms in blood and bind them with my soul."

"With the moon as our witness I press my terms in blood and bind them with my soul," she followed after his silence. She felt a small prick in her hands as she spoke that she shook off as a nervous cramp.

He continued, *"The terms of the first party are as follows: We receive the knowledge on how to duplicate an alchemical stone to a perfect replica of itself in a continuous manner. We will make an informal arrest of the second party should this not be delivered."*

When he finished speaking, Harley once again took the initiative to follow with her part of the contract, *"the terms of the second party are as follows: upon deliverance of the alchemical knowledge the first party seeks, I will receive my freedom from the crime of witnessing clandestine auger business as well as the freedom of my associate, William Rushings."* She felt a sting in the palm of her hand again as she started to speak. It grew sharper with every word she said until she was wincing her way to the end, desperate to let go of the contract.

"With the terms defined, I, speaker of the first party, sign my name; Victor Redding."

"I, speaker of the second party, sign my name; Harley Abernathy."

By now the auger's hair had been completely taken over by the deep red. He somehow made Harley even more uncomfortable than he already did. His eyes had returned to normal however as he blinked and then pulled the paper from her hands. He unfurled it to scan the legislature. He nodded at it approvingly while Harley looked at her palm. It was shaking, had a large gash in the middle and was dripping blood. She tore a shred from her dress sleeve and wrapped it gently over the wound hoping nothing would fester.

Victor was just holding his gash in the fountain, letting the red spread out through the water in a cloud as he finished appraising the writing. It was red, of course, being written in the blood from their hand's. It said exactly what they had and bound their actions under a blood moon's curse. Harley was not entirely sure what that denoted but she fully intended to uphold her end, so it mattered not.

When he was finished reading he held the contract out and Mary approached again to hold it for him. He pulled some bandages from his coat, wrapped them around his hand and held them with a pin, before returning them to his pockets as well as the contract.

"You should pull out some more paper. And actual ink," Mary advised, "we should like to take note of what Harley shows us."

"Yes, good idea," Victor agreed reaching into his coat once more.

"Actually," Harley reached into her own pocket of treasures by pulling a furled up piece of paper from between the jars in the basket. "It's all here. List of ingredients too- hey!"

"Thank you." The moment Abernathy had produced the instructions, the auger had swiped them from her hand and claimed them for himself. He even swooped into a standing position with the ingredients basket hooked under his arm.

"D-don't you want proof that it works?" Mary whispered to her boss.

"Actually," he replied sincerely, "I believe that your earlier advice was sound. All the proof I need is in Magellan's dislike for me being so prominent that he would eagerly hand over accurate information. If not him, then whatever alchemist the whore had procured the ingredients from. We have saved a pretty penny here, let us not spend unnecessary time in its place."

Mary opened her mouth to argue but closed it just as quickly. She knew that he was set in this decision and so she just crossed her arms, nodded and gave an affirmative, "m'lord."

"Whatever," Harley interrupted, "can I just have Will back... please."

"Besides," the auger hissed turning to face the whore in question, "her disease will take her over sooner than later. A blood moon curse is the least of her worries if this does not work out..."

Harley took that on the chin and simply glowered back at Redding. "Please can I have my friend back." Her repeated words were hard but vulnerable.

Before the man could say something else just as acidic, Mary took her cue to stand in again. "Of course," she said. She looked expectingly at her boss and he eventually relinquished the bottle. He pointed it at Mary and uncorked the stopper.

"Go on then. And take your time with it..." Harley looked in awe at the bottle wondering what secrets the swirling vortex inside held. She looked to see what was meant to be happening to Mary only to see that she was no longer where she was once stood. She had vanished. She turned in concern to look at the man holding the bottle but he seemed to have found his smile again. "After all, I need to have a little chat with our friend here about Adam Sunvale."

Abernathy

Harley had honestly not thought about Adam since her drunken adventure with Will. The only exception being a brief second when she was sleeping on the streets just the night before and considering knocking on his door for asylum.

She had quickly put that idea out the moment she realised that not only would Victor go snooping there, Adam would just as happily sell her out to him...

So while her instincts told her to rebuke Victor's demand by saying that they are no longer associated she simply moved the conversation forward to the quickest way of ending it. She wasn't ready to face that part of her past yet, not until the whole ancercy matter was resolved anyway.

"What about him?"

Redding seemed displeased to have not struck a discordant string in her but pushed on none the less. "Are the rumours correct that the man is an opiate dealer?"

"Yes," she replied. And because she simply could not bite her tongue back from moving, she added, "why?"

That enjoyed Victor. "Because I am in need of one," he pulled the alchemist's stone from his cape. He gently placed it on top of the basket of ingredients before looking at Harley with a mock innocence in his eyes. "I'm sure you can imagine why."

Harley looked at the confession presented in front of her. She thought about it for a moment considering the scale of what exactly she might be involved in. And she simply shook her head, letting any ponderings on the matter fall away, "I don't care."

"Then would you be so kind as to give me his address?" He was starting to look impatient.

She nodded. "Annum's Lane. Just down from the butcher's, the house with the boarded windows."

"Ah. So close to the Happy Whore."

"*Huntress*," she corrected with a grunt. She immediately felt ashamed when he grinned in self-satisfaction.

"Of course," his voice curled out, "my deepest apologies.'

She opened her mouth then to try and hit him by pointing out that his chase couldn't have been quite that good if he hadn't searched her closest friend's house

He even raised a quizzical eyebrow at her starting words as if ready to refute at a moment's notice, only for them both to whip around at the sight of Mary Culver's concerningly quick return.

She had come out of the bottle a few steps away, exactly the same place where she entered, except she was now sprawled on the floor, protecting her fall with her arms.

She was breathing heavily and looked up at the square around her to assure herself of her reality. She seemed to calm down, the wideness of her eyes receding, as she ascertained her surroundings and finally locked on to her master and Harley. Victor had stepped back, deeply embarrassed to be seen in public with a panicking woman. Harley had stepped back with him except out of fear. This world – the alchemy and the paganism and the devils – was one she did not belong in.

Mary slowly stood up, her limbs shaking, and looked back and forth between her two acquaintances unsure on which to elaborate to until eventually she looked Harley in the eyes. She tilted her head and softened her face as if Harley were the one panicking and just managed to whisper something to her.

"Speak up, woman," the auger urged.

"I'm so sorry," she huffed out again not looking away from Harley.

She didn't know how to react to that and simply stood there allowing Victor to take charge. He stomped over and grabbed Mary by the shoulders and practically shook her. Harley had considered leaving just then if not for the fact that Mary had failed to produce her friend.

Oh god, Will! she thought.

After her body had been forced rigid by her boss, Mary finally managed to splutter out an explanation.

"It was all dark in there... except for this great planet in the sky... it was like the sun except red... it was like it was watching me."

"Have you gone quite mad?" Redding hissed under his voice.

But Mary just kept her eyes dead ahead as if she was still seeing into the bottle world, "it made the bricks look orange... it made the blood look black."

"Blood?" Abernathy rushed over then, "blood? What happened, is he okay?"

Mary released an uncontrolled and guttural 'hah!' She looked at the auger, intent flashing across her eyes, and he raised his head in ascension as a look of knowing crossed his eyes.

"It wasn't Will's blood."

"That's quite enough, Miss Culver," with a straight arm he ushered her away, "I can finish your thoughts."

"Where is Will? What happened!" Harley demanded.

"Oh, my dear. It appears that your friend has succumbed to his disease. William Rushings has been killed by his ancercy." He whispered the last part of his sentence, as if not to startle Harley, "as was his daemon guard, it appears."

Harley, by then, had clutched at her chest as she found herself moving to sit on the edge of the fountain. She took her deep breaths and tried to grasp her grief as it surrounded her like a consuming darkness. She turned around to see Mary, with her lips slightly parted, as her own breathing returned to normal. She had an expression that basically screamed 'sorry.'

And then she realised that what she felt was not grief in the slightest. She had only recently met William and had spent even less time as his associate. She had come to be so close to him in their few hours as friends, trusting him with herself as they bonded over fucking away the past. But she did not grieve him. Because she did not know him. Not as a person – not every day, not in highs and not when it was so boring that she thought his presence was normal. No, all he was to her was a bright light that in a few moments had managed to light up her life.

What she felt was not grief. It was anger. She had let that light go dark... and now she had to fight to bring it back.

"In that case, I suppose the matter is over-"

Victor tried to herd Mary away from the woman on the fountain whose breathing was getting deeper and harsher only to be stopped when she rose again and pointed at his cape.

"Give me the bottle," she demanded.

"Excuse me?"

"The bottle! Where William is trapped. I want it!"

He laughed at that, "well I am afraid you most certainly shall not have it. Come, Miss culver." He turned, allowing his cape to swish in her face as he stalked out of Saint Mungo's square.

Harley watched with clenched fists ready to fight the man if she had to. In a second, she listed off how she had absolutely nothing left to lose. Her money, her parlour, her love... all gone, and soon her life would follow. She had decided that it was time to throw herself at the auger and force the bottle from him or die trying. She stepped forward, a manic feeling rushing to her head as her entire body suddenly sharpened and her vision closed in on him. Everything seemed so focused, so clear. She knew she could do it...

Then her mind caught up, becoming just as sharp as her muscles. She exhaled and coughed in doing so, not realising she was holding her breath. A realisation came that there might just be one more option.

She raised her voice so they could hear her from across the square, "and what about the blood moon's curse?"

Victor stopped in his tracks and Mary stopped a moment after, not even hearing Abernathy's voice.

The auger turned, growling at the woman and quickly stormed back over. He stood over her, his teeth grinding as he searched for a response to that.

She continued anyway, "Will has not received his freedom, per the terms of the contract."

"I could not give *'Will'* his freedom," he snarled. Mary caught up to him but stayed quiet watching with her lips pursed in curiosity.

"You could," Harley answered. Her hand was tensing, opening and closing, as she tried to dispel the rush of energy in her body. She gestured out to the square with the other one, "Will is not technically dead. You can still grant his freedom."

Victor chuckled nervously at that, "I am not releasing a beast in the middle of Summerset, *Harlot*, it would be insane to do so."

She moved the held-out hand to point it towards him. She indicated that she was ready to grasp the parchment of the blood contract by pulling free the make-shift bandage. She didn't laud the hold she had over him, she simply looked with a deadly serious urgency that implored him to weigh his response. "If not... I would be happy to change the terms of the deal to accept the bottle in his place."

Her eye flickered to Mary to judge her standing in the situation but only saw a woman deeply enjoying herself.

"This is a matter far beyond your ken," the auger warned, drawing her attention back. "You should think carefully before you do this."

Harley stared back into his eyes hardly and with great content. "So which is it?"

He frowned in a very miserly manner, before reaching into his cape and pulling the parchment back out. He swatted it into her hand and she gripped it tightly, with great determination. They swore on the moon's witness again and moved to edit the clauses from before, the red ink being drawn from their respective veins:

'If William Rushings cannot be set free, then the first party will offer the bottle where he is imprisoned as compensation.'

But before he signed off, Victor insisted on one more clause:

'Upon either the curing of William Rushing's ancercy or his death, the bottle will be returned to the office of the Royal Auger in Okhram.'

Harley frowned but agreed to the term, believing it to be only fair. When they finished, she pulled her palm close to her chest as she quickly reapplied the torn shred of fabric to the cut. Victor didn't bother with any healing this time as Mary was both too intimidated and entertained to step in. He simply reached to store the parchment back in his cape. When he pulled his hand out again it was gripping the bottle. He held it out to Harley and the blood from his palm dripped down the glass in a slow trail.

She swallowed nervously and stored it under her arm, still not quite sure what to do with all her pent up energy.

And, apparently satisfied to a degree, Victor turned on his heel and made another attempt at storming off. That is when Mary stepped in, "now, hold on," she requested. Victor stopped, threw his head back and groaned very loudly. He did not actually turn to face them.

"Harley," she offered, "would you like to ride with us back to Whitley Moor? It's only fair, seeing as we, ah, drove you out in the first place."

Harley could feel her emotions rushing to her head so she simply nodded her appreciation. If she had spoken she might have sobbed as the next part of her daunting quest caught up to her and she realised she actually had to cure ancercy now. And with but a few days, maybe hours, left to live herself.

"She won't be doing that," the auger declared. He still didn't turn around, not fully. He just looked over his shoulder with cruel, narrowed eyes. He had not looked at Harley though, but Mary.

"Now, why not?" She said in return, making a shaky stand.

"Because she doesn't want to."

"But she-"

"Oh, Miss Culver. Why on earth would Miss Abernathy here want to ride in a carriage with you of all people?"

"Victor..." Mary warned. Her wobbling defence quickly shifted to fear. He liked that and carried on.

"After all, you are the one who sent the daemon that gave her ancercy, are you not?"

He didn't wait for the response. He simply left back towards where he had parked the carriage with the intention to leave whether Mary caught up or not.

She didn't look at Harley but she could feel that the other woman had stalked over to her with an aura that made her hairs stand on end.

For the second time that day she made a pathetic attempt to whisper something to her fellow woman.

"*What was that?*" Harley insisted.

"I'm so sorry."

Culver

"You're sorry?"

The words bit Mary. They didn't sound like words that flew out on one's breath. They were the words that had climbed from the throat, spoken not with the mind but the visceral organs of the body.

"I honestly, truly am." She turned and faced her victim. Harley did not look angry. She held the bottle in one hand, her arms both hanging at her sides. She was completely still, like she had shut herself down to prevent her conscious body from doing something she really did not want to do.

"Why?" Her words were pragmatic again.

"Because," Mary sobbed. When she answered she struggled to form the words. No, she knew exactly what to say, she just struggled to say it. The words came to her mind fine; it was the effort to push them from her mouth that hurt. Each syllable stung her eyes and every other one caught in her throat. Guilt or fear, she didn't know which, but something was trying desperately to dam her lips. "Because... our research. To figure this out, ancercy, we needed to set up- up different situations. Like an experiment, honestly! Each of the whores I sent a daemon to-"

"YOU DID THIS TO OTHERS?" Harley roared, her fingers squeaking as she tightened around the red stained glass of the bottle.

Mary stumbled away from her two steps and finally let the tears welling in her eyes fall down. "I- I did."

"WHY!"

"Because I needed to find out what would happen-"

Harley stomped over and leaned closely into Mary's face. Not Victor close. Victor only got close enough to frighten you. The proximity of Harleys scowl in that moment was enough to calcify Mary's bones. Their foreheads touched and her words, while just a whisper, sounded like the shrillest shout.

"They would get ancercy. That's what would happen."

"They were... they were circumstantial," she sobbed, "l-like yours! Your daemon was instructed only to perform oral tasks. Perhaps you would not have been infected in that case, that was the experiment!"

Harley responded by rolling her head to the left. It was a slow, intentional movement that forced Marys head to roll with her to see what she was looking at. Slowly she pulled up her sleeves, making Mary bear witness to the scales on her arm. Fortunately, they had not yet crossed the palm, but they had gone all the way upwards, far past her shoulders. In no way could Culver look away from it. It was everything in that moment. Her own body started shaking.

"Well look at that... it turns out I *was* infected."

"I know that now..."

"But you didn't then."

Mary just sobbed some more and let loose another barrage of 'so, so sorry.'

Harley leaned back to stand up straight, freeing Mary's body. She didn't realise it but that connection was all that had been keeping her upright. She buckled and fell down to her knees in a pile of red dress. She looked up at Harley like a pilgrim and held both her hands to cover her quivering mouth.

Harley shook her head at the sight before her. "The thing is you don't even understand what you did... not really."

Mary didn't know how to respond to that without incriminating herself further.

"*This*," Harley pointed sharply at her scales, "is going to kill me; *this* pushed away the man I love; *this* took over a great friend of mine; *this* has caused my place of work to be ransacked; *this* has not only mutated my body BUT MY WHOLE LIFE."

Her chest heaved up and down as her voice grew. Mary's hands just clutched tighter as she blocked any more words from leaving her mouth and shrivelled in on herself.

"And you will never get that. Sat there, crying yourself away. I bet you feel so bad for yourself, don't you. But you still don't know what *this* feels like. What it feels like to not only slowly approach your death but know that as you do so, everything you've done in life is becoming undone along the way. You've erased me, Mary Culver. I hope you feel good about that. You've wiped history clean of Harley Abernathy."

She turned and walked away, moving to be mixed in with the crowd and shake off her fury elsewhere. For if she had stayed, she feared, Mary too would have become a casualty of her disease.

Once she was from sight, though, Mary was safe to finally collapse, curling in on herself and clutching her stomach. She shouted at the ground below her, screaming into the stones to vent her head of all emotions. She felt horrid and she never wanted to feel like that again.

During the entire encounter – the blood contracts, the bottle and the arguing – people had just come and gone. As curfew approached, people moved from taverns and workplaces to their home and so there had been a fair few witnesses to the events that had transpired.

But nobody seemed to be bothered. They were just another strange band of pagans and then a pair of women bickering over something and finally a peculiar girl crying into the floor.

Again, no one's business.

And while she was not physically sick, Mary could feel some form of change from her expulsion. She had continued her screeching into the square, saliva flying everywhere, and was noticing that her head and heart had started to feel hollowed out. She didn't want to return to a positive place, she had decided: a place from where she could fall again. She just wanted to go somewhere quiet – not good nor bad. Amoral. Indifferent.

Quiet.

Everything was so loud to her and so she emptied the sound from her body until her throat had been run raw. When a fit of coughs was brought on, she sat back up on her knees trying to right herself and alleviate the pain in her core.

With the coughing done, she opened her mouth to keep crying.

Nothing came out.

Just a dry, itchy throat.

She twisted around and leant back against the edge of the fountain cutting an image not dissimilar to a drunkard. She stared up at the darkening sky as a piece of inconsequential spit dribbled from the corner of her lips.

She saw the beginnings of stars like pinpricks in the deep grey. She saw the falling sun and rising moon. She remembered the red, fiery planet in the auger's bottle. She thought the astroglobe was so beautiful. She reached out to it, longing to be a part of such a desolate world – a world where celestial bodies shifted mechanically. A world where everything aligned so perfectly. And a world where everything was oh so quiet. She yearned for it and pulled herself to stand up as if she could rise to the heavens.

But she knew she couldn't. She was Engelland's foremost expert on knowing that she couldn't. So why did she try? What's drawing her there? What's... tempting her?

The thought of temptation made her hand recoil, the word going hand in hand with sin. Why not aspiration? Why not ambition?

She tried those words in her mind's eye but they did not push her arm quite as far. When she blinked and looked at the stars again with inclination that they tempt her so desperately she found that she could spread her outstretched hand farther than she thought. It was a motion that moved her whole body, from her tip-toes to her watering eyes.

It tempted her.

So what was anchoring her.

She fell down from her tip toeing and landed to sit on the edge of the fountain. She considered that Ahmar might be her anchor. She thought what she would do when they reunited. She frowned as she realised that she would simply slap him;

"Here's a 'what if' for you. What if you, the esteemed Mary Culver, turn this down and the matter ends up in the hands of an actually bad person. An actual heretic, an actual traitor? What if, by doing this yourself, you aren't serving any dark purpose but controlling it and maintaining some light in there?"

She laughed then as she recalled his words. She was the actually bad person. She was a traitor. Definitely a heretic. Certainly serving a dark purpose. She had enabled a man to spread ancercy on a wide scale. To do to hundreds of people what she had done to that poor woman, Harley.

No... there was no actually bad person. Just Mary Culver.

* * *

It only took five minutes to find her again. Harley didn't actually know what to do once she had acquired Will. So when Mary chased she found that the woman was just staring listlessly at the bottle in her hands on a nearby street corner.

She looked up from the bottle immediately noticing the red frills in the corner of her eyes. She clutched the bottle tightly and shot a dead stare at Culver who came with her arms held up.

"I have something for you," she implored.

"Another disease?"

"Please."

"What."

Mary nodded quickly as she lowered her hands. She folded them in her lap as she slowly walked closer. Talking was strange now, her words felt so light. Not just physically as they swam from inside but mentally too. As if she had unchained them and knocked down any damming effort.

"I wanted to help you," she gestured at the bottle.

"How?"

"I don't have a cure," she said in precursor, "but I have an idea of where to start."

Harley continued to stare through her but she simply didn't feel the affect. She continued her proposal, "ancercy is an affliction of the soul – a disease of the spirit. These are what we call curses," she flicked into teacher mode as she explained, making Harley sneer slightly at how condescending it sounded. "Curses, therefore, usually have supernatural symptoms rather than natural ones. Bad luck perhaps or a repulsive aura."

"Oh, like yours."

"Thank you," she kissed her teeth. "Ancercy, however, is different. In that it does manifest naturally. That's why its status as a curse rather than a disease has eluded most people."

Harley crossed her arms impatiently, "what's the point of this?"

"The point is that unlike other curses, this one might be able to be, not cured, but supressed. You can fight the symptoms unlike with most curses. Throughout history, people have gone to churches, witches and witchers, warlocks and even cultists in search of a cure, never mind alchemists and doctors. But no one appears to have tried simply fighting the- the scales or the red fur or the tentacles or whatever! They have tried to fight the ancercy. Everyone tries to cut off the head of the snake all while ignoring the tail that's wrapped around their throat. I'm just suggesting that maybe freeing yourself from the grasp can give you the chance at the head."

Harley nodded at that genuinely appreciating the wisdom. "Alright... just one question."

"Of course."

"Do you think this makes up for what you've done?"

Mary's eye twitched. 'YES' she wanted to scream. She wanted to grab Harley by the hair and shout 'YES, YES, YES' in her face because it was true! It would. This was her redemption. She was going to balance the scales by helping develop the cure and ultimately undermining Victor's efforts.

She would balance her heart against itself and become free to rise from the ashes.

"Of course not," she lied amiably.

Harley nodded again. "Whatever."

"I suggest you head to an alchemist. I- I don't know exactly what to look for, but clearly the ancercy gives a daemonic form. Perhaps look for something that might repel a daemon. A physical, tangible thing that has gone untried."

"I will." Harley answered. Mary was ready to suggest something else, but clearly the other woman had heard enough. She took off at a moment's notice and headed through Saint Mungo's square and down some other street with a purpose beyond Mary.

A moment ago she might have been flummoxed by such rudeness but now... 'it is what it is.' That was her thought on the matter.

That was her new maxim.

She did what she did. Everyone else did what they did. And the world still turned. All of them did – the seven above Etherium. The ones beyond that and even within.

The thought made her smile.

She walked out into the open area again to find that it was vastly beginning to clear. She held up both hands to the heavens as if to cradle it, allowing the open area to emulate the space in her mind.

"Oh stars above, I have a confession. I have found myself, as a member of human society, to be... lacking."

She moved forward, possessed. She kept her hands up like she was delivering a mighty sermon. She did not even trip over the lip of the fountain once she reached it. Instead she stepped elegantly over it and placed her feet in the low pool. It went just up her shin and cause the bottom of her dress to fan out around her liking a blossoming flower.

"I have found that in serving others in life I have only lead myself to my own displeasure. In trying to be good, in trying to be bad I am... so displeased. Morality has been nothing but a weight on my soul – a burden on my shoulders, whichever side of it I find myself on. The better or the worse. It's just so loud."

"But the truth is that there is no light and there is no dark. No good or evil. No God or Satan. No Old King or Pale Lady. No Anaximander or Mara. At least not in the way we devise them. A lord of light may reside in your ranks and He may even call Himself God, but it is men who write His scripture. There may be a mouthpiece of the devil, but it is Mara no more, for she is long dead. The truth of the world is warped by mythology. Even a whore can be seen as a victim, crying with the disease she caught by being a whore."

Her arms fell to her side.

"So where does that leave me?"

As the sun fled across the last breadths of the sky, and the grey became dark grey, the water below her turned into a reflection of the night. It sent a euphoric feeling through her body as she felt even closer to the heavens than before.

"I can answer in terms of action and inaction. Of moral or immoral. But that would be a further mythologization. No. I did what I did, motivated by a petty feeling of gratification from a *man*. That is the fact of it. I am beyond such wrappings now – no longer will I call a state of matter as 'working to prevent someone worse.' I will be worse because I am Mary Culver. And I will be better, also, for Victor will lionise my help. BECAUSE IT'S ALL JUST HUMAN ISN'T IT? Those little semantic pairings, they're just that. Human. Good and evil. Light and dark. God and Satan. A messiah on either face of the same coin. It's all just human."

Her screams from earlier rang in her mind. It made her clutch at her heart as she recalled how Harley had made her feel. It ached her organs to remember that low point of her life and how it had scraped every remnant of her soul away.

"And I hate being a human. It hurts- HAH! Even now I call it pain, that feeling of emptiness. But in the time, I thought it a blessing as it finally ended the grief I felt."

She fell to her knees, letting the water go up to her waist as she hugged her stomach and then moved to clutch at her head. She looked down at her reflection in the backdrop of the galaxy and groaned out through gritted teeth. Each feeling she felt was marred by arbitrary distinctions. Her pain was as much cathartic as it was punishment. Her mind became muddled as she hated to hate and hated that she hated even that.

"But what can I say..." she sobbed, unable to escape the noise that accompanied each thought in her head. "I will never be anything other than human."

Lobelia

"It was simply wonderful!" Thomas applauded. By the time the excitement had started to die down, Lolita had turned a tad shy. She blushed as Thomas and Alex both hounded her with congratulations.

Meanwhile, everyone else had fanned out to their own bubbles of conversation. The archbishop had been the first to leave, muttering about councils and meetings and women or something bitter like that. Her mother had moved out of earshot to talk to the Viscount about the vision while his wife sat obediently on a nearby pew.

The mayor was dangling by the door waiting for an opportunity to excuse himself and the bishop was dangling near to the princess so that he could keep a stern eye on his acolyte.

"He's right, I loved to see it!" Alex added.

With the other girl's praise came a realisation across Lolita's face. She looked down at her, "oh, right. I do hope this future of mine isn't going to be stepping on any toes."

The acolyte shook her head and took Lolita's hands in her own, "not at all. It isn't a competition, after all. Us girls should be brilliant together!"

"Alex!" Barked the bishop. "Keep your hands to yourself."

"Sorry, father," she muttered. Her hands fell sheepishly to her side as she looked to her fidgeting shoes. That made both girls frown so the princess, ignoring the holy man's command, took Alex' hands again. What would he do, scold *her*?

"You're exactly right," Lolita agreed, "I rejoice for the day I can call you sister."

Alex beamed and nodded enthusiastically. Her embarrassed flush grew into a great heat of pride on her red face. Next to them, Thomas nodded approvingly, making both the girls giggle and pull him into a hug as the trio continued to discuss the various aspects her vision in the pool.

Through it all, the princess had taken the occasional glance around to see if she could locate Cyrus, but the man was nowhere to be seen.

She shrugged away any concern that that notion brought and continued to mill with her friends.

Katherine, on the other side of the chamber, spoke with apprehensive authority to Viscount Azalea. His face was hardened once more, any shock from the visions being chiselled out of his features as he addressed his queen.

"I suppose..." she began, "that if ever there were a royal baptism worthy of the emperor's attention, it would be this one."

"I couldn't agree more." The viscount's voice was deeply masculine. It made him sound astute in whatever he said. "On the morrow, I will take the first transport I can to the capital to ensure he is informed."

"Of course..." Katherine rarely felt powerless like she had then in front of the auspicious Viscount. But she also felt aspiration amidst it: for her daughter's prospective career. The worry of how hard her daughter would struggle was quickly dawning, however, and ruining that hope. Lolita's a princess after all. What does she know of work, of not being handed something? She was going to have to fight to make that vision a reality. The queen thought it might be a comfort to know that the vision is indeterminably accurate, but all that makes her certain of is that her daughter will fight. She will go through the turmoil. She will be broken down before she is built up to that status. It terrified Katherine. So much so that she hadn't even considered the mortal implication of her son ascending the throne at such a young age.

Once the Viscount was satisfied with their formalities, he made his bow and left ahead to his manor house where he would retire early. His staff would welcome the Lobelias once they followed.

Before going to collect Lolita, she moved to address the increasingly anxious mayor and alleviate his restlessness.

His words got ahead of him as she approached, "m-ma'am. It was a wonderful ceremony, absolutely wonderful. I was honoured to have been present. I thank you a thousand times for inviting me but now I must be off. I am needed at Whitley."

She smiled down at him with sympathy. She could only see the lost son when she looked at Theodore and in her swelling of emotions for her own spawn she could not bring herself to just let him leave.

"I don't think we can have that," she announced. It made Theodore stiffen and stand up straight, terrified that he had misspoken. "Instead, I will send a pigeon to Whitley. Your intermediaries can make do for a few days longer."

He seemed to relax a bit. "In that case... what am I to do, ma'am."

"Relax," she explained. "Take residence in the Azalea house with me and... well just relax."

He nodded at that. "Of course."

"And, Theodore." Her voice stopped low and soft, "I am sorry about your son."

He stared blankly at her, processing the comment. She was worried that she might have triggered a breaking of the dam inside him but after a few moments he finally answered with a wide smile. "Oh, do not make any thoughts for him, ma'am! He is just out being a boy. When I return home, he will be back in bed... my boy will be all tucked in bed."

The words made her nauseated. Every time she tried to make herself explain what had happened to Will, to tell him that the ancercy had probably taken him by now, she simply couldn't. It was only then that she started to think of Aaron again. About how if she knew he had a disease she wouldn't picture him slowly losing himself. She would cradle herself and remember him, her little boy, all tucked into bed.

She would not rob the mayor of the same privilege.

"My son can be quite the same," she acquiesced. "We must just let boys be boys, hadn't we."

That seemed to genuinely make him smile, the first piece of genuine emotion she had seen from the man since before they left Whitley.

He thanked her again after that and excused himself as he too made his way out to the carriages where he would ride on to the Azalea manor house.

She moved then to collect Lolita, walking over to her daughter's little grouping and causing their jubilant conversation to quickly quiet down. "I think it's our turn to leave, sweetheart."

Thomas looked around the room, past the queen. Alex knew a command when she heard one and gave a polite curtsey before taking leave. She waved at her fellow teenagers as she rejoined the bishop and they both stalked into the darkness of the cathedral.

"Where is mother? And also father?" Thomas muttered, poking his around. He frowned to realise that he couldn't find them. Katherine had no choice but to relent and invite him to join their group.

"Come," she said herding the pair, "you can ride with us back to the manor.

Thomas' frown remained as he nodded his thanks.

The queen lead the way out with the other two trailing just close enough that they could chatter in whispers. Being ever the optimist, the Azalea heir chose to wipe his smile away and reengage his friend, "you know, when we get home you simply must catch me up on whatever happened down in Whitley."

"Hm? What do you mean?"

"That delicious boy you were talking about, he was the mayor's son, right?"

"Oh right, we were interrupted by Mary, weren't we? No, I'll certainly tell you."

He grinned, "you always know how to cheer me up, Lolly."

She grinned back, "of course!"

* * *

It was too dark to see much outside but Lolita still tried her best to peer through the carriage windows to see the looming approach of the Azalea's home.

Lanship house stood elevated with a great doorway at the end of a circling driveway. To each side was a series of staircases even larger than the grand one back in the mayoral house. It stood atop its bricks and pillars in a perfectly symmetrical two tiered building. With the two rows of large, arced windows on each tier, Lolita could only imagine what secrets inside she had yet to uncover.

For even she had had not roamed the entire grounds of Lanship as of yet – it still awed her each time she visited, herself still being accustomed to the spire palace rather than horizontal architecture. Unfortunately, each time she came, her treasure hunting efforts were squashed when her mother corralled her into her best behaviour.

In the past, her and Thomas had snuck down to the kitchens and even made attempts at finding hidden passageways in the library, but all to no avail. In the years, neither had managed to discover something new, always thwarted by overly secure parents or incredibly strict butlers.

So every time they pulled in or out of the long winded entrance path, or every time they simply walked to picnic in the gardens, the two would try to scale up where the inside rooms matched up with the outside. Both of them, but Thomas especially, were convinced that things didn't quite align. Although neither could quite put their fingers on why.

Even now, Lolita was staring at the outline in the black, starry sky and trying to count windows. When they got too close to see the entire scale from her window, she sat back down and giggled to herself, thinking about how she had just been baptised into a woman, only to immediately keep acting like a child.

She might have felt shame, had she not loved the feeling of exploring with her best friend. But when she turned to him, he was no longer humming happily to himself on the journey or trying to peak the building's structural inconsistencies. He just grew quieter and perhaps smaller as they approached.

When they came to a halt, he alighted the car followed by the queen and then her daughter. He whispered something to her about getting ready and then, after a polite bow, dashed into the house alone.

Katherine did not appear to care, relaxing if anything to see him leave, and simply wrapped her arm around Lolita as they walked behind the butler inside the house.

"You know," she muttered, leaning in slightly as they trotted up the stairs, "I'm very proud of you for today."

Lolita blushed, "really? I didn't do much, mother."

The queen chuckled at that. "You were brave. That's what you did."

"I was scared," she corrected, "terrified. The only thing that kept me focused was, well, knowing Aaron would be there with me in the future. Even if it's just watching down from a church window."

That made Katherine feel warm inside, to see her two children get along. They had squabbled like any siblings when they were younger but once their dad passed they had become rather close.

"Being scared is the only time you can be brave, dear."

"Oh, mum!" she scoffed, "I am no longer a kid, the fairy tale idioms are embarrassing!"

Katherine really laughed at that. "Oh, sweetie. I wasn't quoting a story book." She stopped then and crouched down, holding a hand on each of Lolita's shoulders and coming face to face with her. "A story book might say something like bravery comes from within or you must find bravery in your heart. And as admirable as that may be, I have never thought it true."

Lolita copied her smile now, although more sheepishly. "That's a bit damp, don't you think?"

Katherine shook her head. "I think you get bravery from the other people in your life. Some people think it's shameful to need someone else to stand on, or to have your goodness come from another person but do you know what I think? That those people, utterly alone in the dark, would have been eaten by the whisps today. You weren't. My precious Lolita found faith in her brother and came through the darkness. And one day, when he is at his lowest, his faith will come from you. And he can do that, he can lean on you, only because you leant on him first. Do you understand?"

Lolita, mouth slightly parted in awe of her mother, nodded. It wasn't just her words that filled the princess with warmth, but her face, haloed by both the dark and the flickering of distant torches. She was a beautiful person.

"I do."

"Good," Katherine stood up again. She didn't wrap her arms around her daughter this time so instead Lolita took the initiative and took her mother's arm in her own. This surprised the queen, but she was grateful for it. The two walked into the manor together, with the night left behind them.

Culver

Victor was already in the forest by the time Mary had caught up. He was stood up straight with his arms crossed and glaring ruefully at his carriage. The two horses mindlessly grazed at the floor. Mary watched pitifully as the gaunt creatures strained to lift their necks.

When she finally came to his side he remained quiet, the only sound being the wet frills of her dress rustling against the grass as she walked.

He lazily turned his eyes to look her up and down, noticing how she was completely sodden from the waist down. While she was no longer dripping he could imagine that she had left a damp trail behind her through the streets of Summerset. Her shoes were collecting mud and her lower body was feeling quite a bite of cold.

"What happened to you?" He asked absently.

She shook her head, "just reconnecting with myself. I noticed you waited for me."

"I didn't wait for you," he replied brusquely, "I was waiting for him. To leave." He pointed at his carriage standing before them, specifically to the window.

"Who? The curtains are drawn, I can't see."

Victor rolled his eyes at her for that and just barely supressed a groan. "So mundane."

She was simply going to ignore him but found she didn't need to. The word didn't stick into her, causing a need to ignore. It just slipped off, leaving her stood indifferent. She truly didn't care.

"Well, we have work to do." She moved on, "so kick him out, whomever he is."

He mumbled an 'I suppose' as he trudged across the crunching forest floor towards his vehicle. Mary followed at a cautious distance, keeping a contrite figure as she stood up straight and kept her hands in front of her. It made the auger uncomfortable and twice he turned around to ascertain that this was in fact the same woman he had left behind.

After the third time he shook his head and cursed himself for reading all those foreign stories about shape changers and other maladies of the desert continent that possessed or controlled a person's body. It made him shiver to think of them again and decided simply that Mary was just under some sort of womanly spell. The full moon is in the air soon, is it not?

"Not you," he hissed. He had one hand on the carriage door and held the other outwards at her. "Just wait here whilst I deal with this."

She nodded and simply stood in place waiting for him to call her again. For the fourth time, he shot a dumbfounded look at the obedience in her and started to question if it was even obedience at all.

As he slowly pulled the door open in his thinking, he decided that the man inside was a much bigger burden than Mary Culver. He turned his head to look at him sat snidely on one of the seats and waiting patiently for his audience.

"Hello again, Redding." The man leaned forward so that he was visible through the door. "Miss Culver," he nodded.

She nodded back, "greetings. Magellan, was it?"

Cyrus grinned, "flattered that you remember."

Whatever Mary was going to say next went unheard as Victor took his place opposite the other witcher, slamming the carriage door in the process.

"That wasn't very polite," Cyrus quipped.

Victor simply glowered at him.

"Not chatty then? Very well," he cleared his throat, "I have a favour to ask of you."

"Get out."

Cyrus took a deep breath in. "Now, now. Hear me out."

"I believe I've done enough of that today already."

"Delightfully blithe as ever," Magellan's bright façade was becoming harder to maintain as the other man continued to sap the life from the air.

"I'm sorry," Victor said without meaning it in the slightest, "but why exactly should I feel compelled to help you with something after how you have royally interrupted me today, hm?"

"Actually, aha, I believe that if it weren't for me all you would have is two pox-ridden prisoners and still no way of duplicating your alchemist's stone." He didn't say it proudly, trying not to further irk his rival, but he was trying to elevate his importance. "I believe you do owe me."

That tugged Victor's snarl of malfeasance into a displeasured frown, "well... we can't be having that can we."

"No..." Cyrus took cautionary steps to keep the other man's anger lukewarm at worst, "so, would you at least listen to my proposition?"

Victor didn't break from his upside down expression and didn't speak in response either. He just stared in deep animosity.

"I'll presume that I can, then, without you setting alight a rune just to be rid of me," he coughed nervously. Before he continued, he pulled his own bottle out from inside his coat and held it atop his lap. He looked seriously now at Redding as he made his proposal. "I would like us to switch bottles... no questions asked about what's happening inside them."

Victor blinked unsurely at him. He turned a quick glance through the carriage window, pulling it to so he could glimpse at Mary who was waiting patiently and leant against a tree. He wondered, for a moment, if at some point in traipsing through the woods he might have fallen through some sort of rift into a realm adjacent to his own...

"Just stories," he grumbled.

"Pardon?"

"Nothing," he coughed. He picked up his words and returned to the world, whatever world it may be, and answered contritely, "while I have no interest in whatever's inside your little bottle, I do have to ask why there is a sudden interest in swapping? Are you taking my advice perhaps?"

"Perhaps," he replied. "Perhaps I just need to cover my tracks while I scamper off somewhere," Cyrus looked into the air dreamily, "perhaps I shall sail to Levie... purchase myself one of those lovely, clifftop castles..."

Victor snorted, "as if." He leant forward on his knees and clasped his hands together, "now, I can't give you mine at the moment. Perhaps you should seek asylum in one of your former colleague's homes, eh?"

"Oh?" Cyrus scowled, "maybe like the one on Rewbridge road?"

All that did was earn a scowl back. The two men sized each other up in growls before leaning back respectively to hold an air of their own betterances.

Magellan continued the talks, "go on then. What happened to your bottle that makes it so indisposed?"

Victor shrugged, not willing to justify the other man's attempts to drive the knife in, "I lost it." He spoke matter-of-factly and cared not about Magellan's slight expressions of judgement. After all, he is the one here to beg. "Blood contract. A temporary matter. You know how things get."

"Hm..." Cyrus appraised the testament, "it appears that wench really did you in then."

"Oh she is on a leash, I promise you that," the auger threatened. "Now, tell me what you saw at the baptism."

"Quite a change of subject don't you think."

"Oh, do dispense of the frivolities, man," he scoffed, "clearly something in that cathedral has you with your tail between your legs."

Cyrus narrowed his eyes, cooking a new idea up in his head. "You think you're so clever."

"I am so clever."

"Tell me, Redding, were you the auger for the Lobelias during her firstborn's baptism?"

"No."

"You lie so plainly it makes me feel dreadful for miss Culver out there," he smirked. He too took a turn to finger the curtain open just slightly. When he did, he saw that Mary was looking directly at him. His smile waned with a shudder as he let the curtain fall back shut.

"Do you have a problem with my choice of employee, Mr Magellan?"

He shrugged, "not particularly. She still has... potential."

"Yes..." Victor agreed hesitantly, although he suspected that the two of them meant different things when they spoke of 'potential.'

"Anyhow," he turned back to look at Redding, "what I want to know, in exchange for the knowledge of what happened in Miss Lolita's baptism, is what happened in her brother's? What did Aaron Lobelia see?"

Victor tried to supress a smile but couldn't stop the corner of his mouth from tugging up, "you are grasping at threads now aren't you?"

"Will you tell me, or won't you?" He frowned, "I might add that Lolita's future might be a degree of interest to you."

"Oh, alright then. If a man begs, who am I not to put him out of his misery..."

"*Redding*," Cyrus warned.

Victor smirked then. "Aaron Lobelia's future was hazy and unsure. But what it showed was determinable. Aaron saw that he would one day marry; he would find his true love at the altar and they would live happily together."

Cyrus was disappointed to hear this. "The king will find a wife," he replied deadpan. "That's not exactly news is it?"

"Ah, but the vision said nothing about Aaron becoming king... a matter that I found to be rather interesting."

"But you said it was wavering, right? One of the more unlikely visions?"

"Oh?" His voice rose an octave in curiosity, "was his dear sister's a tad more solid then, hm?"

Cyrus was remiss now to impart his fair share of information considering Victor's was not quite so juicy. "It was, actually. In fact, the archbishop declared it to be the most likely future he had ever witnessed."

Victor raised one eyebrow, not impressed, "that is all well and good, but only if what is bound to pass is actually that interesting."

"The princess will become archbishop."

"PAH!" Victor lurched forward with a dry laugh at the other man's words. "You... you're serious! My word, man, that must have sent the current archbishop into a tizzy. I would have loved to have seen it."

"Quite," Cyrus grumbled, "but the point that I believe is of interest to you is where the future archbishop Lolita was standing."

"Oh?"

"Hm. In her vision, the princess-priest was in a cathedral."

"Hardly surprising."

"Let me finish!" Cyrus was now remiss to have entered the carriage at all. "In the back of this cathedral was a large stained glass window depicting the Aaron as a young king."

Victor was not laughing now. "You're sure?"

"I am," he replied just as gravely.

"Well... that is certainly something to ponder. I must say, I feel this chat has benefited me quite well."

With the conversation being brought to a close and the tersity of the air rising sharply, Magellan stood up and let himself out. Victor just sat there staring at him with an eye of observation as he took the first step down from the carriage. As he left, however, Cyrus did not give the fight up just yet. When he spied Mary walking over the vehicle ready to rejoin her master he also spied the opportunity in having the last word and turned finally back to Redding.

"Yes, I'll be leaving you to sit on that little egg for a while. I hope you take it into consideration as you hand those little rocks out in the north of Okhram."

Victor rose with thunder to his feet as his face fell into the kind of angry frown only seen on carnival masks. He started to follow or perhaps open his mouth in refute, demanding to know how Cyrus had guessed at his plans, but before he could do anything the other witcher had swapped places with Mary. Mary, who wanted very much to know why they were planting the seeds of ancercy in their own kingdom.

As she came in, arms crossed and a determination on her face, he realised that what Cyrus knew was irrelevant. The man was more a cad than he would ever be and so he recognised the honour amongst thieves. Yes, he had just wanted to ruffle feathers as he left, and Victor had to commend him for doing it so well.

So he sat back down calmly and gestured at the bench opposite him for Mary to sit. She did so while maintaining her expression.

Before responding in any way, Victor leaned out the window slightly, giving commands to the driver that the magister could not hear before tapping against the roof to indicate an immediate departure. As they started to move, a whirl of dark colours danced from the edges of the curtains and the roots of the auger's hair began to slowly move outwards in a shade of dusty pink.

"Right then," he sighed. "We are going to pick up one Adam Sunvale. He will be our plant – our dealer. We will place him in a few cities of my choosing where he will deal out the stones and cause an epidemic of ancercy."

"Well I had guessed that much," Mary replied. Victor hadn't minded that; it was that she seemed so unperturbed by such an action that made him uncomfortable. It even made him think that she could have some sort of other plan up her sleeves. But, once more, he shook it off as a hypochondriac's musings and reminded himself that she would never be capable of undermining him, especially not at this stage of the operation.

"What I want to know, is why we're doing it in Okhram, I mean…" Mary Culver spoke adamantly, "I knew you were going to attack someone. I just assumed that it would be some sort of new initiative against the Finnick union – the beginning of an effort to reclaim the other kingdoms on the island."

"Interesting," Victor commented. He was curious now, "and why do you think our queen would want to do that?"

Mary continued, her expression betraying nothing to her lord. "For the usual reasons. For glory. To hand a weapon of destruction to the emperor. To reclaim the Old King's rightful territories."

"How… broad."

"That's not it then?"

"No, that's not it. I have to say, Miss Culver, I'm disappointed in your narrow mindedness."

"Then what is it?"

He smiled at her, ever so grimly, as was his greatest talent. "I can't tell you the full extent, but you will be helping with the next operation. So I can tell you that we plan to plant these drugs in the cities on the edge of the border with Northold. Our side, of course, until it becomes empire-wide news that those territories are infected with cases rising at a speed never seen before."

Mary furrowed her brows at that.

"You're still not seeing the whole picture," he sighed. He was disinterested now and had turned to gaze at the myriad colours out the window. "That's fine... all will be revealed soon, Miss Mary Culver."

Lobelia

Thomas stood outside the door to the dining room knowing that everyone was waiting for him inside. His parents had gone on to bed for the early trip tomorrow so it would just be the queen, Lolita, and the mayor. When the door opened and he stepped inside, everyone would be looking at him, their eyes following him to his seat as he made stumbling apologies for taking so long to change into evening wear. They would say nothing but their gaze would tell of having been held up by his delay. They would not talk about it all evening, but as he ate, it would weigh on his heart that they had had to wait for him and it would make every bite of food taste longer. He would look up from his plate to see everyone eating only to know that when he turned back to his own meal people would make faces and whisper about him. It would draw the oxygen from his head and he would turn dizzy as his throat closed up and-

"Hey, Tommy!"

When he finally managed to push the door open, he was greeted by a cheerful Lolita. Her mother was making a trite smile as she gestured for him to sit by them and the mayor was nowhere to be seen. As he walked over, it appeared that the only whisperings Katherine Lobelia took part in was chidings of her daughter for her informality.

When he took his place, his best friend was all too happy to talk with him about the room she had been given at Lanship this time as well as the views she had seen walking her way through the corridors. While the food was brought and they took from the deep serving dishes held out, he came to realise that no one actually cared about the time he arrived... nobody was looking at him.

So while he had been quiet throughout the conversations he had eventually learned how to exhale again; he slowly returned into himself and found, by the end, that he had chatted his way through dinner without any panic attacks or concessions to anxious thoughts. When they reached the desert course, a glamorously dressed parfait with the most succulent strawberry garnishes, the boy had remembered to pick up their last conversation from back at the cathedral.

"Oh, dear, you were going to tell me," he took a quick bite of the pudding on his fork and swallowed delightfully, "tell me about the mayor and Whiteley and all that."

Lolita's eyes went wide, and she didn't respond. She lowered her fork and poked her eyes at her mother who was gently savouring the taste of the Azalea chef's fantastic baking. After a few seconds of silence, Katherine finally noticed what was happening and spoke up.

"Oh, honey, I don't care what you talk about. He's your cousin."

Lolita turned red in embarrassment and Thomas grinned. He clinked his fork back on his plate and rested his chin on both his hands to listen eagerly to what the princess had to say. Meanwhile her mother tucked back in to the parfait truly not listening to what either of the teenagers conversed on.

"In that case," she began, "I told you about his son and the, ahem, problems he is having. Mother simply wanted to invite the man because, well, we all witnessed his deteriorating state as his son fell further away from him. He just needed a break is all, some time to process what's happening."

"I suppose that's why he isn't enjoying such a banquet..." Thomas smiled very sadly as he thought about the poor man losing his whole world. His expression fell even more morose as he thought of his son watching his body twist into something inhuman. It made him feel an odd kinship – an estrangement from his parents that he can't control, a world trying to mould him into something he's not. He knows he can never compare to losing his life in such a tragic way but to live like that at all. Well, it makes him feel terribly morose indeed.

Then he lifted his head again, "oh, you should thank him for coming to your baptism! Give him a good reason to smile."

Lolita opened her mouth to respond but her mother got their first, stabbing her fork in her daughter's direction, "I told you."

Lolita turned red once more and grumbled as she rose to her feet. "If you'll excuse me," she mumbled her words and her mother, too indulged in the sweet treat before her, simply nodded without comment on her daughter's mannerisms. Thomas, afraid to be alone with the Queen of Belgrave, also took the opportunity to excuse himself and walk Lolita out.

As soon as the attendants shut the door behind them they moved in to embrace one another very tightly. They were both tired now from the day's activities and a bit high on the fatigue. They looked into each other's weary expressions and bid a chorus of very good nights.

"I am proud of you, Lolly. Here's to a future where the archbishop of Stourford is not just any woman, but my best friend!"

She laughed at that and mimed cheering with him.

"And I am proud of you. You put on such a brave face every day just to keep yourself safe. And there hasn't been a word on your sixteenth all day..." she frowned as she finished talking.

"Oh, come come. I already said today is about-"

"No! It is just as much about you!"

Thomas leant forward and kissed the shorter girl on the forehead. "If ever we needed proof of your grace," he chuckled. He reached down to take her by the shoulders and spin her around to face the corridor opposite him. "Now go. Give it to a man who really needs it. You have a life ahead of you of doing that, after all."

Lolita nodded. "You know... for such a colourful man, you seem more than content to live your life on the sidelines." She didn't turn around to look at him, she just commented as he remained behind her removing his hands from her side.

"Hm," he mused. "I suppose that's right. I just want to be."

"Then be." She commanded. She walked off, not looking back at her friend as she gave out her first piece of advice in what would hopefully be a long career of speaking the voice of God.

* * *

Theodore Rushings had not managed to find his sleep. It was a talent that had evaded him more and more over the recent days and was leaving him to stare at the ceiling with wide, circular eyes.

And his focus was too sharp. If he drifted, William would come to mind. If he stopped staring, stopped keeping his mind active then it might wander even further into unpleasant territory.

No, he was fine. He was awake! His son was fine and everything was... fine.

It was this heightened state of attention - and the one particular spot on the ceiling that he was channelling as much focus into as possible - that caused him to leap out of his skin the moment a soft but determined rap came at his bedroom door.

When fluttered across his bed sheets his rumpled, striped pyjamas rode across his body as he re-anchored himself to the world around him.

"Mister Mayor?" The princess' soft voice came through the door at the same moment his feet found the floor.

"Just a moment, your highness!" he replied, desperately pulling a warm, brown robe around his waist and fluttering at the floor for a pair of slippers. Upon finding them, he made a quick peek at a bedside mirror to ensure that his hair, which had greyed severely, was in a straightened up form.

Not wanting to keep her, he rushed to the entrance, ironed out his clothes with his hands and switched on his greatest smile as he welcomed her to his room. He noticed that she was unchaperoned, which made him feel a bit uncomfortable, but still closed the door none the less as she made light steps inside.

"Your suite is a very homely," she commented, making the briefest of neck turns to examine it.

"Yes. Yes! The Azaleas are very accommodating," he stammered for a moment, "what exactly is it that I can do for you, ma'am?"

"Right, it is late..." she commented. She faced him and gave him the kind of smile that showed more in the eyes than the mouth. "I just wanted to say thank you. For coming to my baptism. It made me happy to see another kind face watching over me."

The truth is, she forgot he was there until Thomas reminded her.

"Oh, no, ma'am. The honour was all mine!" He puffed his chest out as if witnessing the princess' baptism had been active duty. "It was a sight for the history books, if I may say so."

She nodded. She moved to say her goodnights then, truly ready to retire, before the mayor continued speaking again: "I only wish that rapscallion son of mine were there to see it! Might learn something from a real hard worker."

The thought of a twenty three year old man being called a rapscallion almost brought her to giggles if she hadn't contained herself. An act of self-control that was very hard in the face of imagining Aaron being called one by their mother.

"Well I'm sure he's minding himself now," she commented politely. Upon remembering where he might be, she blushed a bit from shame and tacked on, "wherever he is... right now." The end of her sentence was mumbled.

But Theodore hadn't noticed. "Oh, he's out drinking! Or finding some woman of the night, if you do pardon my language. That boy needs to learn the ropes of the mayoral trade before his galivanting gives me a heart attack!"

She hummed a vague note of interest as she pondered what one could possibly say to something like that. 'Sorry, your son is actually dead right now and it's about time you face reality instead of pretending he's a teenager again because you miss him!'

No, that won't do. But the idea of William's youth did strike some interest in Lolita. "Tell me," she bade, "what was his mother like?"

"Oh," the mayor changed completely at that question. He was brought back to reality then as he began to talk on a topic that he didn't have to falsify for sanity's sake. "Portia was a darling gem, I say. She would have given everything for our boy... she did, in fact. That's why she's not around today."

"I see. Childbirth is a rough course for all women. Portia sounds like a real inspiration."

The mayor blinked at the princess for a meaning, the understanding not glazing over his eyes until just a second too late. "Oh yes, childbirth, of course. Yes, dreadful business. It was actually all overseen by Magellan."

"Cyrus?" Her curiosity snapped to at the mention of the witcher's name, "but he's not a doctor is he?"

"A doctor? Oh no, no. He just, helped things along is all. Some charms and good luck, you know how it is," the princess opened her mouth but the mayor spoke first, "my goodness! I should not be keeping you so late. I'm positively talking your ear off."

He reached behind him for the door knob but Lolita only moved to stand closer to his personal space. He started sweating, and his eyes began to dart around to look anywhere but at the princess'.

"Now, Theodore," she began sternly, "tell me the truth. You aren't talking about Magellan's other business are you?"

"Wha- what other business?"

"The one with all the peculiar tanks."

"I- I-" he tried to formulate a lie or a cover to backtrack on what he had let out but he in fact ended up overcome by a beaming smile of all things. "I am!" He lifted his arms slightly in the air then before he made himself bring them back down. Joyous, he couldn't help but to give a single hearty clap that made Lolita hop back a step. "Oh, I am! It is wonderful to be able to tell someone about it, too!"

"Just to be certain," the princess continued slowly, "your wife visited Cyrus Magellan to give her own life to create William?"

"Yes!" He exclaimed. Then his expression fell, "oh, did you not know about the mother's sacrifice part?"

That question had slapped Lolita in the face. She hadn't even realised that that was what had happened! Perhaps even to every woman who visited Cyrus. She hadn't realised it because she was too focused on the fact that she had been in the same room as William Rushings before. That he was born in a vat like Adam Sunvale and those serving girls but had caused no adverse reaction in her. The man's aura felt as normal as any other regular born humans whereas the people born by Magellan's hand were meant to cause such uncomfortable feelings in her...

"Thank you, Mr Rushings, but I must dash!"

She was out of the door before she could even hear him say goodnight as she ran through Lanship House searching for Cyrus to demand an explanation.

Culver

"I don't know no Harlot Abernathy, thanks."

Adam Sunvale shoved his hands into his pocket and made his best attempt to walk down some alleyway, far from the grasp of Mary. She shook her head but did not pursue knowing what was waiting for the man at the other end of that side-street. Instead, she just crossed her arms and walked a slow pace behind him watching as he very nearly reached the other side.

Just as he did, her friend the auger stepped out. He looked grim. Not menacing or intimidating as he usually tried to purport but just grim. He was staring dead through the man as he lifted up one bent arm to reveal a red stone sat comfortably in his palm. Adam was not all too perturbed by this until the sunlight seemed to just reflect off the vermillion rock and suddenly, in a moment of blindness by the reflected ray, there was a tall creature stood behind Victor.

"The fuck?" Adam whispered stopping in his tracks and back peddling.

The beast that came from the stone this time was no red devil but instead a sort of succubus; a caricature of the female form. Its breasts popped out just too far and curves came just too narrow. Its skin was yellow with orange veins like pools of flowing magma and on its face, beneath four eyes, was the plumpest set of purple lips. Its hair, contrary to the rest of its washed out colour scheme, was blue-black flickering like the night sky with every heavy step it took forward.

This had been Mary's idea. Victor was ready to summon another devilish being to frighten the man into compliance but Mary had suggested something like this instead – a sample of the product he would be selling. Besides, she had added, Adam seemed like the type of man to try and fling himself at a mannish opponent like a fool who thinks he could fight a bear. This would intimidate him far more.

And she was right: after he caught his breath back, the man whipped around to try and run out the other end. And while she did not summon a second daemon, it was now Mary's turn to hold out an alchemists stone in her palm in the same grim way Victor was. The threat was enough to cow the man.

"Fine, fine! I had known her, alright!" Adam begged. Mary tilted her head looking at him. He was sweating nervously and his whole body was moving in fear. On the whole he presented masculinity but he suddenly had a boyish charm when he was ruffled that made the magister curious about herself. She smiled at that thought, wondering why she was having ideas like this now of all times. Perhaps a degree of disdain for Ahmar had liberated her more than she first thought...

"Mr Sunvale," barked Redding. "Please, do shut up!" He tucked the alchemist's stone into his cape and walked up to the man. Both he and Mary stood side by side as he backed into a wall. All he could do was focus on the succubus behind them, its arms crossed as it glowered. The sight confused him. He was scared of it, terrified. But just as much as its strong crossed arms scared him into place he could not help but stare at how they also pushed its breasts to bounce up a tad. He swallowed nervously unable to stop staring, his mind melting in terrified arousal.

"Please pay attention," Mary demanded.

"Sorry, what?" He looked between both of the humans not sure who had been talking.

Victor groaned. "We need to hire you for a job. Can you understand that, street rat?"

Adam nodded, "yeah... yeah."

"It's," Mary started only for Adam to suddenly find more words.

"How much does it pay?"

Redding scoffed, "you would do this for pennies and you know it."

"It's commission," Mary explained.

Adam nodded again. Victor was starting to think that perhaps they could find an easier dealer to patron but the thought of trawling through the kingdom looking for one made him shiver in his skin.

"And what exactly is the job?" His vision landed on Mary as he decided that she was the one he would rather be talking to. And looking at.

She held the red stone in her hand outwards towards him now, causing him to somehow recess further into the brick wall at his back. "Dealing these. You can do that, can't you?"

He frowned. "I can but, what is it?"

"An alchemist's stone," she explained. Victor reached into his cape and pulled out a brown sack as she explained. He loosened the cord to show the man what was inside; a pile more of the vermillion substance. "These ones, all of these ones, do the same thing. They each have the ability for the user to summon seven daemons for the purpose of sleeping with someone, whether it be the summoner or someone else."

"So... that?" He raised a timid finger to point at the succubus behind them. Victor turned his head to look at it and laughed.

"You have Miss Culver to thank for you not meeting the same beastie as Rushings."

"Huh?"

"Nothing," Mary stepped in again to steer the conversation back to topic. "So, do you think you could deal this?"

"Course I can. I can deal anything. Plenty of people want sex and plenty of people want sex with something like... *that*."

"Good." She took a turn to look at the daemon now, doing so uncomfortably. Deciding that it wasn't necessary anymore she commanded it to run off somewhere and sleep with a beggar so it could go back to hell. Adam was disappointed to watch it run off, but he did definitely still watch it until it was completely out of view.

"The question," Victor continued, snapping his fingers to pull Adam's attention back, "is will you?"

"Hm?" Sunvale turned to look at Redding and Culver, his brain working a moment to return to the conversation. Despite her recently found sense of self, even Mary was beginning to lose patience with the man. She gnawed on her bottom lip, decidedly not lashing out at him despite desperately wanting to.

"Will you plant the stones for us?" The auger repeated with more instance.

"Oh right. Well now, hold on a minute," the man put his hands up defensively for a second, "now I'm no fool." Mary coughed to cover a laugh. "Therefore... I know that if I go ahead with this there might be some sort of disease break out. Like big time break out."

"Yes, ancercy. Yes, the consequences of our own actions. It won't be on your head will it? Now are you with us?" Victor spoke with a degree of urgency closer to the edge, his face getting tenser.

"Well, now I might agree with you there about other substances," he replied hesitantly, "this would actually, you know. Kill people.

Victor bared his teeth, ready to threaten or shout at the man. No one would find out which, though, as he was pushed a step back by Mary leaning forward instead. She took Sunvale by the collar and slammed him backwards against the wall. He reached up and grabbed at her arms but was stopped from throwing her away by her harsh words directly in his face.

"Heavens above, man! What you do does kill people! You are a drug dealer. You sell substances to people, hook them on them, and clear your conciseness of it by blaming it on their own free will. But you still enabled them, you still committed the crime, you still literally got people addicted to giving you money. People who have become shells of themselves with no life or cash or family just because you want them to fork over the next coin they get for a gram of whatever you're peddling. Of all the creatures, of all the people, I have seen these past few days not one has been quite as evil as you! So don't you dare pretend this is a moral issue because you are fooling none of us!"

Adam loosened his grip on her wrists and she let go of his collar. She took a step back to be beside the opposite wall to him where she could catch her breath back after her rant and glare indomitably. He straightened his shirt and cleared his throat but found that he had nothing to say in response.

Victor stepped in then and held the bag out to him. Adam looked down at it and snatched it from the auger who nodded and took the younger man with an arm around his shoulder, leading him back to the carriage as he explained the intricacies of what he wanted him to do.

* * *

"I have to say, I did not expect that from you," Victor said as he returned to Mary's side. They were both in the middle of a street now emptied by the impending hunter's hour. The carriage, with its two sickly monochrome horses, was parked right in the middle of it anchored by a runelight lamppost.

"Thank you, m'lord," she mumbled recognising the compliment.

"I agree, for the record." Victor spoke with casual acidity, "drug dealers are scum and I have had the pleasure of hunting down many for her majesty."

"Yeah," Mary listlessly responded. It wasn't until they had begun to feel the sudden sharp chill of the oncoming night time that she focussed herself on a discussion. "Am I now allowed to know why we're planting ancercy? In Okhram?" She added ruefully.

"No." His reply was simple. Not a denial or a satisfactory slam of the door. Just a fact. No. "The queen will tell you that, if she wishes."

She turned her head to look at him with narrowed eyes, "Charlotte?"

"*The queen*, yes." He asserted. Although, his regular roughness was not in it. He seemed tired; cowed by the night time and the pink mane of hair that indicated his exertion. He sighed. "You're a clever girl, though. The stones on the border, empire wide news of infection. Surely you've pieced it together? You do know the history of our nation's borders, do you not?"

"I'm more of a scripture girl," she replied, nervousness on the edge of her words. Even though she felt herself redeemed in assisting Harley with the cure, she still knew that things had to get worse before they got better. That people would have to be infected before they could be cured. It made her both too hateful to talk about the auger's plan and equally as hungry to know.

"Then I suppose you should leave it to time," he replied. "You will find out soon enough, Miss Culver. Soon enough, indeed."

"In that case, could I ask you something else?" He grunted his assent and she continued, "I have been feeling more grounded recently. More myself." She thought of the fountain, of her dance with the stars. Of how boring her life as a good woman had felt and how abhorrent her tenure as a bad person made her feel. She thought of how loud her head felt when she had to face the world, to face people, and thought immediately that she never wanted to be so overwhelmed again.

"That is not a question, Miss Culver."

"I wanted to know what you think about being human." She clutched her arm nervously, "about how we do wrong because we're human; we have animal nature, inherent sin and primal urges. And how we also do right because we're human; we have intelligence, morals and collective knowledge. What exactly is in the middle? What's the balance? Because I've been feeling lately like we just tilt from one to the other until the end."

He grunted again to acknowledge that he heard her as he thought up something to say. "I believe that is the folly of man. We're as evil, as natural, as any other animal on the planet. We are just cursed with knowing that we're evil. Does that mean we have to stop being evil? Or just that we can keep on while knowing it. Embracing it."

"I don't like the black and white," she replied, "I rather think we should be something more grey."

"Well we're not," he snorted. "A grey world is a philosopher's world but it is not ours. We, the working men, do the right thing or the wrong thing. We can't afford to be grey. That's why we have kings and queens and an emperor. People who write the rules and then enforce them – people who are grey for us. So that humanity keeps making food, keeps surviving onward. Being a man isn't about dreams. It's about doing what you must to keep cultivating humankind. Just like any other animal species but with a few extra steps. We keep on marching through time. You do the right thing, you keep on. You do the wrong thing and you are ousted. What, my dear, is grey about that?"

She looked down at her feet guiltily. She worried that she might not be able to escape either world after all. That she had a choice after all this to be the good, working magister or be the bad agent of the crown. But there was no wrong in the former and no right in the latter. Only the teeter between them. Only the overwhelming feeling of facing either world. Ungrateful students; infected victims; cruel teachers; rueful augers.

She looked back up to see Victor walking over the carriage. He pulled the door open and stepped inside. He held a hand out to her in the flickering runelight and stared wondrously. "So are you going to see it through or are you going to go home? Because let me tell you what I think. It doesn't matter whether you choose right or wrong. It matters that when you choose it, you mean it with every burning fibre in your heart."

Ever since working with him, she had not seen him in such a way as she did after that. The light pushed against the faint folds in his skin and he appeared to her as a man whose age did not betray bitterness, but wisdom. Each line showed a path he had fallen down before he realised the truth of the folly. And she was grateful that he had shared that truth with her.

She stepped forward, striding across the cobbles to take his hand in hers as she alighted the carriage once more and chose the path she wanted to go down.

There is salvation in bringing pain to others... in keeping it at arm's length from yourself. The good world only overstimulates *her* every day in choking consequences. The bad world... the self-serving world... well, her goal is to serve herself, is it not? As long as she did not face her victims like she had Harley Abernathy. As long as she never saw her victims as anything worth attention. As long as she kept her head above the water then maybe, for once in her life... she could be the winner.

After all, she knew that she was never to be anything more than human.

After all, she knew that there was no one worse than Mary Culver.

Phoenix Clarke

Abernathy

The bell to Ripley's – that is the Ripley's in Summerset – rang bravely into the dimly lit shop. John rarely bothered to lock the doors until last thing at night before he went back upstairs to his flat. It was very rare for someone to be on the street so late never mind a criminal looking to loot some unguarded alchemist's. Not even the most vile of vagabonds dared to prowl the same streets as the shadow creatures that come victim to the night hunters. Which all in all is why the sound of the bell had made his eyes dart to the ornate time piece on the counter top before anything else. He checked it twice and three times to reassure himself that it was too early for some sort of monster to have wandered into his place of work.

But when he had lurked around the vast pile of engines on the island so that he could shoo away whatever straggler had come to his door he found that he was no longer so sure of his original hypothesis.

The woman before him, who had called herself Harley Abernathy, was now glimmering in his candlelight. All the way up her neck, just stopping at her chin, was a set of prismatic scales. He could see that they were coming from the cuffs of her sleeves too, defiantly treading the skin on her palms. He knew right away what her ailment was and, from not seeing it just earlier, he knew that it was dire.

So he didn't even welcome her in or console her. He simply looked back into her wide eyes and said, "I can't help you with that, I'm afraid."

"You can," she implored.

It was not the first case of its kind he had seen. John slowly backed away to the counter in the corner where he knew a silver athame was hiding in the desk's shelf. The double edged dagger was a family heirloom passed down from the days of his ancestors. Back when witchery was illegal and the Ripleys were forced into the alchemical trade so they could make an honest living. That athame was the last sign of his pagan blood and so whenever he held it his veins ran alight with fire and he knew could defend himself just fine. He had had to many times before, after all. He just had to reach it...

"Please," she whispered, her voice soft but urgent. "I still have all my faculties, there is no need to edge away." He believed her, knowing what madness looked like. He stopped for just a second only to see that under her arm she was holding a bottle with blood staining the glass and stopper. It did not reassure him of her sanity and so he took another step away.

"Please!" She begged again. "Look, I just want to try something out. Won't you give me the chance to try!"

He couldn't understand what she might mean but still took the effort to nod. "I will. If you allow me to defend myself."

Harley nodded in turn but she did not speak. She watched him walk backwards and retrieve the black-handled knife from under his desk and hold it sturdily. With the sight of a man defending himself before her she hand only just come to realise how she might be perceived. She had not thought herself a monster but in remembering that first meeting with Will she knew what it was like to see a person with ancercy.

"I'm sorry."

"It's okay... I think." The clerk replied. "How about you tell me what I can do you for this time? Did your past remedy work?"

She nodded, "yes, it did what I needed it to."

"Good."

"What I need now is..." But she did not know how to finish that. Because she did not know exactly what it is Mary had meant in her explanation. Instead she just relayed the woman's words ending on: '*Perhaps look for something that might repel a daemon. A physical, tangible thing that has gone untried.*'

John Ripley nodded slowly at the wisdom in this before vehemently shaking his head at it.

"Everything has gone tried," he explained, "while the theory is there, there is just no practicality."

Harley looked over to the rack of material bottles at her right. As she tilted her head she felt the skin on her neck scratch the point of the highest scales and squirmed uncomfortably in her own body. "Really?" she asked, "every single thing there has been tried?"

"Well, the obvious ones haven't. I mean rubbing giant hogweed on the symptom is only bound to make things worse in my professional opinion."

She sighed, "so some treatments have not been tested."

"Because it would be lunacy. But if you are so desperate to spend your last minutes self-harming then might I recommend you do it with a different alchemist's material stock, eh?"

"Come on!" She whined, "please have a degree of mercy. You must have some sort of untested daemon repellent."

"Oh yes," the man replied, his arms falling helplessly to his side, "let me cherry pick one of those untested daemon repellents I have lying about. Oh hold on! Some of us have jobs to be doing in the day."

"This is literally your job!" she shouted back through gritted teeth.

"And how do you propose I do my job, hm? Would you like me to apply a salve of brimstone to your affliction?"

"NO!" She grunted again. But then the word brimstone stuck in her mind, and she could not figure why. But it did, it lingered. The image of the triangle with the cross below it hovered in her mind with a feeling as strong as when she hugged that silver cross so tightly. It felt right in her head.

"Then what?"

"Shut up," she whispered.

"Pardon?"

"Shut up, shut up, SHUT UP!" She said in a rather excitable manner as she flapped her hands about. "Right. No. Yes! Look. What is the daemon's bane?"

"God?" He guessed. "Salt, silver, good scents and liturgy?"

"No. I mean yes, but that's not all of them. These methods have been tried to cure ancercy before but what we need is the thing that a daemon cannot stand most of all."

"And that is...?"

"Fire and brimstone!"

His grip tightened on the athame as he lifted it slightly higher. She was gone completely now; he was sure of that. "My dear... that is where daemons live. That is hell."

"Oh for- yes I know! But daemons do not come from hell do they. Daemons come from?"

"Heaven," he finished. "Hell is their punishment, the worst place to be devised by the Lord himself."

"So let us try that!" she enthused. "Come, rub fire and brimstone on my symptoms quick!" She was too excitable to understand his reluctance at literally burning her with the fury of hell. Their theory was only a theory after all. As far as they knew, the remedy might even encourage the affects instead of burn them away.

But another thing he knew, after a life time of the mystical sciences, is that when you had a ridiculous theory that sounded exactly right, like it just might make sense, then you ran with it. Like the reflection of the sun.

So he moved on, slapping some black gloves over his hand as he gathered a largish bowl to the island near his materials. He pulled three bottles down; the one that clearly contained the yellow brimstone; the one that had a thick substance John explained to be the oil of a coconut and a final bottle that had a cyan powder within. The symbol on that one was one that grabbed the attention of Harley for some reason other than the captivating colour of the bottle's contents. It was a circle with a cross in the middle, simple and symmetrical.

"What's that one?" she asked pointing at it.

John cleared his throat as he got to work mixing different measures of the brimstone and oil alongside water and other agents that changed the consistency of the product. The blue powder, which seemed to be shimmering in the light, seemed to be left out of it for now.

"I am mixing the brimstone with oil and thickening agents to create a salve," he explained. When he was satisfied with his concoction, he turned around with the bowl in one gloved hand. He held out the other, miming for her to hand her own arm over.

She did, pulling up her sleeve to expose the infected area as he took her in his grasp.

She winced when the medicine made contact, for it was both cool and stinging. She thought it was uncomfortable and already wished that the treatment was over.

"*This one*," he began to answer her question by picking up the jar of blue powder, "is etherium."

She looked at him confused. "Sorry?"

"Etherium," he repeated.

"Oh. Like, the realm?" she used her free hand to make a gesture indicating a large open space. John snickered at that.

"Yes, like our realm. Etherium is focused ether itself. This powder is very rare, very powerful and very, very delicate. It is useful for writing runes as it can charge itself once the image is complete." When he finished talking, he used his teeth to pull the glove off his right hand while the other still firmly gripped a squirming Harley. He took his middle finger, gently dabbing it on his tongue to moisten the tip. Then he lowered it gently, gently into the jar marked by the crossed circle. He only tickled the top of the powder to collect a dusting of it on his finger which he took to the smooth surface of the salve currently on Harley's wrist. Slowly tracing a symbol, he began to draw.

"What's that?"

"The rune for fire," he explained. He drew a straight line down and then, about two thirds down it, a diagonal one protruding down from it.

"Isn't it meant to be a triangle?" She asked, remembering some poster she had seen on his wall about the matter.

"That is for records and equations. The alchemist's symbol. This is a rune – an invocation. It means lamp, really, but it serves the purpose of combusting the brimstone all the same."

As he spoke, the blue symbol faded into the cream coloured medicine on her wrist as it began to ignite the compound.

"Are you ready?" he asked, knowing it was too late to stop now.

She bit her lip and nodded.

They both stared at it expectingly, waiting for something to happen. It was a slow reaction, with Harley only feeling a slight warmth amongst the stinging then instead of a coolness. Quick enough, the colour of the mixture fell from cream - it began to take an orange tint to it that seemed to ripple across the salve with flecks of yellow like sparks.

"Oh, ow, yeah that's doing something," Harley hissed as it only got hotter and hotter.

"The lamp rune should be igniting the compound and causing a literal fire and brimstone solution to your ancercy problem."

She nodded at him knowing that if she opened her mouth and allowed words to escape, all that would come out are violent curses.

But even then she could not stop herself. Suddenly it felt like she were holding her arm inside a furnace. A very hot furnace that had been raging long and with plenty of fuel. A furnace with heavy flames that hungrily curled towards her skin and licked at the nerves to press pain down on the area that the salve covered.

"FUCK! Fuck, AGH!" she screamed. The hand above the treated wrist was tensed into a claw while her other one cradled the bottom of her arm. She stared down at it, curling around the burning agony, as tears unwillingly streamed from her eyes.

Nervous and unsure on what to do now, John had made sure to keep a good distance, his knife still prepped in case the whole matter went terribly wrong.

Soon enough she lost the ability to form words as spit dribbled from the corners of her mouth. She started to crouch down then, as if she could curl into herself and end the suffering that way. She made garbled noises, snot now trailing with her tears as she wrenched her voice wicked begging the pain on her wrist to stop.

This was hell, she decided then. If this does not punish a daemon then nothing will.

"Take- hah... TAKE IT... hah," she tried to form words as he neck snapped upwards to talk to John. "TAKE IT OFF!" she begged, her voice splitting his ears like scythes in the air. He stared at her dumbfounded for a moment before stumbling over his equipment to grab a grey cloth that had been left atop one of the miscellaneous surfaces. He quickly dunked it in a small bowl of water before kneeling down opposite Abernathy and trying his best to pry her tensed muscles out.

He was struggling greatly to fight her and she too was battling herself to be loose enough to let him hold her. Eventually, after another shriek, she let her arm go so that he could pull it out of her protective position and wipe away all traces of the salve. As he did, he heard her wailing dissipate into the background. Not just because it was slowly being replaced by moans of satisfaction to see the burning washed off, but because he was utterly transfixed by the sight in front of him. As he dabbed and pulled and cleaned off the medicine, he found that underneath was bare skin. Amidst the scales was a patch of ordinary, human skin. And it wasn't even burnt, in fact, it was soft and pale. It was new.

"Oh my, oh my goodness!" She uttered, finally coming down from the high of relief as the last traces of the medicine was removed. She rubbed the cured patch and poked at it and held it right up to her eyes so she could be sure that she was seeing what she was. "It worked, IT WORKED AHAHA!" She lifted up like a spring, bouncing from her crouch and into the air where she enthusiastically hugged John before continuing to prod at her newly healed wrist.

When she stopped her celebrations to catch her breath, she looked at the shop owner and saw that he was busy mixing a larger quantity of materials again. Her smile soon faded when she realised that not only was she going to have to do that again, but over her entire torso too.

Her first instinct was to run. She wanted to dash away and never ever come back, just let the ancercy consume her for all the pain was worth.

She sighed thinking it was a shame that that bottle with the small swirling vortex inside had reminded her exactly what it's worth to see this through.

She grabbed a band from off of the island nearby and tied her hair up into a lazy, high pony tail before beginning to undo the clasps on the back of her dress. She let it fall down to her waist where she could see that the scales had spread from both her wrists up her arms and to the bottom of her chin as well as down to just above her naval. She undid her bra next, letting it fall to the floor to bare her chest, which had become compressed with the scale-takeover, as she presented herself to the Ripley brother before her.

He didn't feel any immodesty at the sight, just pity. She looked beastly.

"Are you ready?" He asked, deadly serious.

"I am. I have to do this," she replied. As he approached and began the process of slathering her, she added a final addendum to her thoughts: *for you.*

Lobelia

The door to her room swung open with verve as she rushed to the desk in front of her curtained window. It was a small thing provided in case one needed to write letters. It was made of a dark, rich wood – very sturdy – and had a candle in a brass holder in one corner. Lolita was too impatient to light it and simply pulled the red threads in front of the window open instead, satisfied that moonlight was all she needed to see by. Taking the provided quill, she dipped it quickly into a pot of ink before scurrying around the drawers for a piece of parchment to draw on. The ink had dribbled off the nib and stained some of the furniture before she finally found a thick, cream sheet that she could illustrate on.

She popped it atop the desk and shrugged off the way she had ruined the wood – she was princess after all, the viscount could live with it.

On the paper she scratched out a circle and then from left to right and back again, she drew a horizontal diamond shape. She drew another inside for the iris of the eye-symbol and then placed the quill back in its holder as she stared down at her drawing. It was crude and blotted but looked close enough to the brass logo that had been in the alleyway.

She leant down on the desk, a hand by either side of the papyrus, as she looked intently into the eye. She stared at it, focussing it entirely in her vision as she attempted to return to the bottle of Cyrus Magellan.

When nothing happened, she made herself blink rapidly and looked around herself, expecting to be somewhere different entirely. All she saw still was the quiet suite at Lanship House.

A moment of anger overcame her as she grunted with futility at the image. She would not give up though and began her second idea by searching the desk drawers once again. She pulled out a matchbox and struck a flame to light that candle after all. She waved the burning matchstick out and let the smoke linger in the air as she grasped the side of her paper. She crouched slightly and she held the eye in front of the flame so that it made the iris dance with a faint orange colour behind it. She stared then as if she were looking through the brass sign at a runelight behind it. Still nothing happened.

"Come on," she whined flapping the paper back and forth as tears of frustration budded in the corner of her eyes. "Come on!" She was urgent but her words were still whispered to respect those sleeping.

"Now where did you learn about a symbol like that, your highness?"

Lolita turned around, the paper falling slowly from her hands, as she looked to the speaker at her door. She saw the

Viscount Azalea, still in his white suit, bowing at the neck to her. His hair was as platinum as his son's and his skin surprisingly unwrinkled for a man in his fifties. If she had not heard the stories Thomas had told of how terrible a father this man was, she might even think he looked respectable.

"Viscount," she murmured, "I'm sorry if I have woken you."

"You haven't. My journey to the capital will be a long one and I would rather be unconscious in the carriage than in my lovely bed."

"I see." She knelt down to retrieve her drawing and looked at it as she continued to speak, "Cyrus employed it as the entrance to his bottle. Oh," she realised, "um, a bottle is-"

The viscount held his hand up to quiet her. "I am more aware of these things than you might think. A lot of us lower houses need a hobby, after all."

"I see..." she repeated unsure on what to think of that.

She watched as he walked over to her and held his hand out to receive the paper. She looked down at it then back at him again before holding it out. He kept it held out for them both to see.

"This is more than just an arbitrary symbol chosen by your witcher, ma'am. It is the eye of Mara. It is the heraldry chosen by her family."

"Who is Mara's family?"

"The family of Mara," he continued with a cold smile, "are a group of devilists. They live by her creed rather like how those of us in the light live by the rule of the Old King."

"And who was she?"

"She was the avatar of sin. Communicator with the dark lord himself and antithesis of our own Anaximander. Some call her Mara. Others, the Pale Lady. Her symbol takes the form of the eye with which she watches us all now from her palace in hell. It is said, amongst their circles, that she will crawl back up from the fire one day into a new body and displace God's rule over Engelland. Perhaps even the entirety of Britton."

She took a step back from him, "and how would you know what is said in their circles," she accused.

He simply smiled again and waved his hand gently. "Nothing like that, ma'am. I just have a rather expansive library, is all. I seriously doubt the family of Mara even operates these days. It is accepted that they most likely disappeared around the same time as the Templar order. Both remnants of a more... divine age."

She nodded, accepting his explanation. "In that case," she moved closer, looking again at the eye. "Why would Cyrus choose to employ such a horrid image?"

"Well, to pose a guess," the viscount pondered aloud, "I'd say that... well, if I had to choose a logo to be an emergency entrance to my bottle, I would choose one that had not been used for hundreds of years. One that is rare and long dead. One that, even if people learned of it, would be considered too unholy to be worth the risk of drawing."

"That sounds a tad risky, especially for him." That explanation did not satisfy her. "Imagine if the family were still about. Surely then the logo would be plastered all over their crypts and cults."

Azalea laughed at that. "Oh, ma'am. You certainly do have an inquisitive mind. I admire that deeply; you Lobelias do make good company."

"Th-thanks," she stumbled, unsure if that was an insult or not.

"But I have to say I agree... although," he grabbed his chin and looked at the symbol more deeply. "Although, if that were true, then not only would Magellan still have a scarcely used symbol at his disposal, but he would also have a window into every lair of the occultists right at his fingertips."

"Is it not two ways?"

"Not if they don't know its linked to a bottle," he explained.

That roused something in her. She had all the intention to go and find the witcher so that she could politely demand he explains the matter in full, especially as to why William didn't make her feel the same as the other vat-borns did.

But now she hungered for more than that. She can guess what his ties are and she can guess now where he might have acquired his spell... she just needed the missing piece. And she was going to get it.

"Mr Azalea," she asked, standing up straight and performing the role of princess once more. "It appears that I require your assistance."

He smiled again, bowing his head in understanding of what she meant. "Here," he said, holding the paper up, this time to the backdrop of the moonlit window. "Try this instead. A flame on its own has very little magical potency but the moon swims through the raw ether of our cosmos."

She moved around his outstretched hand to line the silver sphere in the sky up behind the image. She slowly saw it fill the iris of the eye and then fill the entire circle with a bright silver light that glimmered for just a second long enough to force her to blink. She stumbled backwards and rubbed her eyes of the spark ready to talk to the viscount again about trying another method, but she found, when she opened her eyes, that he was not there.

She had made it back into the dimly lit, dungeon-like room of Magellan's bottle.

Something about it felt darker this time though.

From around the corner, where she knew the vats stood in two rows of three, came a heavy breathing from a woman's startled throat, too startled sounding to form words.

She saw, splashed on the wall, a shadow of two melded figures but could not discern from it who they were nor what position they were in.

As she stalked closer to the edge of her side of the wall, she could hear the female voice grunting and groaning as whoever it belonged to clearly struggled. It was a young voice too, of an age close to her own.

She assessed – with as much optimism as she could muster – that the shadows showed that the two people were looking away from her. She chose to risk peaking her head around the bend and was thankful to see them turned.

She was not surprised to see that the man stood up above the woman was Cyrus Magellan. She could not see his face but his hands were tense, the muscles and veins both rippling as they gripped the girl by her long brown hair.

"Stop it, stop!" The girl begged. Lolita recognised the voice and promptly stepped from the shadows to call the name of who it belonged to, hoping to save them from whatever Cyrus was doing.

"Alex!" She shouted, stepping into the light and drawing the faces of the two of them to stare in shock. Alex's once soft face was stained by tears as she gripped tightly to the floor below her trying to push herself away from the tank Magellan was dragging her to. She looked at Lolita with a plea in her wide, wet eyes that did all the begging she needed.

Magellan on the other hand simply remained where he was, moving only his neck to face the princess. He still gripped his victim furiously by the hair as he spat viciously through his gritted teeth at Lolita.

"You *really* shouldn't be here, little girl."

Abernathy

Harley woke up on the floor of Ripley's. Sweat had formed a gruesome layer over her skin as she felt her muscles aching with movement. She had been unconscious for thirty minutes, she was told, but it felt to her like a blink.

And in those thirty minutes everything had changed. The pain of igniting the serum over her body may have knocked her out but it was worth it to feel her own human skin again in its place. While she was out, John had taken to rubbing the mixture off of her and then quickly covering her exposed torso with a brown blanket. He then waited patiently for her to return to the world again.

As she sat up, cursing her body's pain, she let the blanket fall completely into her lap. She didn't pay any mind to the shop keep as he tilted his blushing face away from her again. Instead she trailed her fingers over every part of exposed skin to check for scales. She found that there were none. As she traced her arms and then her shoulders she relished in the feeling of her own soft – albeit sticky – skin. She pawed at her chin and groped around her chest feeling every crevice as she well and truly confirmed the best.

She held her arms out and went from investigation of her form to admiration as she declared, "I am cured!"

John turned to look at her to explain the situation only to wince at the smell. Musk mixed with brimstone. All that thrashing was as if she had been working all day. He pulled away to grab a bucket of water and a fresh towel so that she could clean herself up properly now.

After agreeing with him, and washing herself down with the provided tools, he started to tell her the truth of the 'cure.'

"It's like your friend said. This is just an attack on the symptoms really. Your soul is still damned, I'm afraid."

"Right," Harley pushed the towel thoroughly against her arms, not for a deep clean but just to be one hundred percent sure her skin was her own. She was satisfied to feel the grating sensation of the rough cloth. "She is not my friend. And also I am alright with that. I mean," she chuckled, "I was going to hell anyway for the whole prostitution thing, never mind the involuntary daemon sex."

After finishing up and taking a last appreciative look down at her reformed self, she finally redid her dress up. Mr Ripley could stop being so flustered now and look her in the eye.

"In that case, all that's left to say is... thank you, Miss Abernathy."

"Aha, what for?" She replied nervously. It wouldn't be the first time someone has forced themselves on her while she was asleep and then had the nerve to thank her for it when she awoke.

She measured him as he replied, deciding whether it would be safer to smack him or run away. "For this," he pointed at the work station, "you have given me, what I fully intend to brand as, a cure to ancercy. I am going to be rich!"

"Oh," she replied, not really thinking about that aspect of it as she calmed herself down. "Well, sure. It was a team effort, I'd say."

That seemed to make him smile genuinely. "It was a team effort." He cleared his throat, "that's why I have a proposal for you."

"I hope not literally," she laughed, falling back into nervous.

That only made him grin, though. "But would that be the worst thing? Look, I am going to be deeply successful now. There is nobody I would rather share that with than the person who helped me get there."

"A love match, perhaps?" she suggested, "maybe a woman whose... scales you haven't already seen."

He shook his head at her. "The world of women has evaded me. I am a man of my work. That's why I believe you would be perfect! Let me look after you, dear. Let me thank you for what you've done for me, let me give you children, the gift of motherhood, please!"

If this man had not literally just helped to save her life then she may have been inclined to point out that what he had really just offered her was a life of dependence on him, his actual seed in her vagina, and the job of raising their children without his help.

So instead she just stammered, "honestly, I'm fine, thanks. I just want to help out my friend for now."

He frowned, "look, I know I am getting on in years. But this, I think, is the best opportunity I'll have for a happy family life." He took both her hands in his and pleaded with a look.

She remained fixed on him, her face twisted into an uncomfortable smile as she searched and searched for a polite way to tell him that just maybe this wasn't what was best for *her*. She continued to stare despondently as the words failed her until he finally got the point on his own.

"I see," he replied, dejected. He dropped her hands and let his own fingers fiddle with the things on his table for no apparent reason other than to keep them busy.

She felt guilty for just a second until she mentally slapped herself into remembering that she had no reason to.

"If you do want to thank me," she said, bringing him back to attention, "then I require a large amount of the salve and some of that etherium powder. My friend that I was talking about, he has turned all the way. I have to try and save him now," she laughed at that, "I suppose this whole matter was the easy bit."

He snorted quietly, a gentle laugh in response. "I would be happy to. In fact, dear, you can come by for anything you ever need from me." He smiled at her before walking away to one of the rooms at the back. She peaked just behind him and saw that inside was a mess of storage that she presumed would have larger quantities of materials for whatever he needs.

The first thing she decided to do while waiting for John, was to take the washcloth again and wipe away the dried blood on the bottle. She smeared it clean off and tried her best at the cork as well. While the whole thing seemed to be sparkling after, she could not fix the dark patches now on the stopper. She didn't really care either, to be honest, as it was Victor's own fault anyway.

Then she cradled the object in her arms staring deeply at the universe within. She wasn't quite sure what lay in store there nor what Will might even look like. She had no attack plan or proper methodology for how she would both smear the salve on him and then ignite it. And at the end she decided that she simply did not care. She could have gone to the local guild and asked a hunter for help only she decided that they just wouldn't get it and deem it better to kill her friend. No, she had to do this alone.

She also didn't want to leave it for too long, worrying that her friend might lose even more of himself with the time to come. She had still been in control of all her faculties as her disease reached the latter hours but she was not totally sure that Will had any left at all.

Even if she could cure his body, could she cure his mind?

Either way, she had to try.

And she had to do it now, while her mind was ready and the echoes of the pain on her skin were still invigorating her to the challenge.

She was so indulged in the idea of action that she hadn't even noticed John return with two bottles in his hand and a large hemp bag. It was burly and thick – inside the two jars lay side by side. The larger one was as wide as the bottle in her hand but just a third shorter. It one was filled with the yellow-flecked solution of brimstone cream. The other was a small jar that could fit in one's hand. It was half-full of the blue powder she would need to draw the lamp rune. This one was resting atop the bigger one so that there was space next to it for Victor's bottle.

She placed it inside and took the bag from him, happy to have a convenient luggage for everything.

"Thank you. For everything," she said sweetly to the man. She raised on her toes to kiss him on the cheek. She even became slightly grateful to see that he didn't blush or misinterpret the gesture. He just smiled back, kindness in his eyes as he watched her go.

"All I have to say is thank you in return. Please, do come back to Ripley's if you're about."

She smiled and waved as she walked once more through the bell and out of the alchemist's shop.

She had decided to make her way back to the fountain in St Mungo's Square so that she could be isolated as she psyched herself up to enter the bottle.

She would be in trouble and then corralled to an indoor hostel, or maybe even an alleyway, if she was found out this late. But it did not matter, for soon she would disappear.

She slung one of the handles of her new bag down her arm so that she could reach inside with her other hand to pull the witcher's bottle out and stare ruefully at the stopper. Before uncorking it, she also made the decision to pull the lid off of the other jars, ready to do what was needed. She traced the lamp symbol in the air a few times to finalise her memory of it before standing up and taking a very large lungful of night time air.

Then she pulled the stopper clear and braced herself for travel.

She stared down inside the bottle mesmerised wholly by the raw sight of the vortex within. She expected that it might suck her down and wash over her like a cold wave. When nothing happened, to her disappointment, she replaced the stopper and turned back up to the fountain to try and figure out how to make work of the pagan tool.

Where the fountain had stood before her was now the comparatively small room of Victor's personal holding cell.

She jumped backwards, her back hitting a wall behind her.

These walls were made of golden bricks and the jail was lined by thick steel bars. At least, she thought that might have been the regular case were it not for the beating red sun directly outside the window. It peered into the realm like a scorching eye and cast a blood-red light on the entire room. It made the actual blood that stained the walls and floor look a horrid black colour. It melted the shadows on the body of the devil guard – that now lay in three or four different pieces – to obscure its true shape and cut a more horrid outline. It even turned the yellow bricks into a sad, orange colour as if the whole room were lamenting what had happened within its walls.

She looked around for Will but found nothing yet. Behind her she saw that there was only a simple bell on a hook. The wall surrounding the bell was the bloodiest as if a large body had been thrown against it and exploded all across the surface.

So instead she stalked forwards, scrutinising the shadows as she went. One hand was inside her bag and hovering above the open salve jar ready to dip into it and grab a thick coating of cream.

As she took slow, heavy steps, she saw that the red devil, now a colour similar to the piercing shadows themselves, had not been cut apart but rather rent. There lay the right half in the corner of the cell, slumped and staring at her through its dead, yellow eye. There lay the other half on the other side of the room; and that half was torn into two again in some messy tear through the middle. It left an arm attached through some vicarious bits of daemon flesh to half a head. Somewhere in the middle of the room was a leg in a puddle of what must have been the rest of the torso.

When she finally managed to walk the league of the room, the looming red star following her the whole way, she realised that there was nothing else. She had thought she might turn around and see a disfigured tentacle creature that was once her friend leap from a hiding spot at her face and maul her. But as she did turn, she saw that there was no hiding space.

There was nothing else here.

As the night hunters prowled the streets of Belgrave, she had come to the harrowing realisation that William Rushings had escaped the bottle at some point.

And he could be anywhere in the kingdom by now.

Lobelia

"Tell me," she said, still holding her head high such as the princess should. "Where did you learn about the spell to do this?"

The witcher sneered at her. He looked to her like a different man entirely. He was contorted, perverted. His mask of servitude to the powers above had shattered as he so evidently grabbed Alex' hair with great intent. "Some old friends of mine had a spell that could edit a person's blood. I adapted it, made it better and turned it into my maternity spell. Is that *quite* alright with you?"

She tried her best to keep a straight expression although even she could not help the disgust from warping her. "And it is infernal, is it?"

"It is holy."

"Then why is she crying!"

"Because her consent does not matter," he said, fully and irrevocably believing himself. "God's will that she be a mother."

"Her- her consent does not matter," Lolita echoed with a choke.

"What are you doing here, princess?" When he spoke he was using the same muscles required to shout. His throat was tearing at itself as the words escaped but they did not come out loud. Just terse and seething.

She refused to be hammered down, still maintaining a straight spine and air of bravery despite her quivering knees.

"To be honest, I just needed to ask you something." He stared at her through black eyes awaiting her elaboration. Alex just continued to fruitlessly squirm in his grasp. "William Rushings. He is born of your experiments, correct? So tell me why he did not incite the same violent feelings that your other products have? Well?"

The question seemed to cause a veneer to cover his eyes – the momentary glossy sign that his mind had gone beyond his reach for just a second as the anger her words - and the betrayal of Theodore - had caused. "How about..." he coughed, doing his best to maintain his composure, "how about I show you."

He let go of the acolyte's hair for just a second so that he could grab her head in his hands instead. She writhed beneath him, kicking at the floor and smacking his arm as he pushed her towards the vat that she was knelt before. Lolita didn't even bother to help her, knowing that she had no power to, even if she could overcome the petrifying fear.

Instead she just had to swallow back bile as she witnessed the girl's face being pushed up against the cold bronze; tears pouring into Alex' own choking mouth. Cyrus' hair started to turn pure black growing out all the way to the end as the surface of the vat began to glow blue in all the areas that Alex was touching it. Soon enough, her body began to meld with the tank as she seemingly passed through the metal and her body disappeared with nothing to show inside. Soon enough, her energy was too depleted to even scream and she just slowly fell more limp as her form was absorbed completely.

It wasn't until Lolita managed to find words that her own tears fell down her cheek, "why her? Why her of all people, WHY HER?"

"Because she had some insane notion of being a priest one day. She wished so eagerly to pursue a career that required her celibacy." When she finished merging into the silo, Cyrus stepped back and gestured for Lolita to look through that small circular window. She did, stepping forward to see a much smaller, shrivelled and less humanoid foetus like the one she knew was floating in the tank at the corner of the room.

She could not describe the feeling in her own stomach as she saw how Alex had been sacrificed to make... that.

"We can't be having women like that," Magellan finished. "So sometimes, when I see a pathetic girl trying to be a holy woman; when I see a girl who is homeless and loveless; a girl who is choosing not to marry; a girl whose body just isn't working as God intended it to... I take them all down here and push them into my vats. And they create new daughters who can breed a litter or new sons who can change the world."

Lolita turned to him mechanically, having to individually push each muscle in her body to turn and face him. Her words came out in between sobs, halted by each escaping emotion. "Alex... was... going to... change... the world. She was going to help people, damn it!"

He laughed at her statement. It was not a reactionary laugh or an involuntary chuckle but an actual guffaw at her. "To answer your question about Mr Rushings. Sometimes, when I tell women about what I'm doing, their eyes light up and they come with me willingly. I like those women. One such was Theodore's wife. Nobly determined to do her duty, she found herself lacking and so was all too happy to give her life to birth William in one of these very vats."

Lolita raised her chin at him, knowing exactly what he meant. "So it is not the unnatural state of these people's births that have been setting my heart alight but rather the circumstances of how some were born from force rather than willingness."

"Apparently so," he snarled. "I can't think why. Perhaps your mother fucked a warlock at some point and dirtied the Old King's blood."

Lolita sniffled, refusing to rise to his accusations. "Are you implying that there is something infernal about- about me? And not the other way around?"

"Why else would your body call blackness to God's will, eh? He made you lot to bear children and I am merely enacting that. It is literally what you're for, just one simple, easy thing. Still, some of you bitches can't even get that right."

"No," she retorted with passion, "God is love! God wants his creations to be as he created them. If He created Alex to spread his word, if he created those serving maid's mothers to be infertile, then that is how he created them! You are the failure for holding all humans to the same standard as one man and one woman from the beginning of a silly book!"

"A silly book? You seem to be failing in your vision already, archbishop Lobelia." He slowly started to move his arm inside his coat to grab something as the two of them spoke.

"Actually, I think I am only living up to it. Our faith is not about what's written in the pages. They are stories and we know they are stories! To be a follower of the Holy Paradigm is to practice love. Forgiveness. For every single human. That is it, just those two things. If a person can do those two things, then they are holy and nothing else matters!" She looked not in fear but just disappointment as Magellan pulled an unremarkable silver short sword from his coat. "And it appears you are practicing neither."

The witcher lunged at her with the blade, foregoing everything just to see her head on its tip. She managed with surprising deftness to role under his swing and crawl away to the wall. The action made him laugh as he saw the realisation come to her eyes that she had cornered herself.

"Everything you say is wrong."

"You're a pagan," she shouted, "you believe in such a vast pantheon yet you cling to my God like an Extenic!"

He tilted his head as if he were looking down at a yapping dog. "It is the simple fact of nature that girls birth and men protect. My pantheon, as you say, has only ever reinforced that. You breed and you die and you shut the fuck up about it, do you understand me?"

Lolita flinched away as his sword stabbed in a spark at the brick wall behind her. She knew that she would not be able to fluke another dodge away from him again and saw in the smile of his eyes that she was right. He was playing with her.

She looked around for an escape but saw none. Just the window above her where that corner tank was incubating a foetus. Where another woman had sold her life to this man so she could provide the world with another baby.

Another lonely baby.

Another... baby, she realised.

She stood up defiantly once more staring through an angered expression at the witcher. He watched amused at how she might articulate herself next. He wanted to know where her misplaced determination was coming from that she might see the outside of this room again.

"Cyrus Magellan. All these vats. That spell you use so wrongly. This whole bottle. Your plans, your philosophies, your morals. Your very perception of the human race. They are all engines of the devil." She took a deep breath in and then out again. "And you would do right to fear the devil's enemies."

"Is a prayer the best you have?"

"Yes. But not for you." She turned around now as if she were completely alone, just her and that corner vat. She looked through the window again to see the foetus from before. She recognised the faintly forming shapes of limbs. Of a head. She still thought it was beautiful, however it happened. And she placed a hand on either side of the cold metal and she addressed only the foetus inside. "Whoever you were. I am sorry."

Cyrus growled and charged her, his sword outstretched. But nothing connected as when he got too close he was blasted away by a sudden blue light. The light spanned from the tank where Lolita was touching it with her two hands. She moved to press her entire body up against it, the blue light expanding to encompass her entire form as she guessed her way at how the spell worked.

Magellan thought she was a fool making a last ditch attempt to not die by his hands. How little he knew.

For when the spell started to take effect, it was not Lolita who melded with the tank. As she cast her spell and a single highlight of her hair cascaded into a midnight black colour, it was the foetus inside that became absorbed. The witcher watched with a degree of both awe and revulsion as the princes reversed his spell to take the baby into her own body.

When it was gone, she fell to the floor clutching at her stomach. She wrapped around herself tightly with raw strength as she began to wheeze and then make spluttering coughs. Drops of blood came next, spattering from her mouth and into a dry pool on the floor. She choked up more with bile and phlegm that also ran from her nose. Her eyes watered profusely. Her whole body curled in on itself, retching and heaving to accommodate her shifting insides.

Eventually, when she was finished, she wiped her face and her mouth on both her sleeves. And when she had stood up and pulled away both her arms there was a subtle bump on her stomach where her potential baby was resting inside.

She stared with the same defiance at the witcher again as this time he grinned. He sheathed his sword in his coat and allowed her to leave alive. After all, he had approved of her new decision and would not harm a pregnant woman.

Culver

Adam had been deposited in the north-east of Okhram in a town called Highcourt. It was where the borders of Okhram, Northold and the capital met. He was commanded to move west from there, until an ancercy epidemic had spread across the entire length of the Okhram-Northold border. He was told to sell cheaply so that the stones would end up in as many hands as possible, a fact that only made him happy once Victor told him that he could keep all of the profit. He would then report back to a rendezvous point in each town where Victor and Mary would be waiting for him so that they could produce and pass on more alchemist's stones. It was an expensive ordeal, buying all the alchemical components to perform the duplication process hundreds of times but they had a queen's treasury behind them, so the matter was moot.

Their quest had been successful.

Their final stop, before lodging at the inn in Highcourt, was to reconvene with the royal camp. There was a train that had travelled to a lone hilltop overlooking the fields and farms that lead into the town. There, the queen had come to meet with her auger and listen to his report as they look down on their first target.

Upon arriving on the outskirts of the camp they both were met by two royal guards. They were wearing large sets of pure black armour with a deep purple tunic over the top. Embroidered into the thick fabric was the silver logo of House Iris: the reaver.

Victor showed these men his letter of marque and the pair were allowed inside. There, they walked amongst a whole gaggle of soldiers and servants running from tent to tent performing various complex duties. As they went on towards the biggest tent of the bunch, Victor had explained to Mary how the entire campsite was basically one big, living being. Every person played their part, like organs, to ensure that Charlotte Iris was not sacrificing any of her creature comforts to be out in the countryside like this.

Once they did reach the royal tent, he informed her to wait outside whilst he told their majesty every little detail of their working together. She wondered if he might tell her even the stranger parts, the perhaps more incriminating parts. She realised she didn't care so much either way.

Once five minutes had gone by the cold night time air sent a chill through her body pushing her to move around a bit. She yawned as she searched for a new post to stand at, the late night catching up to her.

As she walked, she looked up at the stars in the sky, watching as if they lead her somewhere new. She let their purple drawings across the moonlit heavens draw her to the edge of the encampment where she watched above the horizon of the nearby town like it was two halves of a magnificent painting.

In fact, she truly believed that there was not, nor ever will there be, a human who can capture a scene quite like the one she was had witnessed then.

Especially because no painter could capture what was happening in the night down there. They could masterfully stroke the colours of the landscape as much as they wanted but it would never capture Adam Sunvale acting as her plant. Their intricate portrayal of the galactic night sky would never hint at what's to come if the queen's plans are successful.

No, no painter could depict the shadow over Highcourt.

Even she could not predict what is to come. She knew that this could be attributed to her lack of personal foresight as her own future was one even more mystifying than that of her kingdom's. Yes, she would spend two or three weeks riding across the border towns helping Victor and Adam plant stones, but then what? Would she just traipse back to The Spire and retake her post as magister from Ahmar?

If there was anything she did know, it's that she was a different person entirely. Marred by both lives of good and bad she wished only to find a state of equilibrium until Redding had dashed even that from her. Maybe she would embrace the temptation of sin. She had spent nearly thirty years doing everything so right. Maybe, as she contributed to the end of lives and spreading of plague, she could let herself just be human in that guttural sense for once; finally, she would abandon consequence for pure, concentrated experience. No more good or bad. Just actions; her own.

"I think I'd rather like that," she commented on her thoughts.

She remembered how to smile then.

"How delightful indeed..."

"Isn't it?" Her comments were added to by a sudden feminine voice over her shoulder. Mary turned around to see a goddess of a woman smiling with sharpness at the view in front of them both, Victor at her heels. She realised, after setting her head straight, that this woman had meant the view and not her thoughts. At least she hoped.

And as to the identity of this woman, well, that was made obscenely clear by the reddening auger who was mouthing the word 'curtsy! Curtsy!' very aggressively at her from behind the woman's back.

So Mary did as she was commanded and fell into a very low, sweeping curtsy, holding her still slightly damp dress out. A while ago, she had wrapped the grey shawl around her shoulders that Princess Lolita had thrown her way to protect from the bite of the evening's chill. And of course that too had stains of mud on it making her feel like she cut quite the horrid figure in the presence of the queen.

"Your majesty," she greeted.

"Rise," Charlotte commanded and Mary did so. The queen was wearing a purple dress but not one that looked like belonged in that century. It was short and made with little fabric. It had silver specks of glitter across the royal purple material and was incredibly form-fitting. She believed that not even a whore in a back alley would wear something quite so feminine. Of course, Mary had dared not say that. And clearly, no one else had ever dared to as the queen wore it with an obvious pride in her gait. The tight sleeves ended just before her wrist and the bottom hems floated above the ankle where it was clear to see that she had black shoes on. Black shoes that were just as slim as her dress with some sort of long, thin heel attached to the bottom. Her hair was partly tied up in a complex pattern that mimicked a bush of flowers and her face had evidence of a subtle use of powder to pretty up her contours. Even her lips had been rouged. And from her ears dangled two thin, silver piercings that ended in a small amethysts that were just the right size to look elegant rather than bawdy.

Of course, atop her head, rested the amethyst crown itself. That gemstone *was* bawdy, and rightfully so. It was large, it was shining and it had a colour found nowhere else in the empire, possibly the world. It was the crown jewel of the queen of Okhram, head of House Iris.

"Victor here has been telling me of your exploits in great detail." When she spoke her voice was inerrably smooth. But it was thick too. It was heard not just pleasantly but with authority. Her words were fact. Which is why it made Mary's heart seize for a second when the queen said, "I am happy with your work."

"Tha- thank you, ma'am."

"Go on then," she continued, her smile turning coy. "Tell me what my plan is."

"Pardon?" she exhaled not daring to presume anything about her.

The queen just turned back to survey Highcourt once more. "In that case... tell me. Do you know the history of Engelland's borders?"

Mary did know but as soon as the question left her majesty's lips, all knowledge fell out of her head. Mary felt like she was choking on nothing as she scrambled around in her own mind trying to find the wandering response. The queen waited patiently for her reply and Victor just looked embarrassed on Mary's behalf.

"They were chosen on purpose," she finally answered. "The capital was put in the middle of its five kingdoms as a message. That even surrounding it, the other five royal houses – *all* the great houses – would never be able to defy the imperial house. House Rose let the empire know that they were worthy of the Old King and his first wife's blood."

"Good," Charlotte cooed. She decided to continue the train of thought for her, "but it was more than just a power statement. The five kingdoms surround the capital in a circle so that each one borders two others. A circle of constituencies."

"It was to discourage war!" Mary said, joining the queen's flow. "If one kingdom invades another then it will invariably have to answer to another on the other side. Unless it makes allies of everyone it will have to fight a war on two fronts, a war that it would surely lose."

The queen folded her hands together and let herself look at Mary again, pleased by her answers. "So we have an impenetrable capital and a circle of kingdoms forced to abide by an unofficial agreement. Which makes me wonder... what would happen if a city next to the capital suddenly experienced an outbreak of ancercy. One that was seen spreading to other nearby towns, hm?"

Mary nodded, picking up what she meant, "then House Rose would have to intervene. The emperor would take temporary occupation of the infested towns until he could sort them out and restore order."

"And what would happen to the borders then?"

"The capital borders would temporarily stretch outwards to encompass the epidemic as soldiers enforced the rehabilitation."

"And if that epidemic stretched across the edge of the Okhram-Northold border?"

"Then there would be a line of capital defences between the two kingdoms." Mary's head suddenly felt lighter. She was dizzy, her body swimming as she comprehended the queen's plan at last. "Then... if Okhram were to make a move, the people of Northold couldn't stop them without moving on capital territory." She looked up at the queen's face against the backdrop of the stars and it appeared to fit there perfectly. "You're going to invade Belgrave."

"Invade Belgrave?" Charlotte tilted her head and narrowed her eyes with her widening smile. What had once been elegant cruelty was now widening into spiteful sadism. "That miserable kingdom is not just filled with Revolutist heretics but also the spineless Extenics who enable their folly." She leant down and cupped the magister's chin, "no, my dear, I am not going to invade Belgrave. I am going to *burn* Belgrave."

TO BE

CONTINUED...

Etherium book two:

Engines of the Devil

coming 2026

About the Author

Phoenix Clarke was born in Worcester and grew in Derby where he worked in various hospitality jobs while he worked on his writing.

He lives now in Scotland with his partner and continues to not only write for his books every day but also work on scripts, comics, and managing his own independent publishing.

He hopes to continue writing exponentially more SFF novels in the future to contribute to the fantastic ecosystem of stories that have inspired his creativity.

Visit Phoenix Clarke online at:
Author website - phoenixclarke.co.uk
Instagram + Tik Tok - @phoenixclarke_ _